What's Michael?

Michael's Mambo

Written and Illustrated:
Makoto Kobayashi

English translation:
Dana Lewis, Jeanne Sather,
and **Toren Smith**

Lettering and art retouching:
L. Lois Buhalis

English version produced by **Studio Proteus** for **Dark Horse Comics, Inc.**

Editor:
David Land

Designer:
Mark Cox

publisher
Mike Richardson
executive vice president
Neil Hankerson
product development
David Scroggy
controller
Andy Karabatsos
general counsel
Mark Anderson
director of editorial
Randy Stradley
director of production & design
Cindy Marks
art director
Mark Cox
computer graphics director
Sean Tierney
director of sales & marketing
Michael Martens
director of licensing
Tod Borleske
director of m.i.s
Dale LaFountain
director of human resources
Kim Haines

What's Michael? Volume Four — Michael's Mambo, January 1998. What's Michael? © 1998 by Makoto Kobayashi. All rights reserved. This material was originally serialized in Comic Morning magazine and published in book form in 1985 by Kodansha Ltd., Tokyo. English translation rights arranged through Kodansha Ltd. New and adapted artwork and text copyright © 1998 by Studio Proteus and Dark Horse Comics, Inc. Dark Horse Comics® and the Dark Horse logo are trademarks of Dark Horse Comics, Inc., registered in various categories and countries. All rights reserved. No portion of this publication may be reproduced or transmitted, in any form or by any means, without the express, written permission of Dark Horse Comics, Inc. Names, characters, places, and incidents featured in this publication are either the product of the author's imagination or used fictitiously. Any resemblance to actual persons (living or dead), events, institutions, or locales, without satiric intent, is coincidental.

Published by
Dark Horse Comics, Inc.
10956 SE Main Street
Milwaukie, OR 97222

First edition: January 1998
ISBN: 1-56971-250-6

10 9 8 7 6 5 4 3 2 1
Printed in Canada

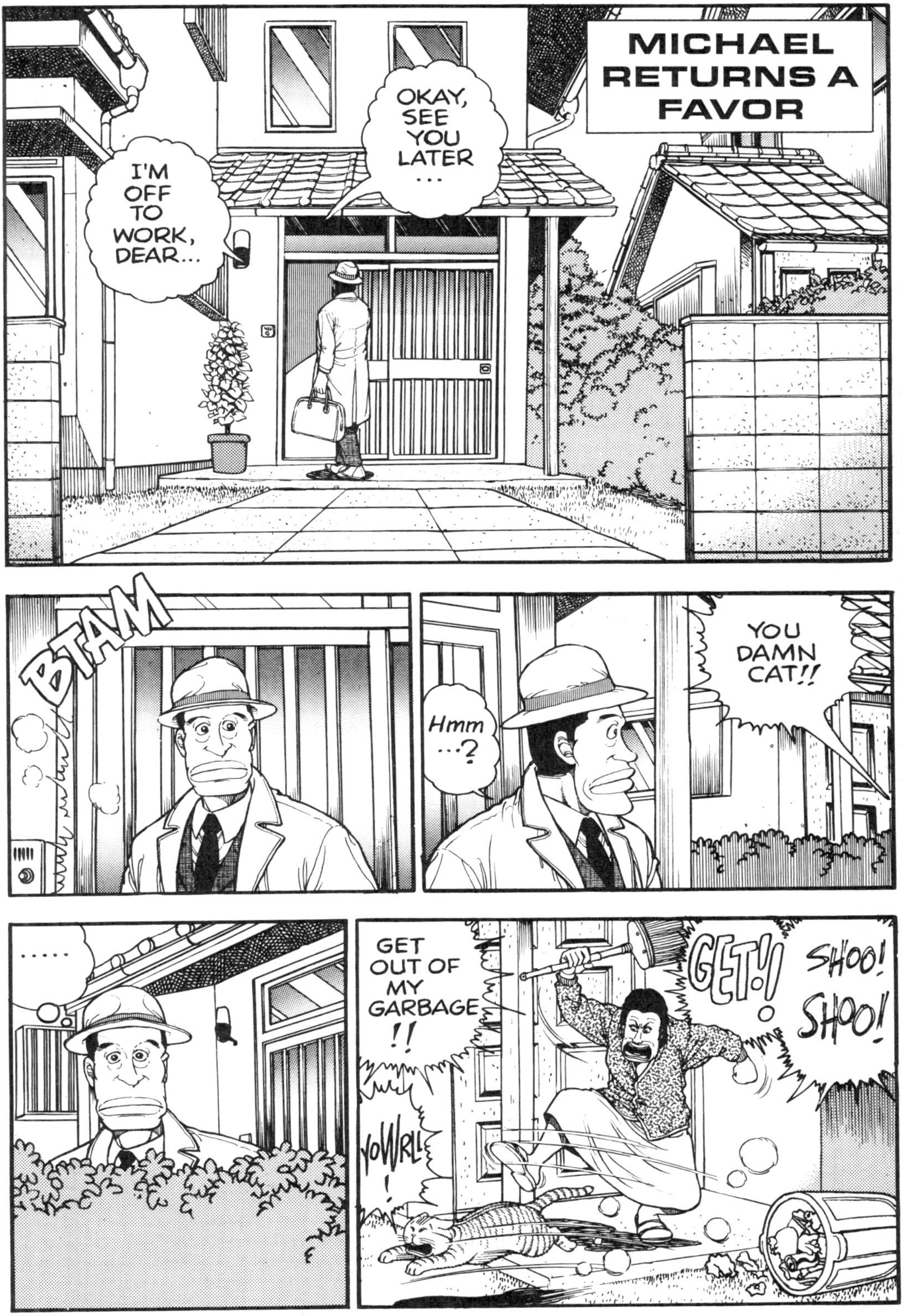
MICHAEL RETURNS A FAVOR
I'M OFF TO WORK, DEAR...
OKAY, SEE YOU LATER ...
BTAM
Hmm ...?
YOU DAMN CAT!!
.....
GET OUT OF MY GARBAGE !!
GET!!
SHOO! SHOO!
YOWRL! !

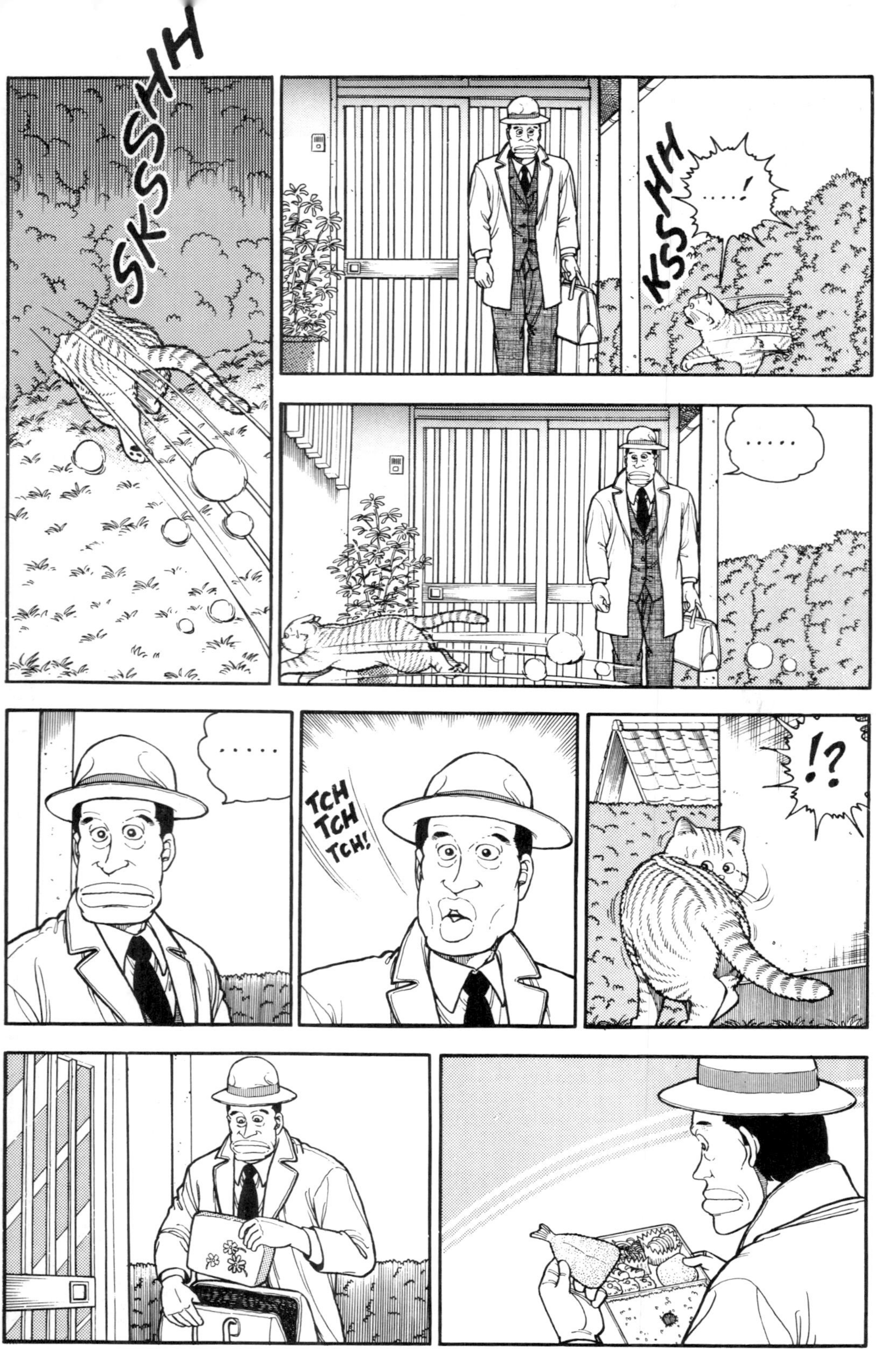
SKSSHH
KSSHH
.....!
.....
.....
TCH TCH TCH!
!?

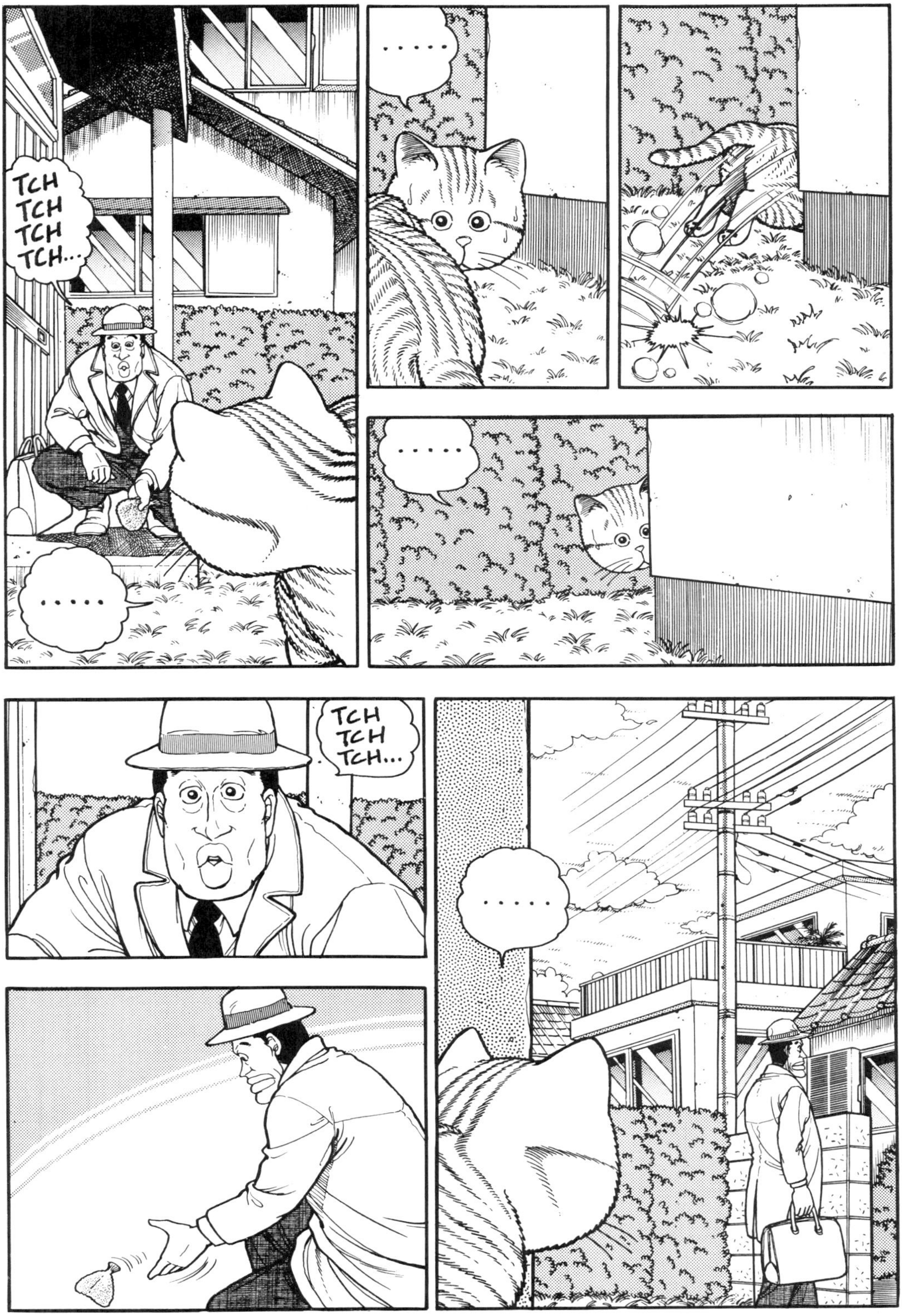
TCH TCH TCH TCH...
.....
.....
.....
TCH TCH TCH...
.....

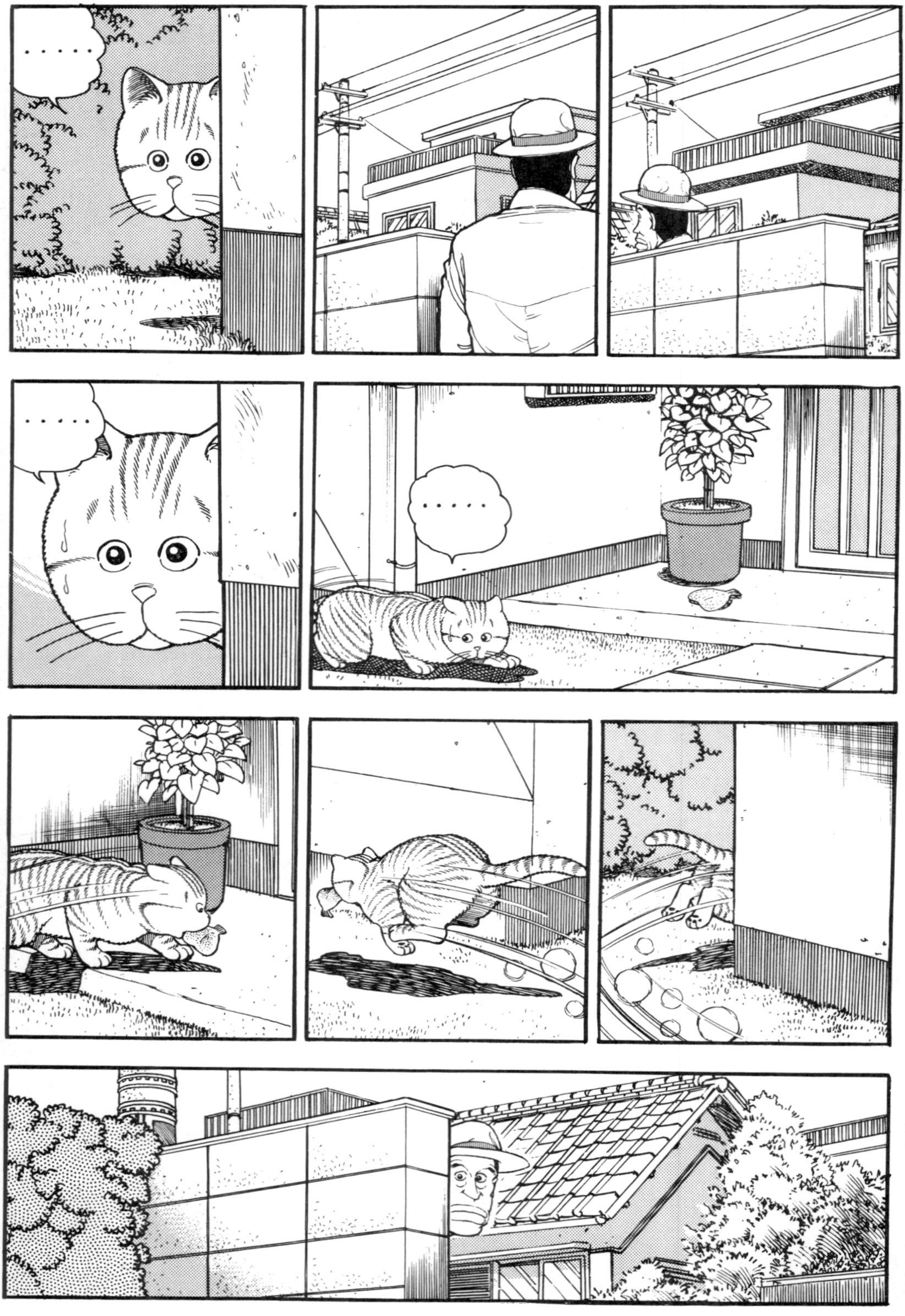
......
......
.....

. . . . . .
THE NEXT MORNING...
`BYE, DEAR...
HURRY HOME...
BTAM
Hmm ?
...?!

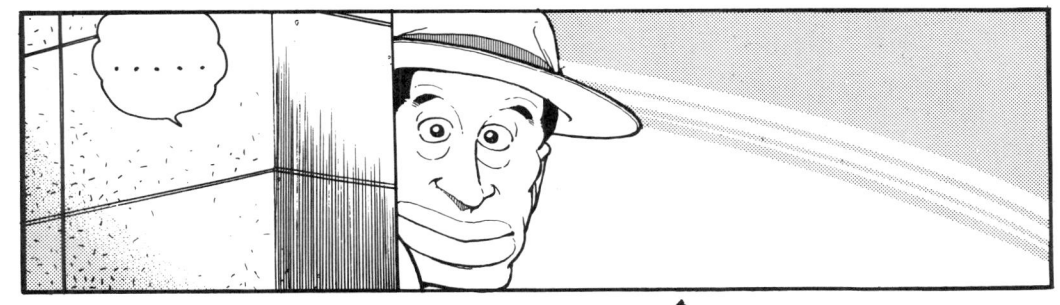

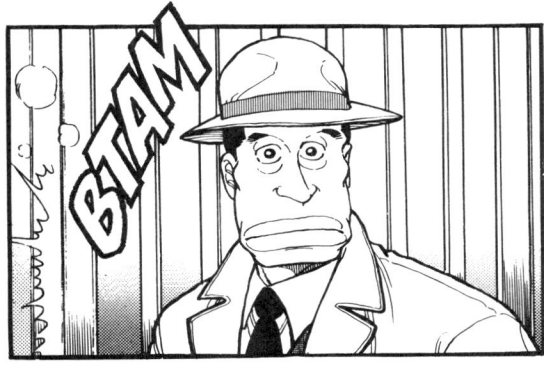

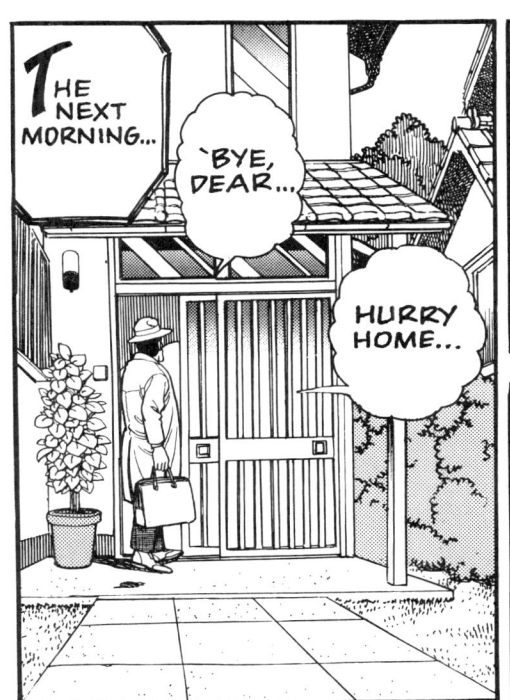

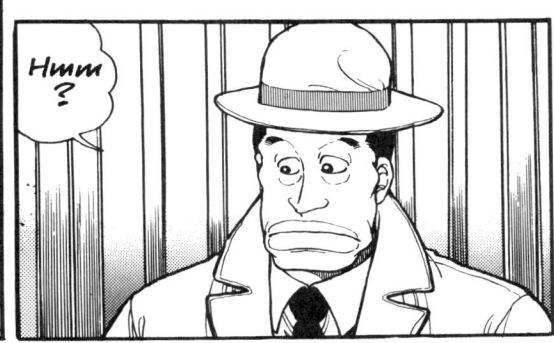

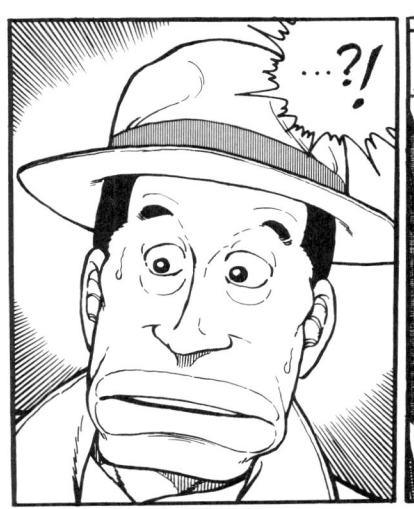

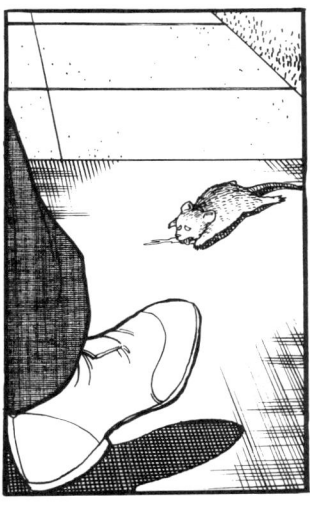

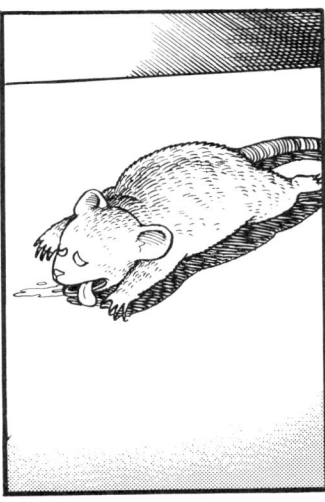

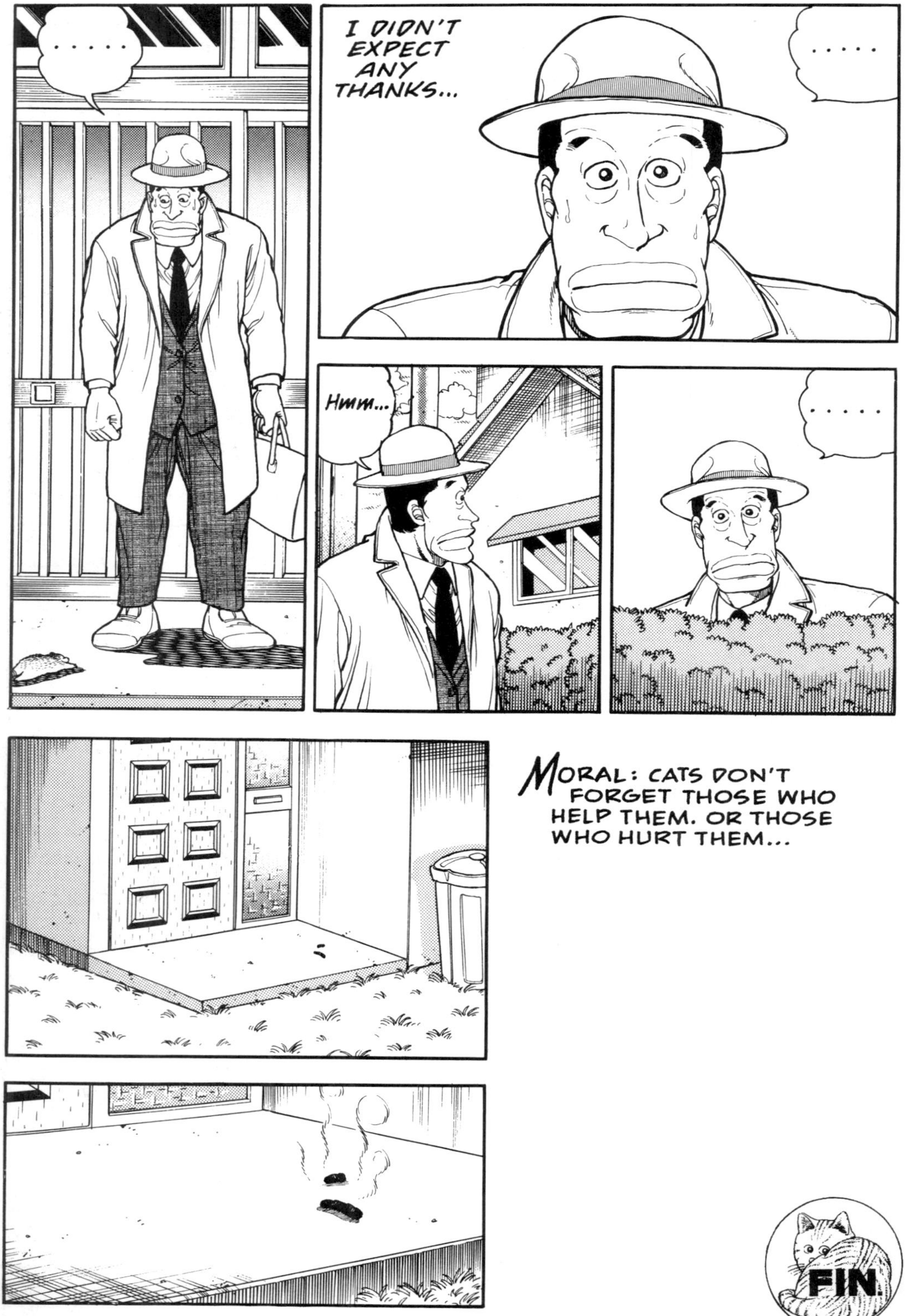
. . . . .
I DIDN'T EXPECT ANY THANKS...
. . . . .
Hmm...
. . . . .
MORAL: CATS DON'T FORGET THOSE WHO HELP THEM. OR THOSE WHO HURT THEM...
FIN

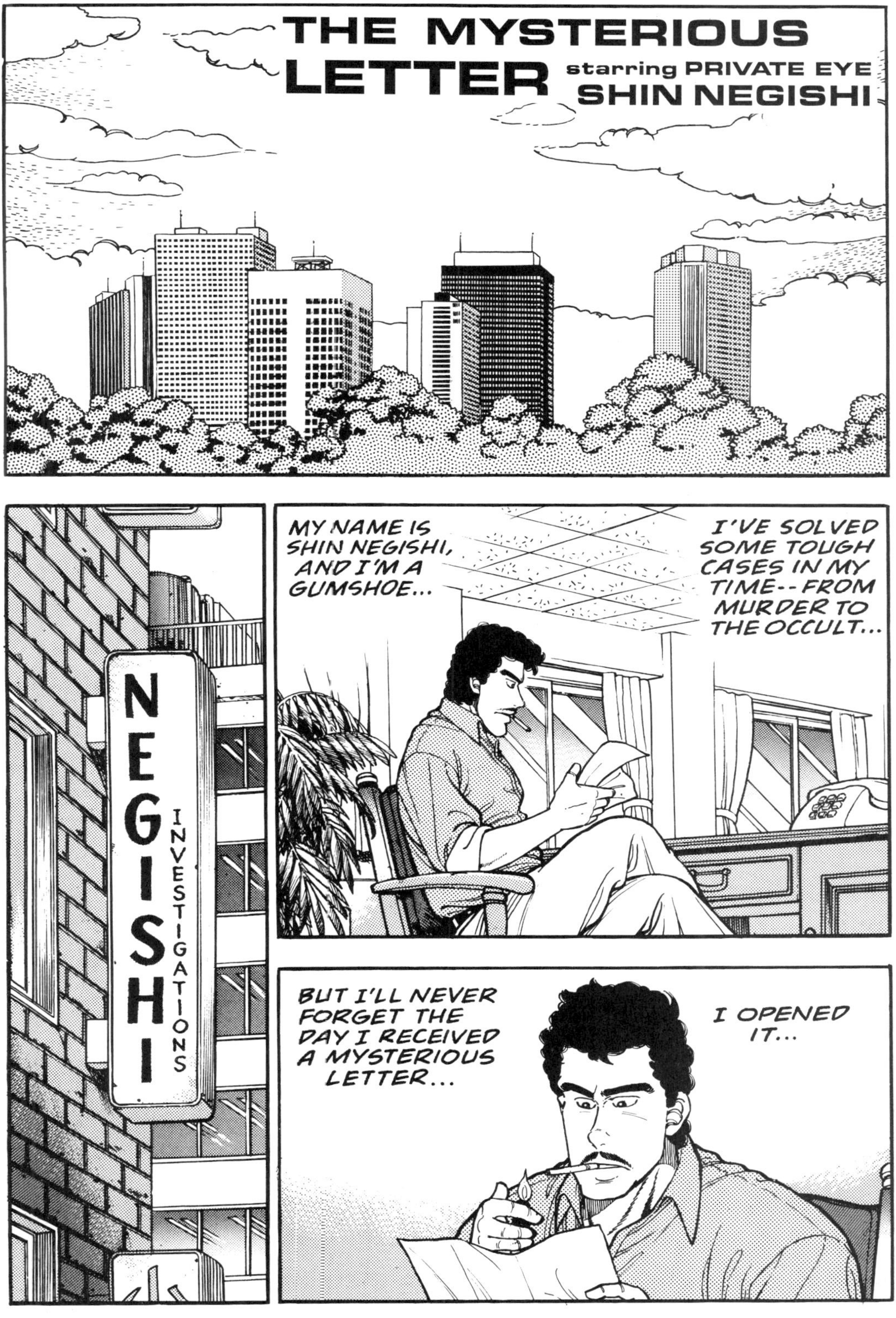
THE MYSTERIOUS LETTER
starring PRIVATE EYE SHIN NEGISHI
NEGISHI INVESTIGATIONS
MY NAME IS SHIN NEGISHI, AND I'M A GUMSHOE...
I'VE SOLVED SOME TOUGH CASES IN MY TIME--FROM MURDER TO THE OCCULT...
BUT I'LL NEVER FORGET THE DAY I RECEIVED A MYSTERIOUS LETTER...
I OPENED IT...

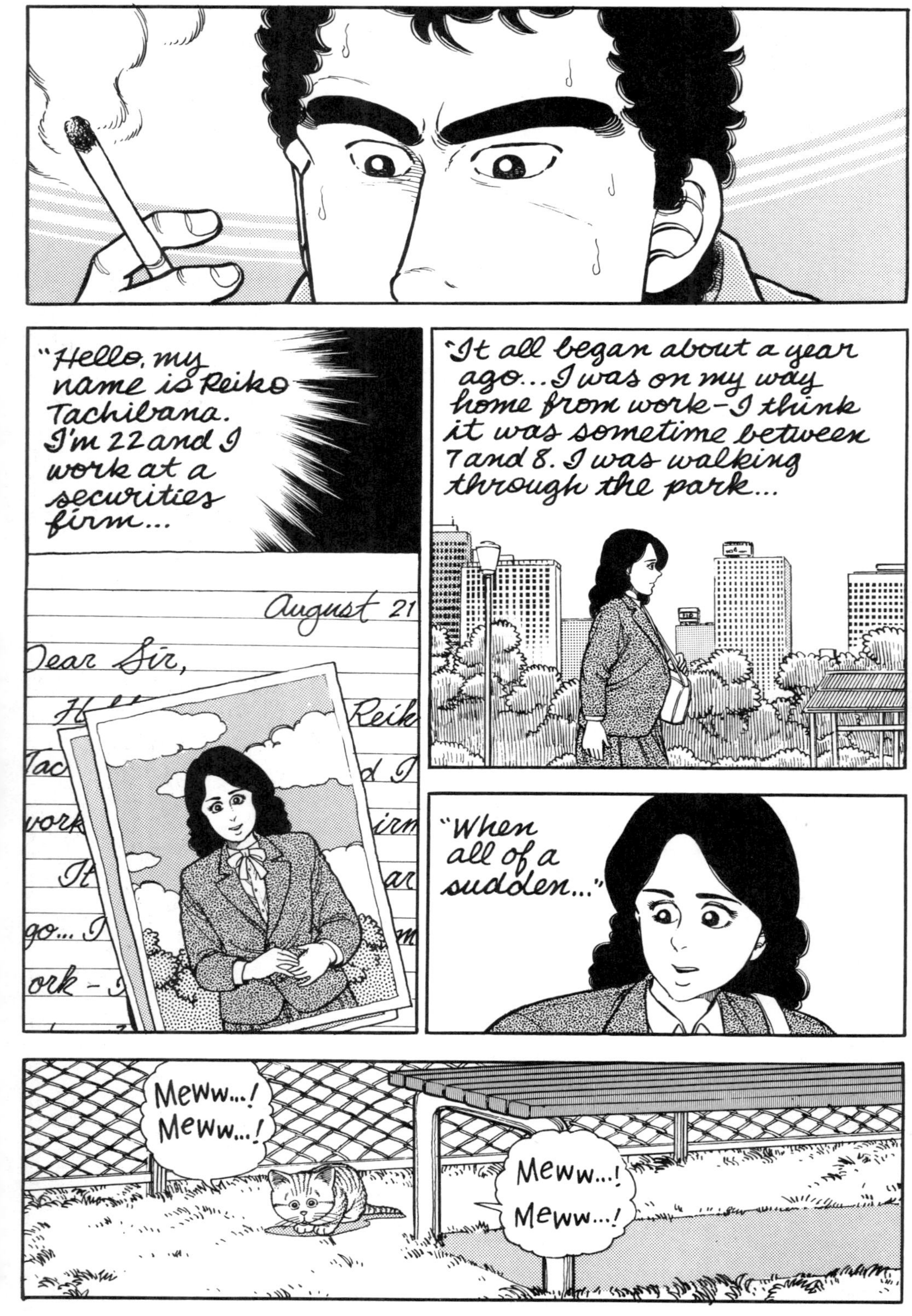
"Hello, my name is Reiko Tachibana. I'm 22 and I work at a securities firm...
"It all began about a year ago... I was on my way home from work - I think it was sometime between 7 and 8. I was walking through the park...
August 21
Dear Sir,
"When all of a sudden..."
Meww...! Meww...!
Meww...! Meww...!

"It was an abandoned kitten, crying with hunger...

Mew...?

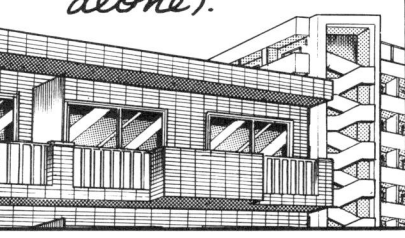

"I couldn't just leave him there, so I took him home to my apartment (where I live alone).

"And I named him Michael.

"But then...

"Well, nothing happened, actually, but he's really cute!

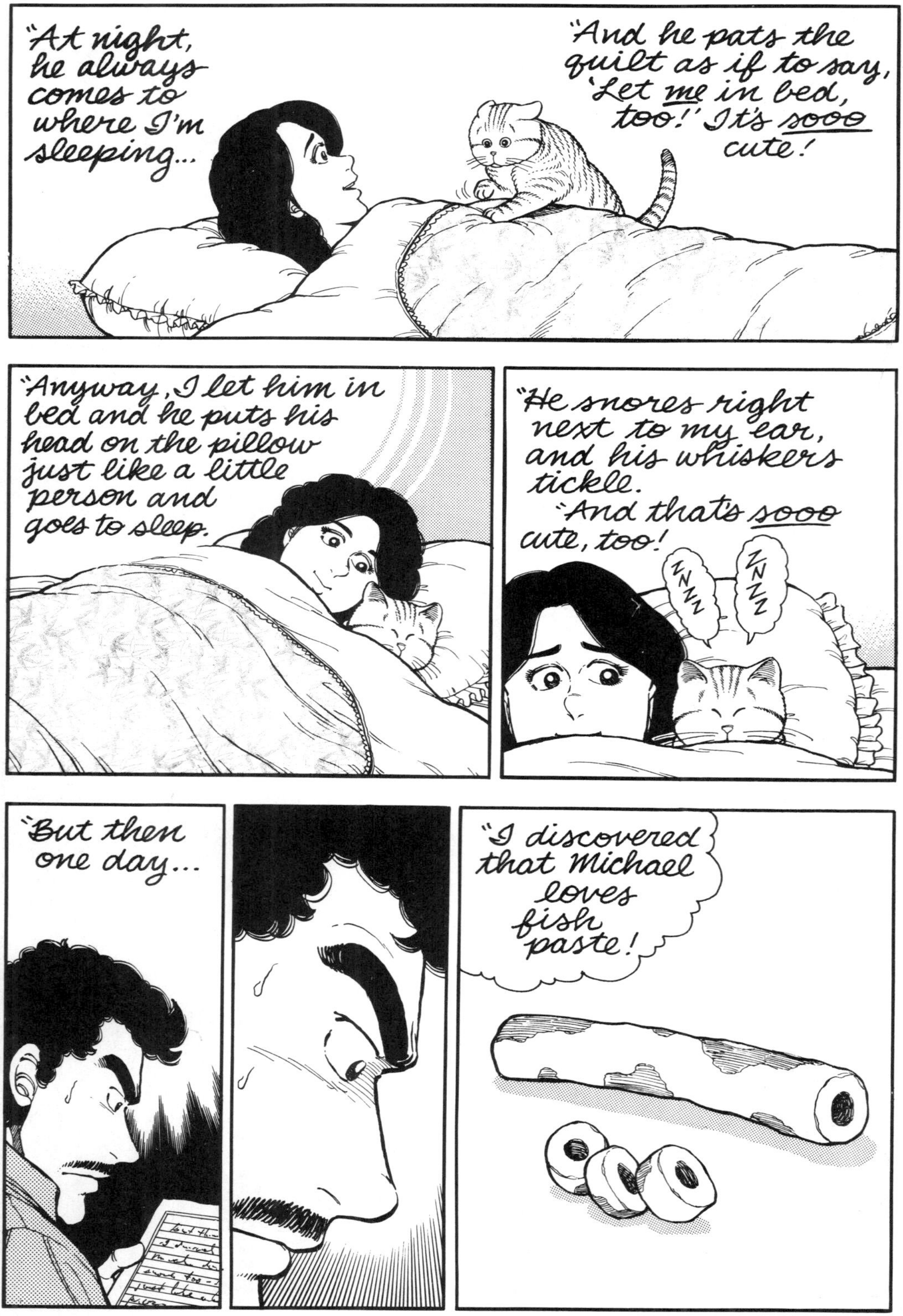
"At night, he always comes to where I'm sleeping...
"And he pats the quilt as if to say, 'Let me in bed, too!' It's sooo cute!
"Anyway, I let him in bed and he puts his head on the pillow just like a little person and goes to sleep.
"He snores right next to my ear, and his whiskers tickle.
"And that's sooo cute, too!
ZNZZ
ZNZZ
"But then one day...
"I discovered that Michael loves fish paste!

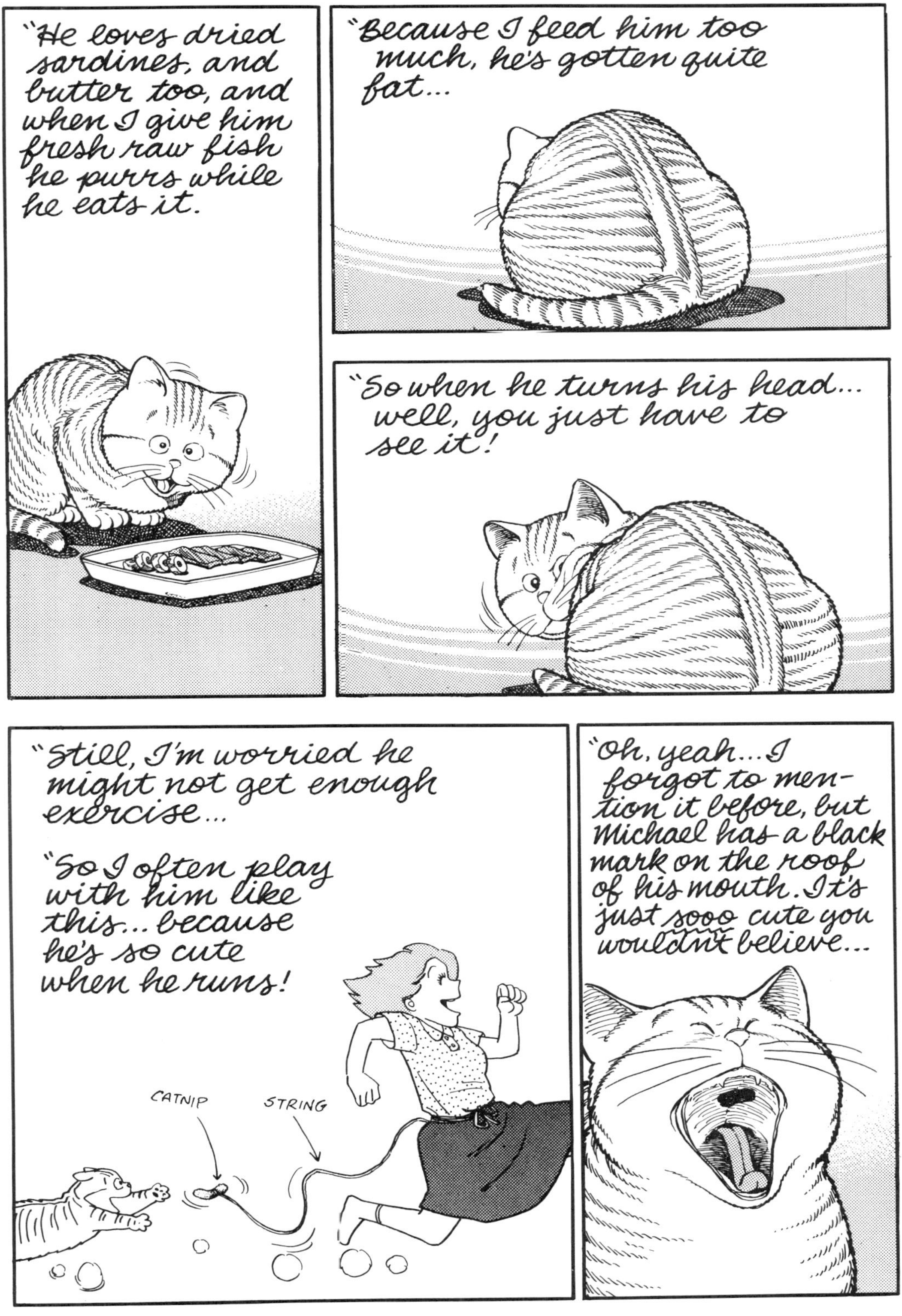
"He loves dried sardines, and butter too, and when I give him fresh raw fish he purrs while he eats it.
"Because I feed him too much, he's gotten quite fat...
"So when he turns his head... well, you just have to see it!
"Still, I'm worried he might not get enough exercise...
"So I often play with him like this... because he's so cute when he runs!
CATNIP
STRING
"Oh, yeah... I forgot to mention it before, but Michael has a black mark on the roof of his mouth. It's just sooo cute you wouldn't believe...

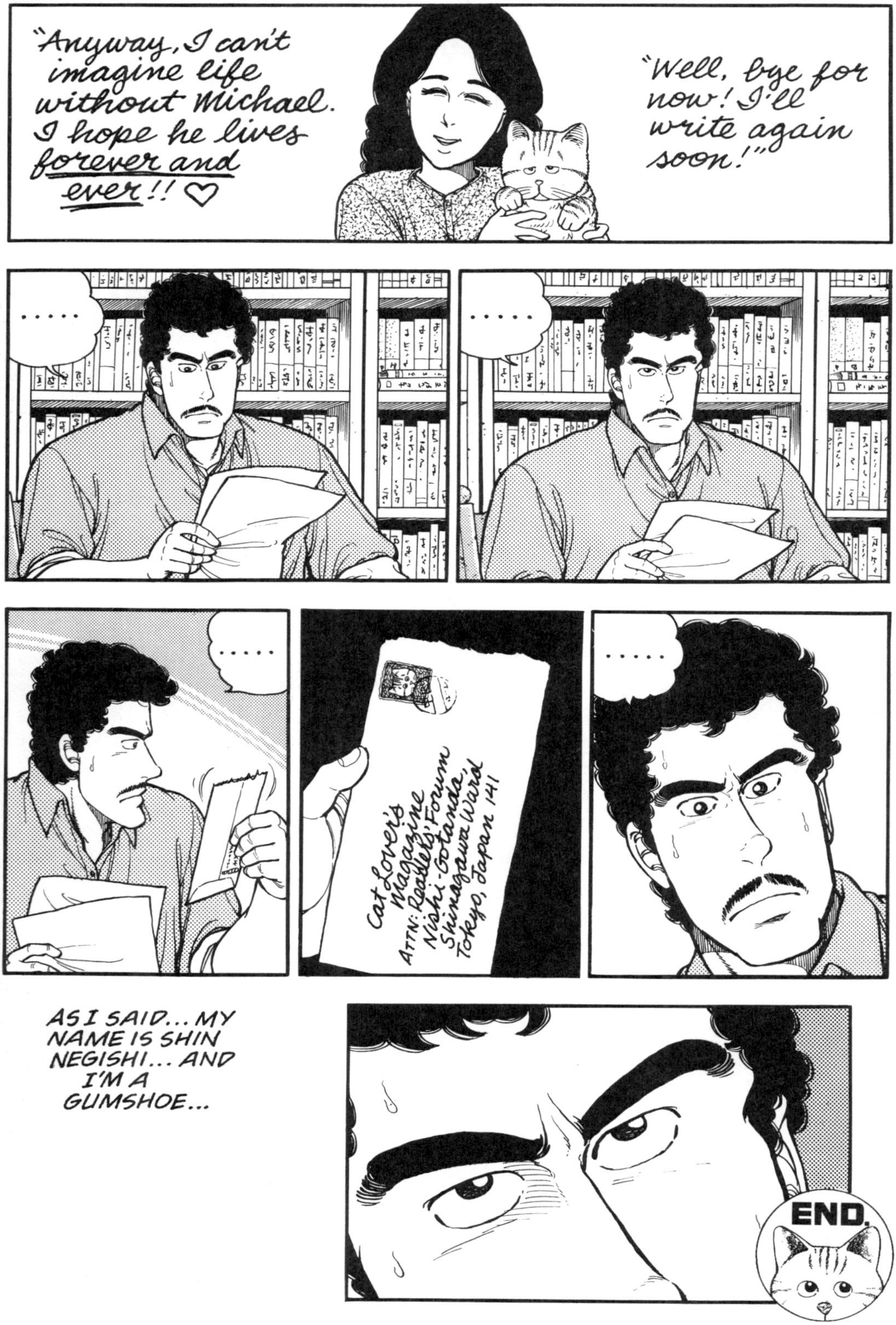
"Anyway, I can't imagine life without Michael. I hope he lives forever and ever!! ♡
"Well, bye for now! I'll write again soon!'"
.....
.....
.....
Cat Lover's Magazine
ATTN: Readers' Forum
Nishi-Gotanda,
Shinagawa Ward
Tokyo, Japan 141
.....
AS I SAID... MY NAME IS SHIN NEGISHI... AND I'M A GUMSHOE...
END.

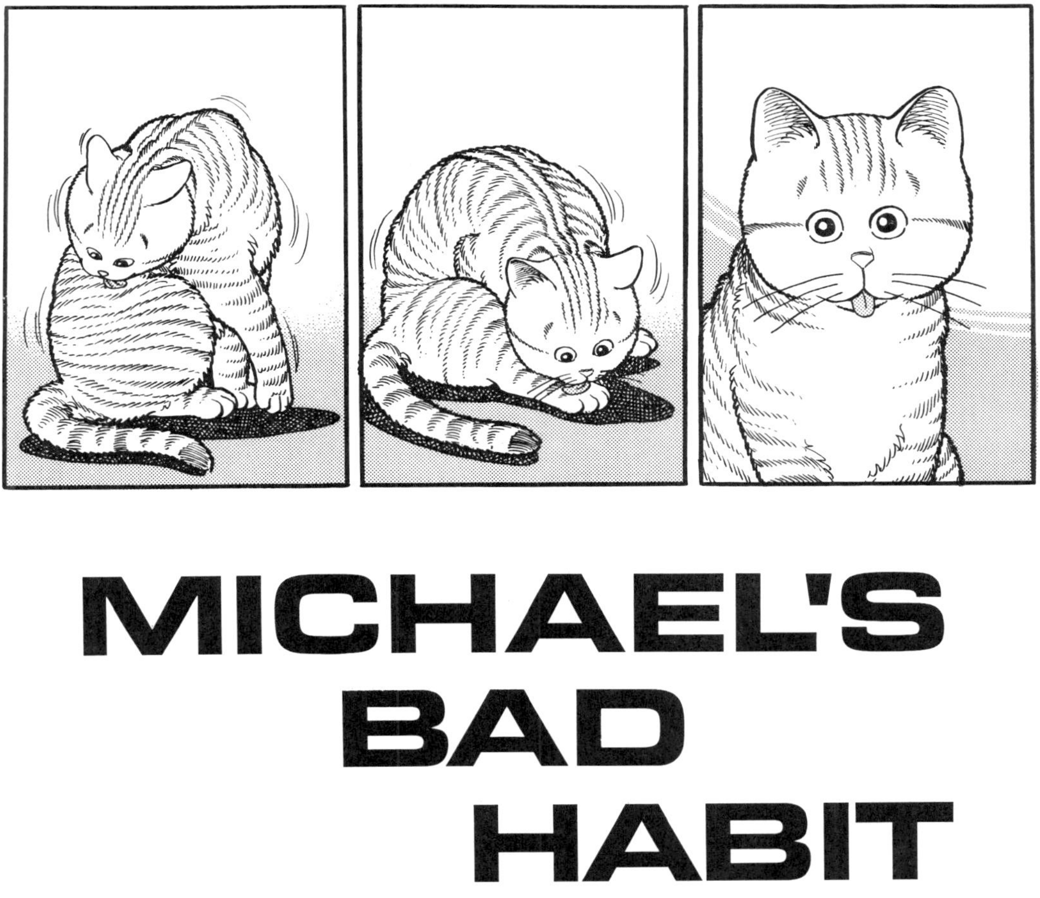

MICHAEL'S BAD HABIT

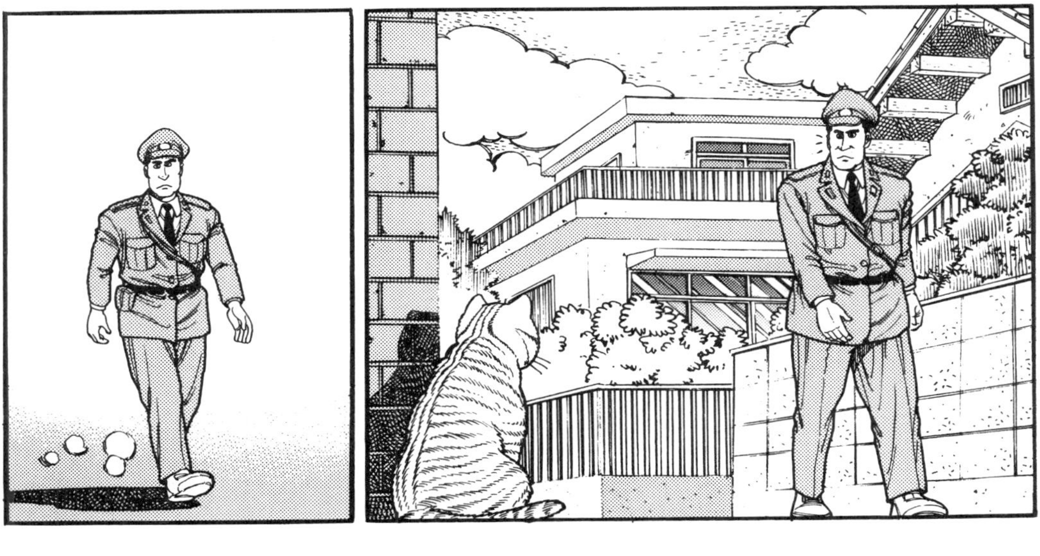

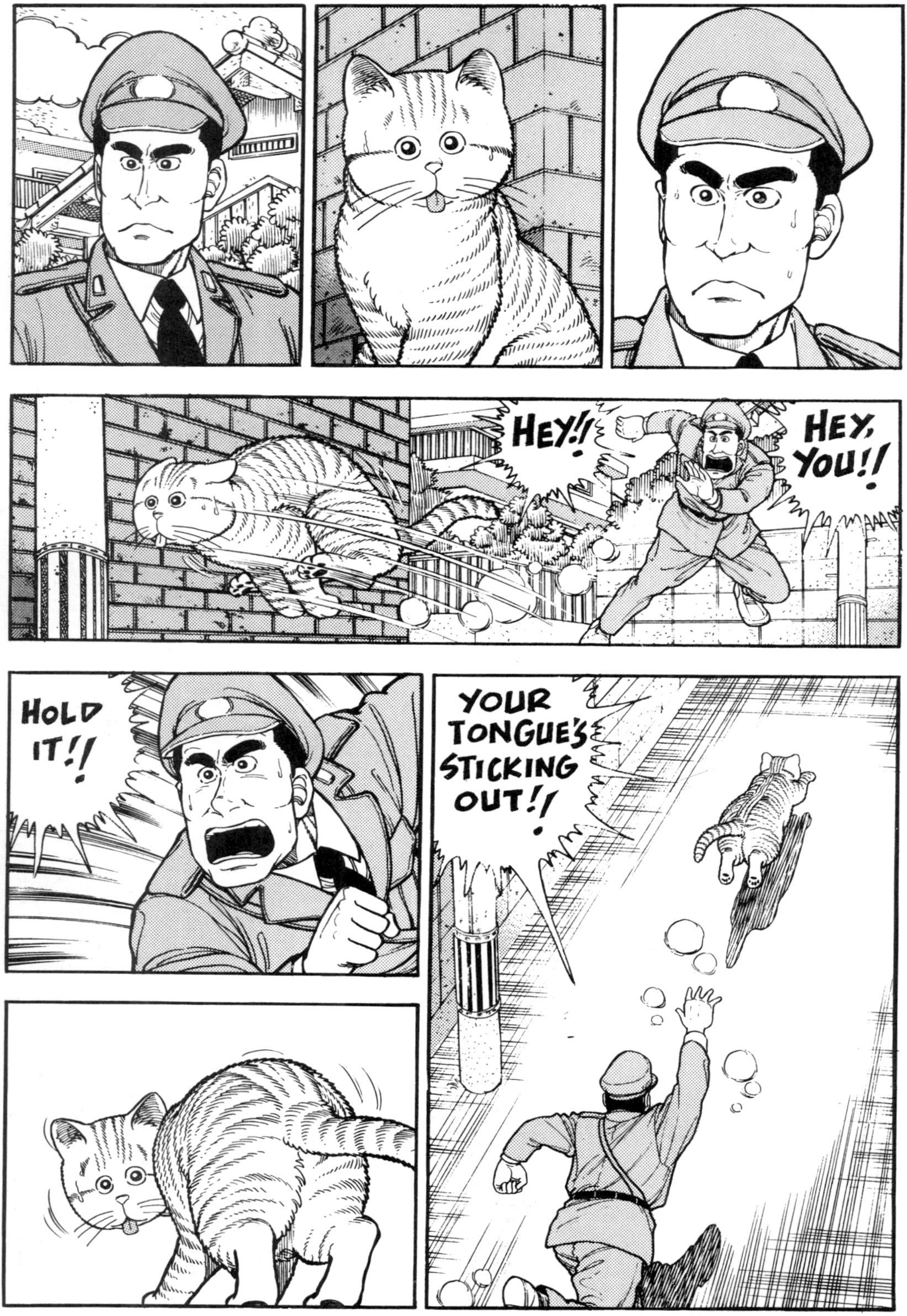
HEY!!
HEY, YOU!!
HOLD IT!!
YOUR TONGUE'S STICKING OUT!!

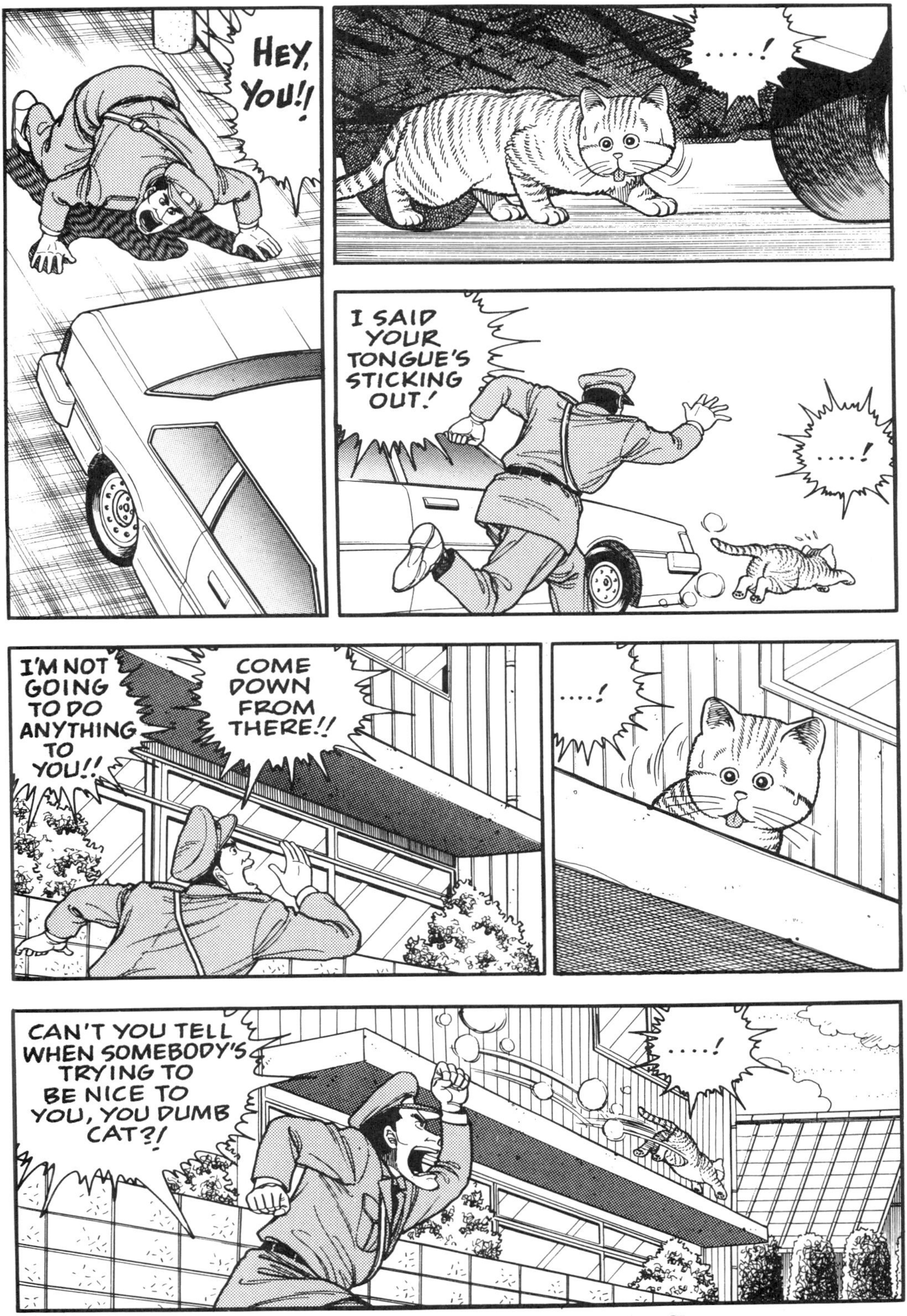

HEY, YOU!!
....!
I SAID YOUR TONGUE'S STICKING OUT!
....!
I'M NOT GOING TO DO ANYTHING TO YOU!!
COME DOWN FROM THERE!!
....!
CAN'T YOU TELL WHEN SOMEBODY'S TRYING TO BE NICE TO YOU, YOU DUMB CAT?!
....!

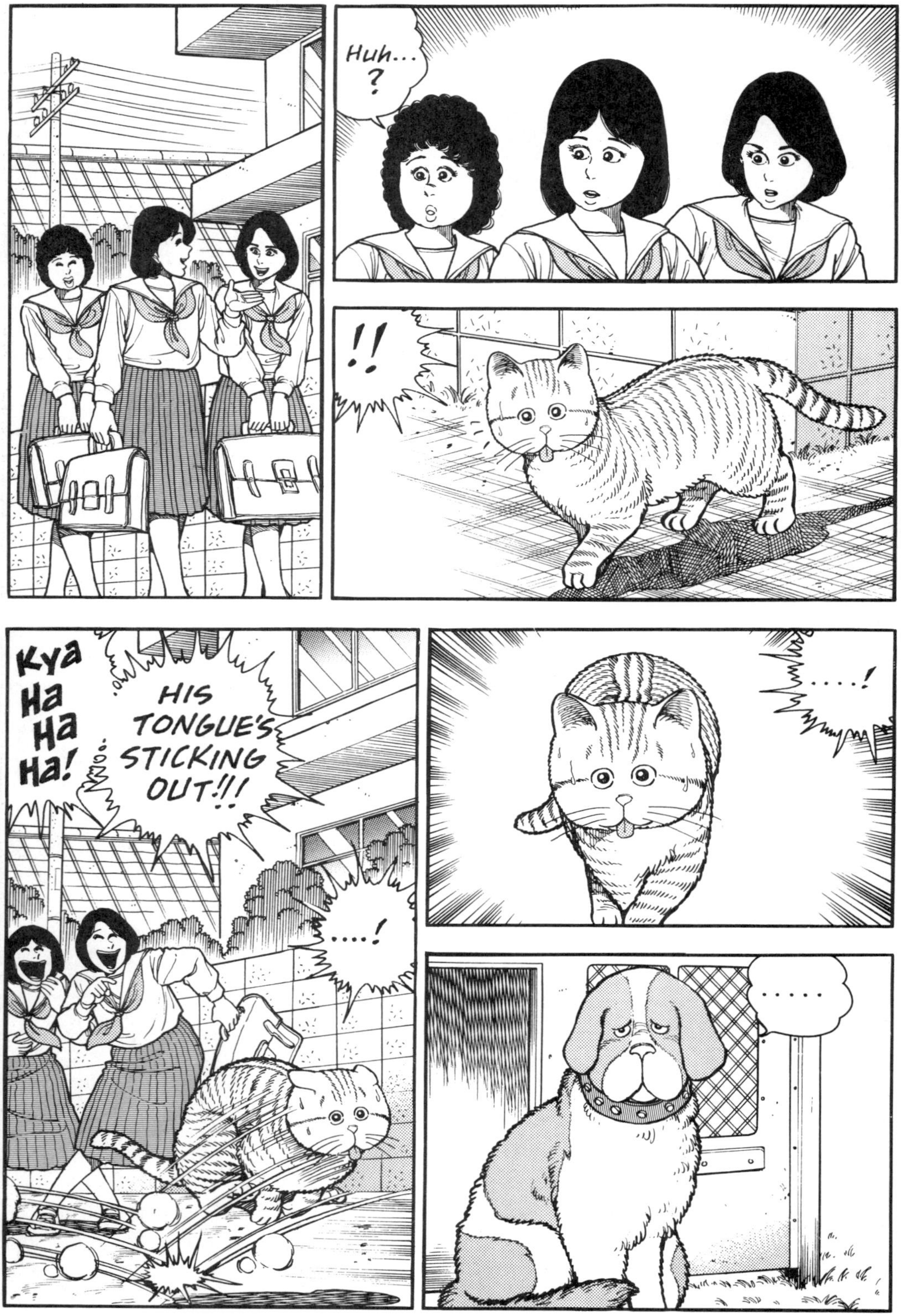
Huh...
?
!!
Kya Ha Ha Ha!
HIS TONGUE'S STICKING OUT!!!
....!
....!
.....

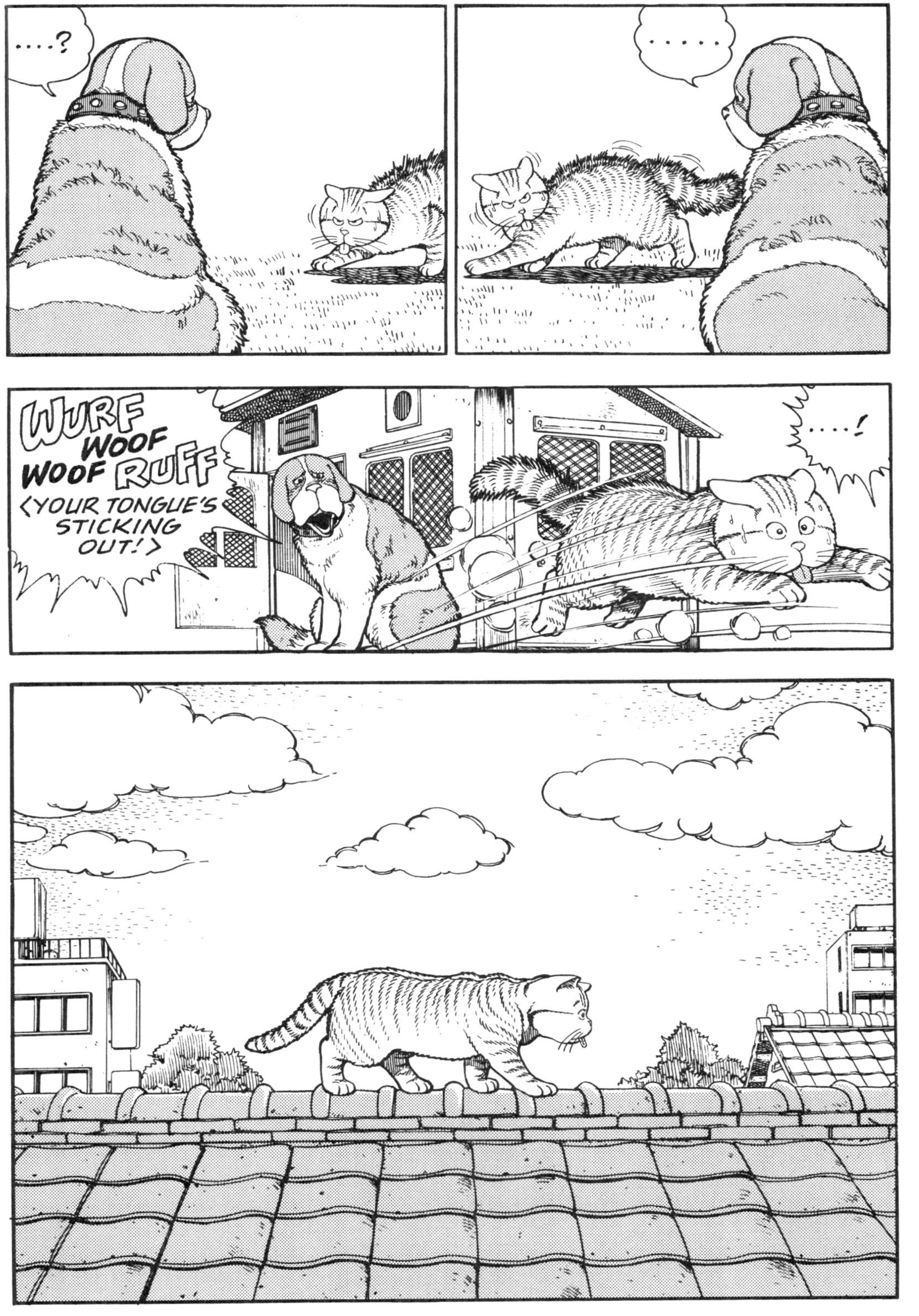

....?
......
WURF WOOF WOOF RUFF
<YOUR TONGUE'S STICKING OUT!>
....!

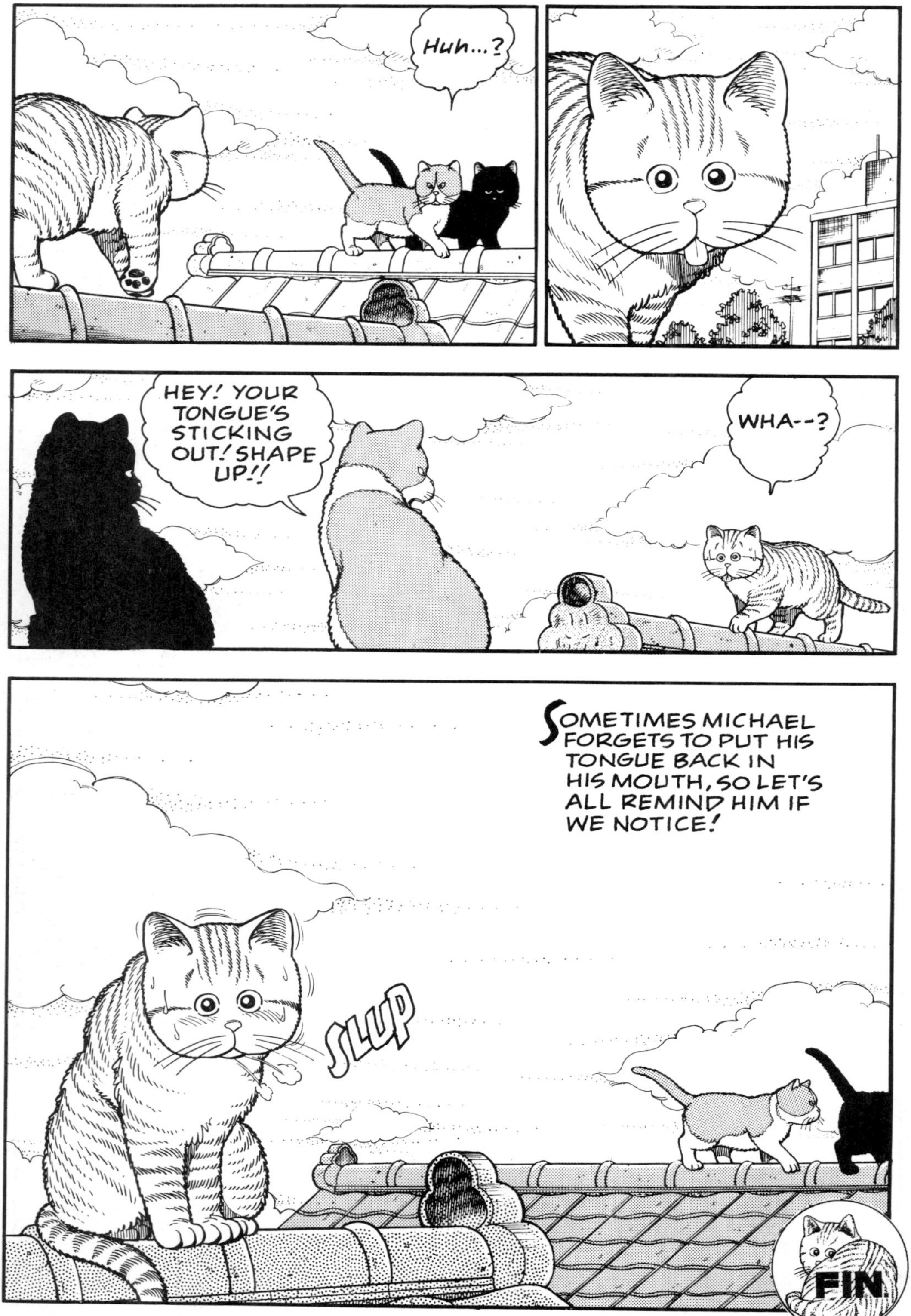
Huh...?
HEY! YOUR TONGUE'S STICKING OUT! SHAPE UP!!
WHA--?
SOMETIMES MICHAEL FORGETS TO PUT HIS TONGUE BACK IN HIS MOUTH, SO LET'S ALL REMIND HIM IF WE NOTICE!
SLUP
FIN.

the CAT BURGLAR

starring
Detective YAMAMURA

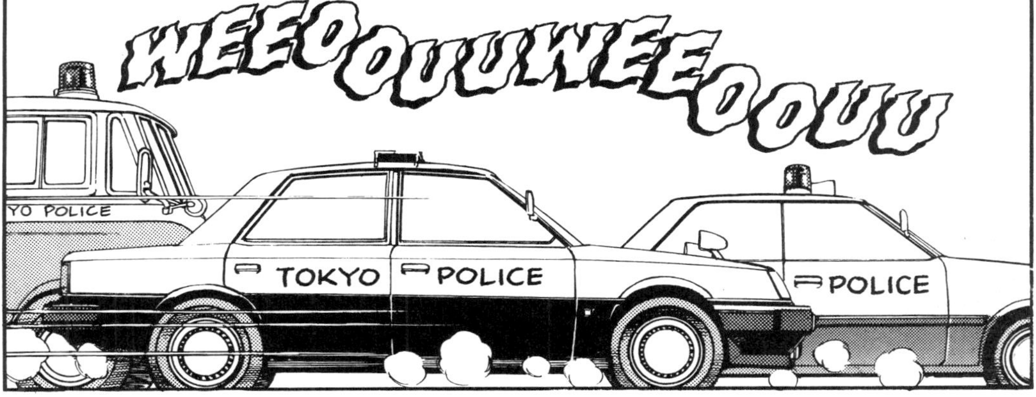
WEEOOUUWEEOOUU
YO POLICE
TOKYO POLICE
POLICE

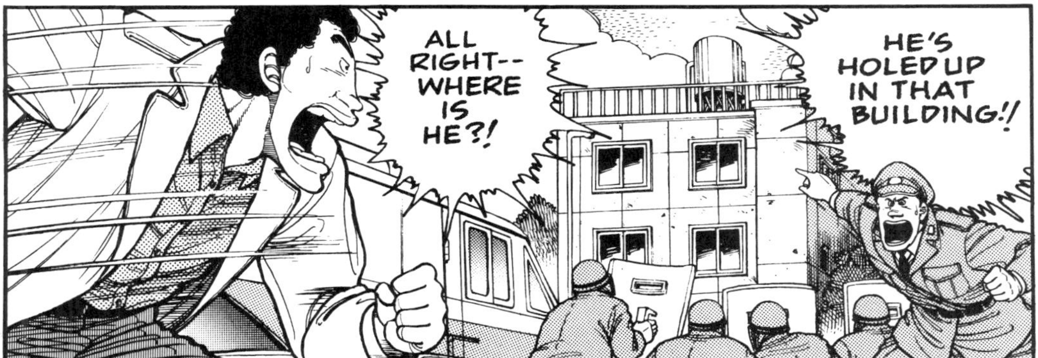
ALL RIGHT-- WHERE IS HE?!
HE'S HOLED UP IN THAT BUILDING!!

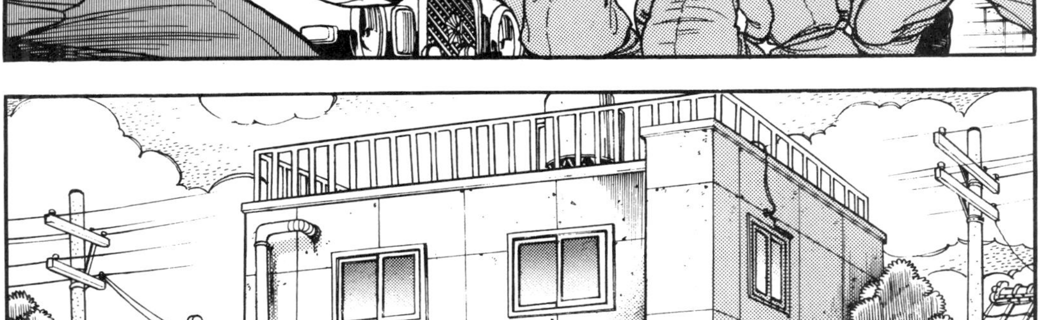

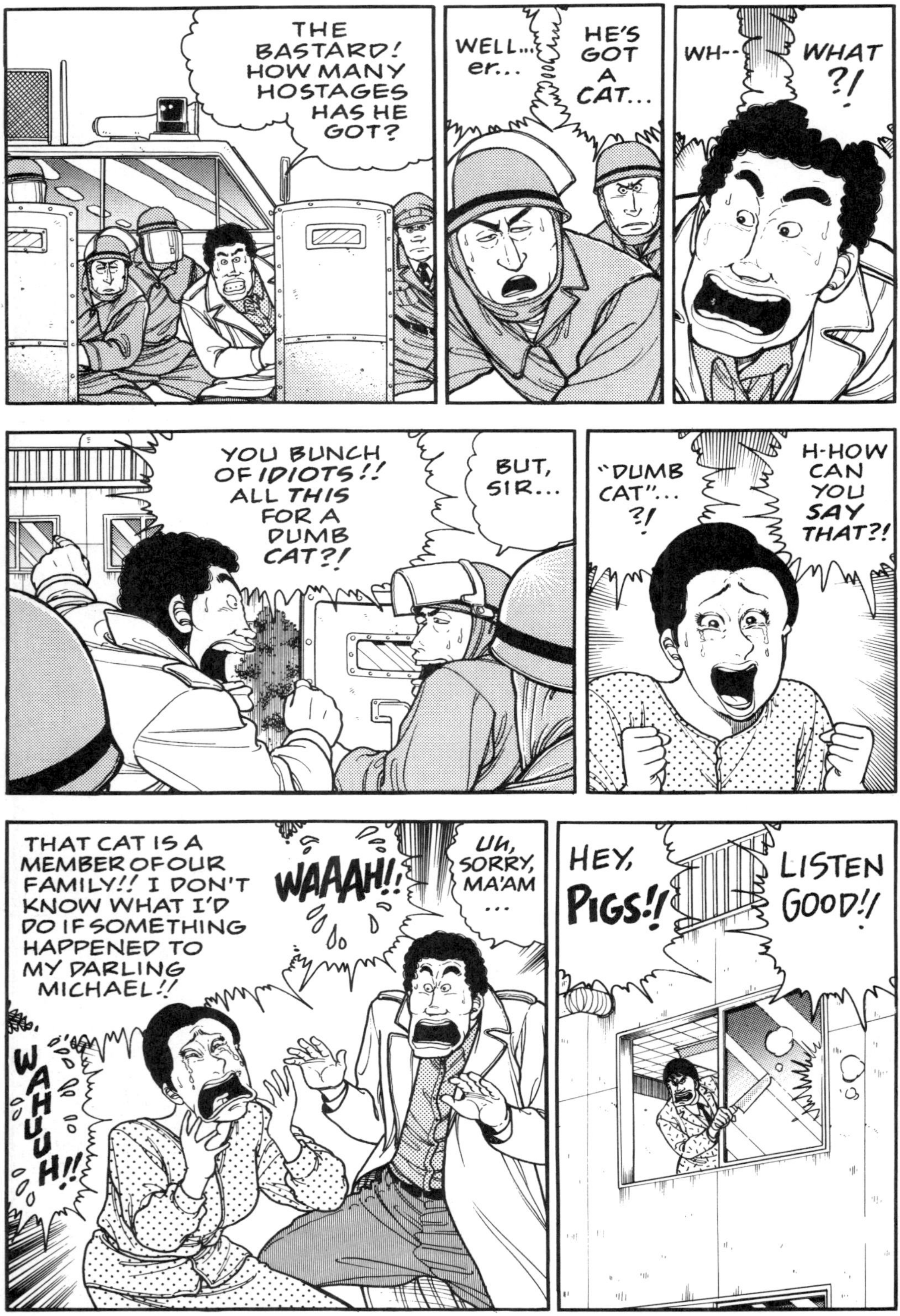
THE BASTARD! HOW MANY HOSTAGES HAS HE GOT?
WELL... er...
HE'S GOT A CAT...
WH--
WHAT ?!
YOU BUNCH OF IDIOTS!! ALL THIS FOR A DUMB CAT?!
BUT, SIR...
"DUMB CAT"... ?!
H-HOW CAN YOU SAY THAT?!
THAT CAT IS A MEMBER OF OUR FAMILY!! I DON'T KNOW WHAT I'D DO IF SOMETHING HAPPENED TO MY DARLING MICHAEL!!
WAAAH!!
UH, SORRY, MA'AM ...
WAHUUH!!
HEY, PIGS!!
LISTEN GOOD!!

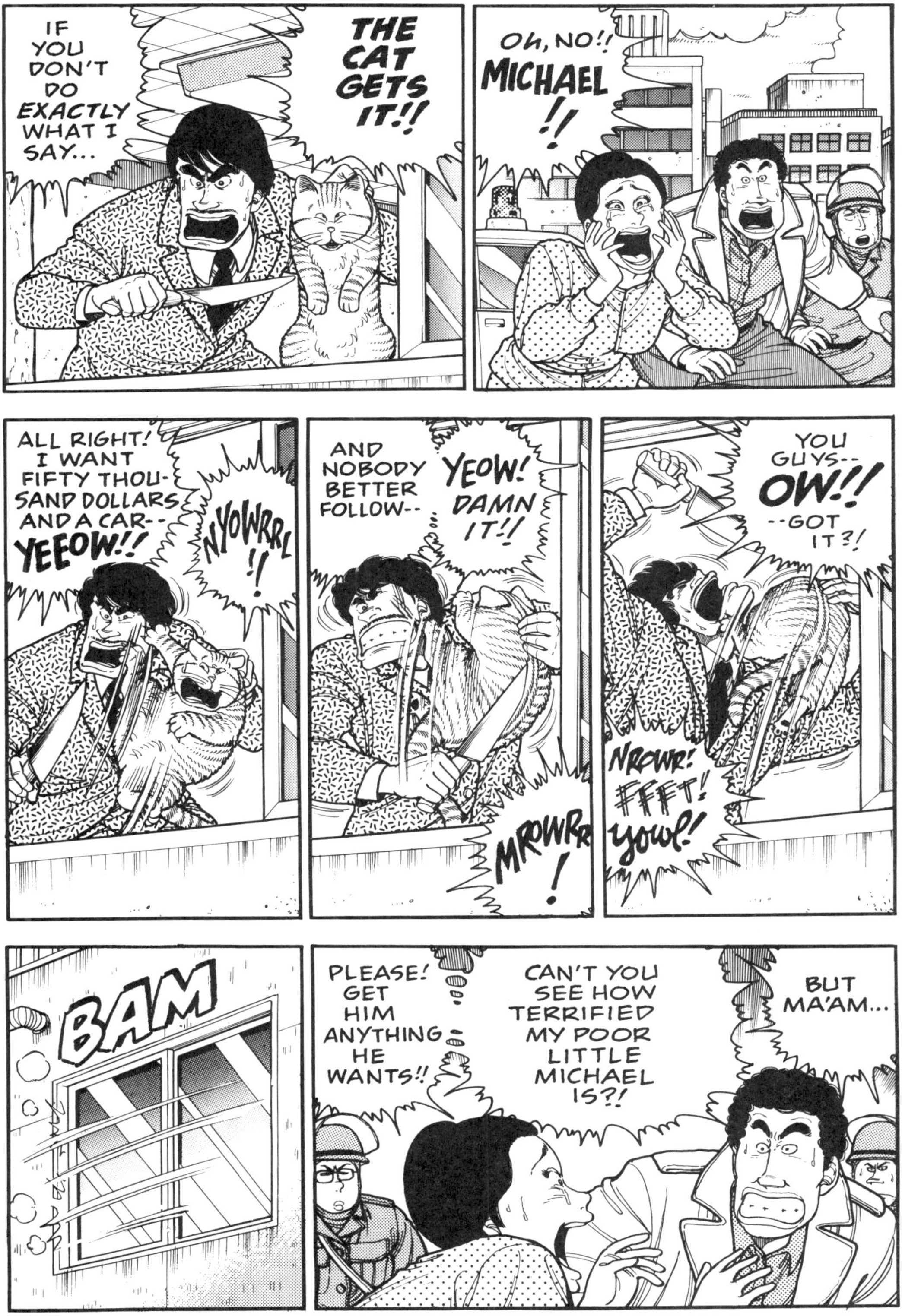
IF YOU DON'T DO EXACTLY WHAT I SAY...
THE CAT GETS IT!!
Oh, NO!! MICHAEL!!
ALL RIGHT! I WANT FIFTY THOUSAND DOLLARS AND A CAR-- YEEOW!!
NYOWRRL!!
AND NOBODY BETTER FOLLOW--
YEOW! DAMN IT!!
MROWRRR!
YOU GUYS-- OW!! --GOT IT?!
NROWR! FFFT! yowl!
BAM
PLEASE! GET HIM ANYTHING HE WANTS!!
CAN'T YOU SEE HOW TERRIFIED MY POOR LITTLE MICHAEL IS?!
BUT MA'AM...

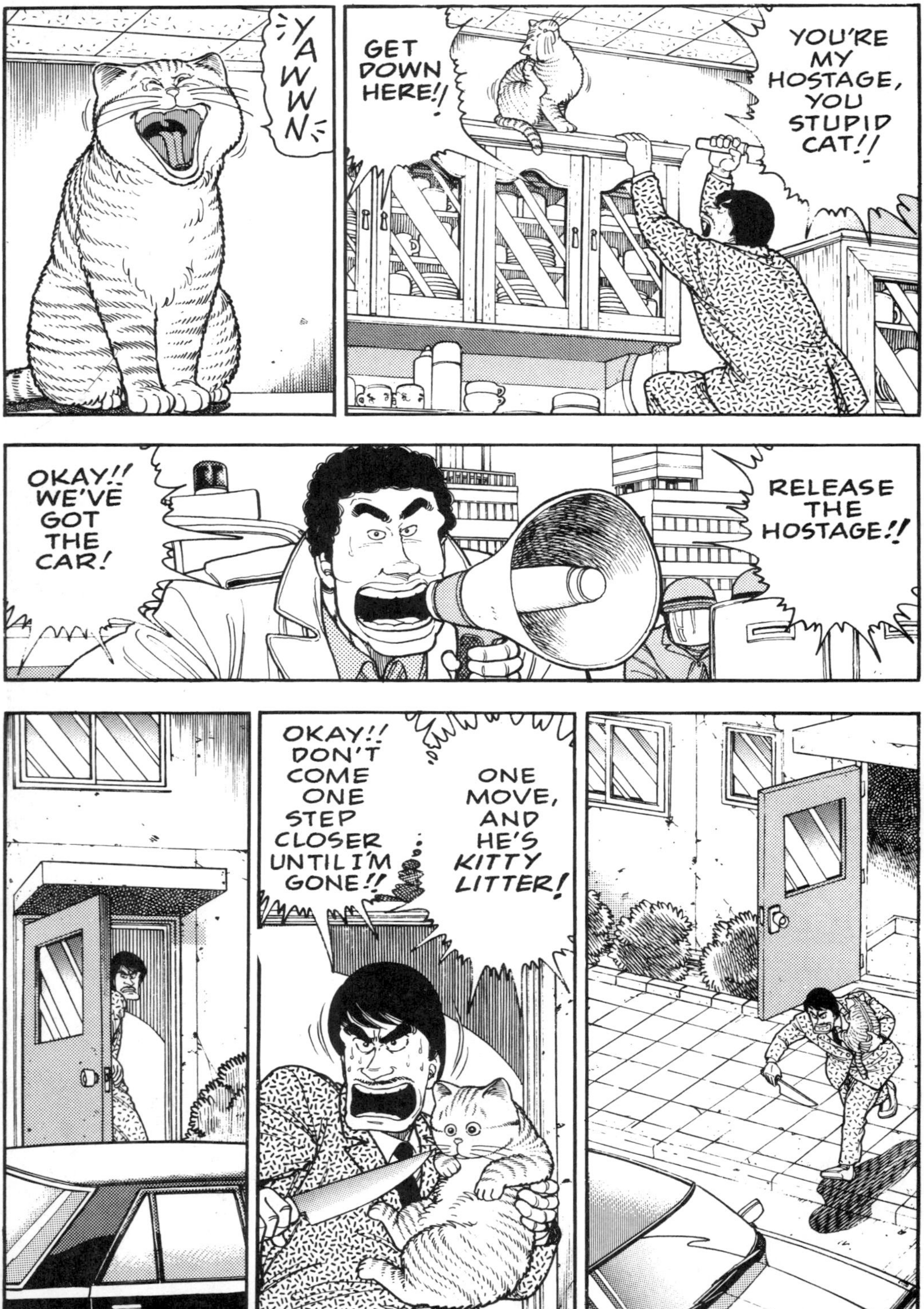
YAWWN
GET DOWN HERE!!
YOU'RE MY HOSTAGE, YOU STUPID CAT!!
OKAY!! WE'VE GOT THE CAR!
RELEASE THE HOSTAGE!!
OKAY!! DON'T COME ONE STEP CLOSER UNTIL I'M GONE!!
ONE MOVE, AND HE'S *KITTY LITTER!*

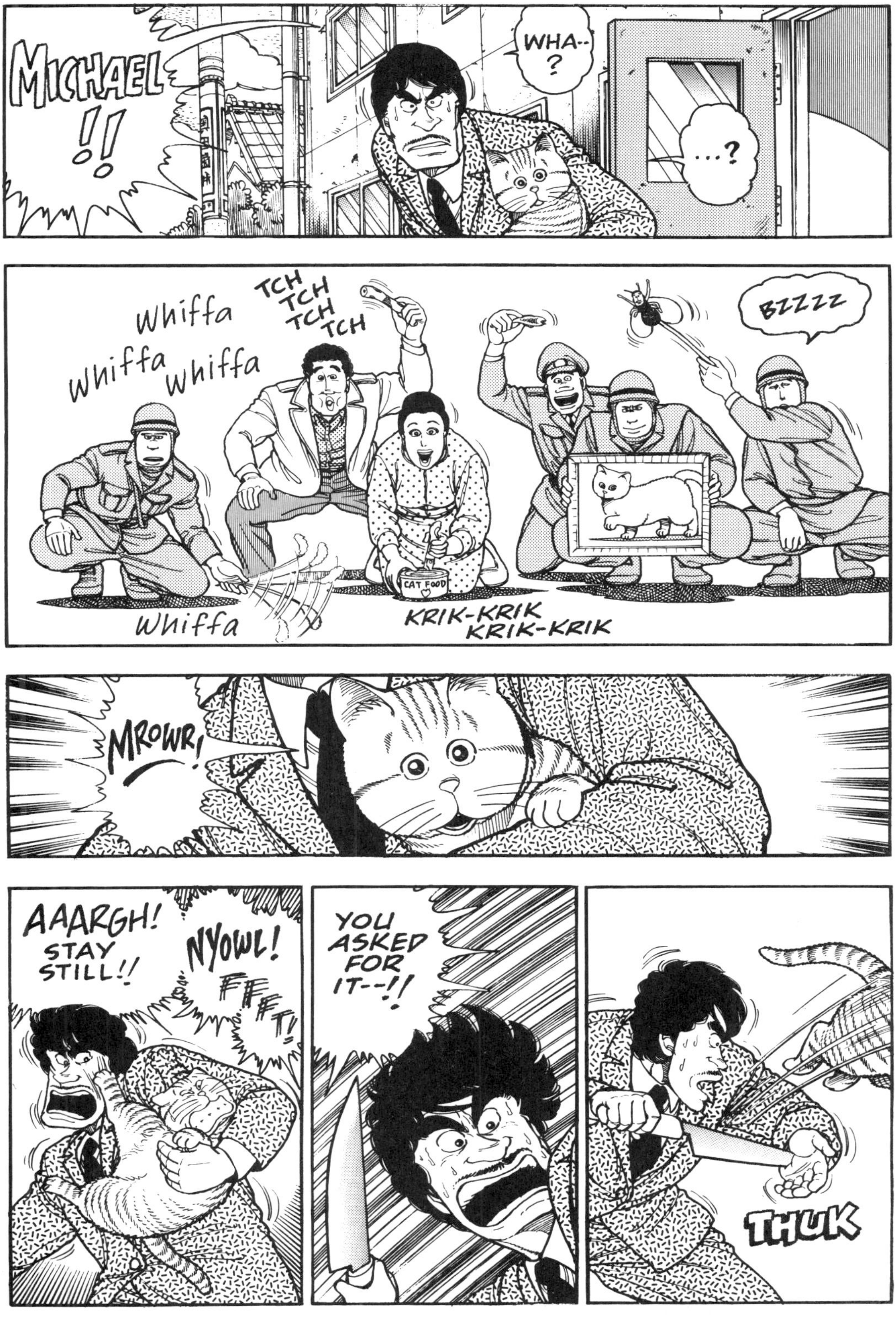
MICHAEL!!
WHA--?
...?
Whiffa whiffa whiffa
TCH TCH TCH TCH
BZZZZ
Whiffa
CAT FOOD
KRIK-KRIK KRIK-KRIK
MROWR!
AAARGH! STAY STILL!!
NYOWL!
FFFFT!!
YOU ASKED FOR IT--!!
THUK

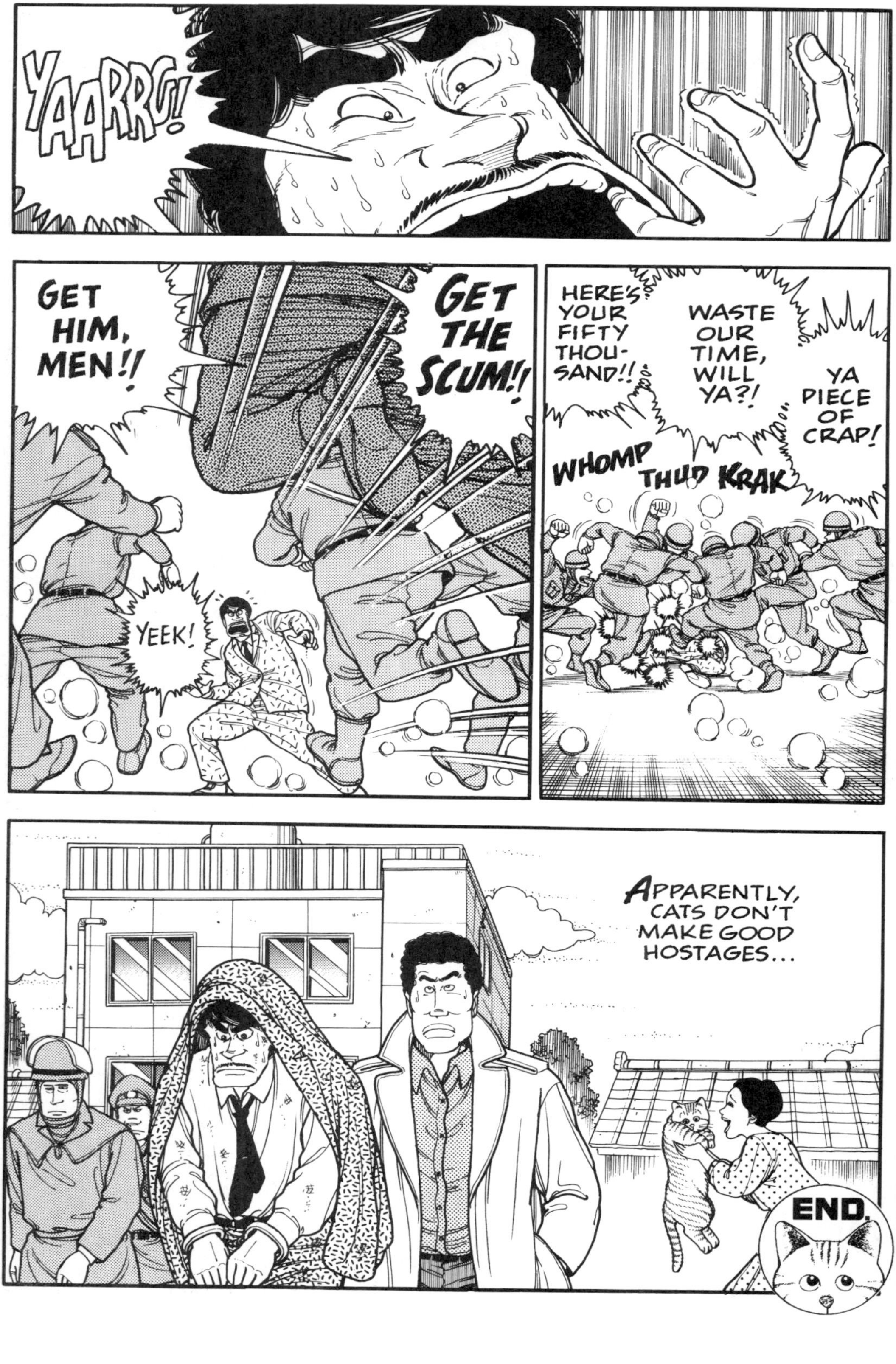
YAARRG!
GET HIM, MEN!!
GET THE SCUM!!
YEEK!
HERE'S YOUR FIFTY THOUSAND!!
WASTE OUR TIME, WILL YA?!
YA PIECE OF CRAP!
WHOMP
THUD
KRAK
APPARENTLY, CATS DON'T MAKE GOOD HOSTAGES...
END.

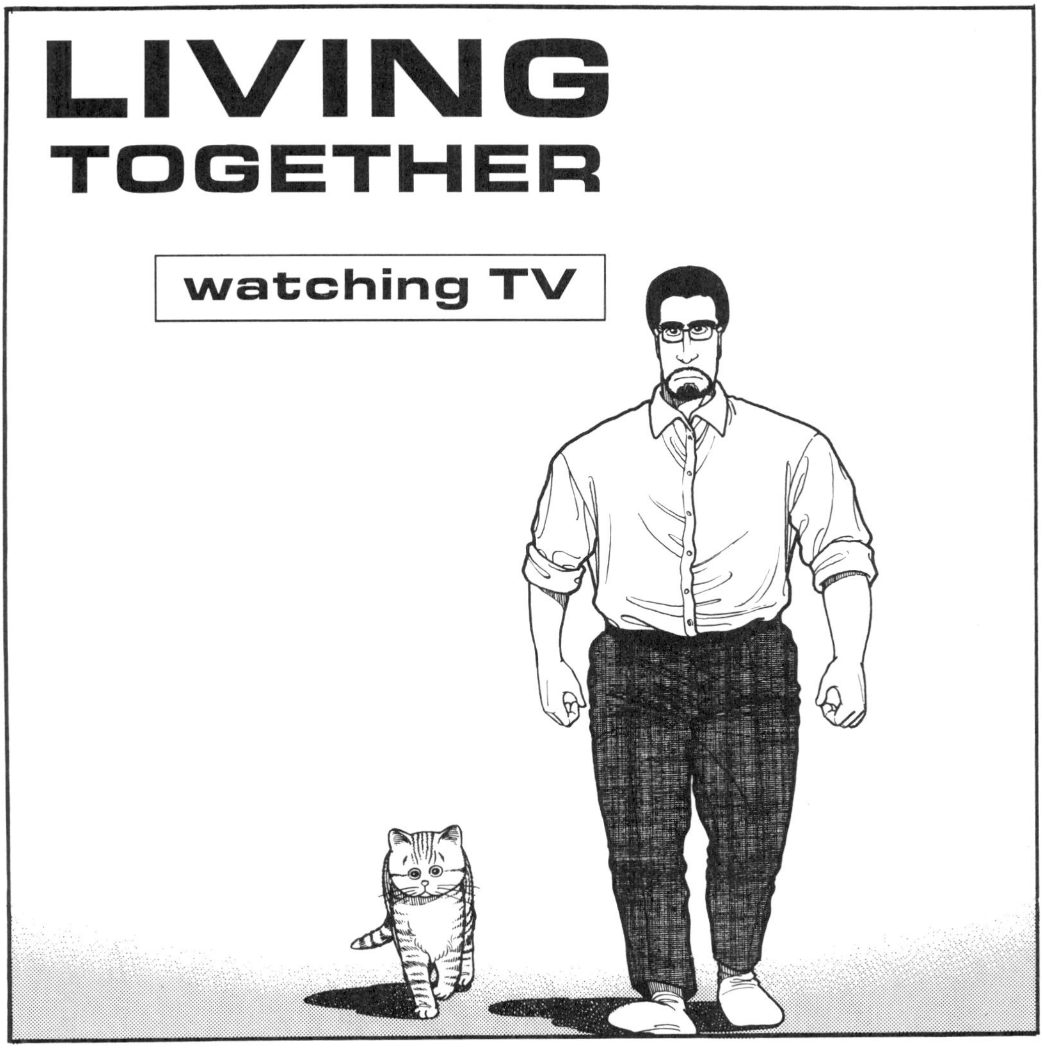
LIVING
TOGETHER
watching TV

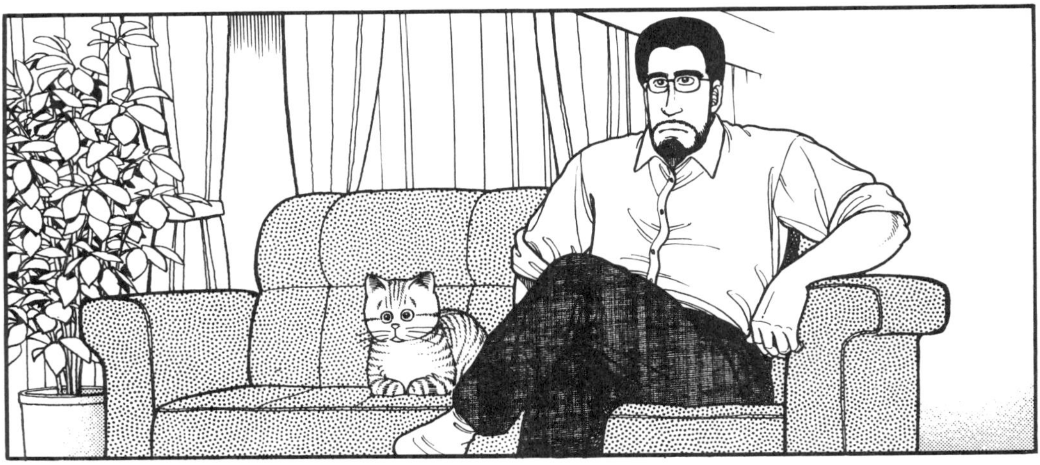

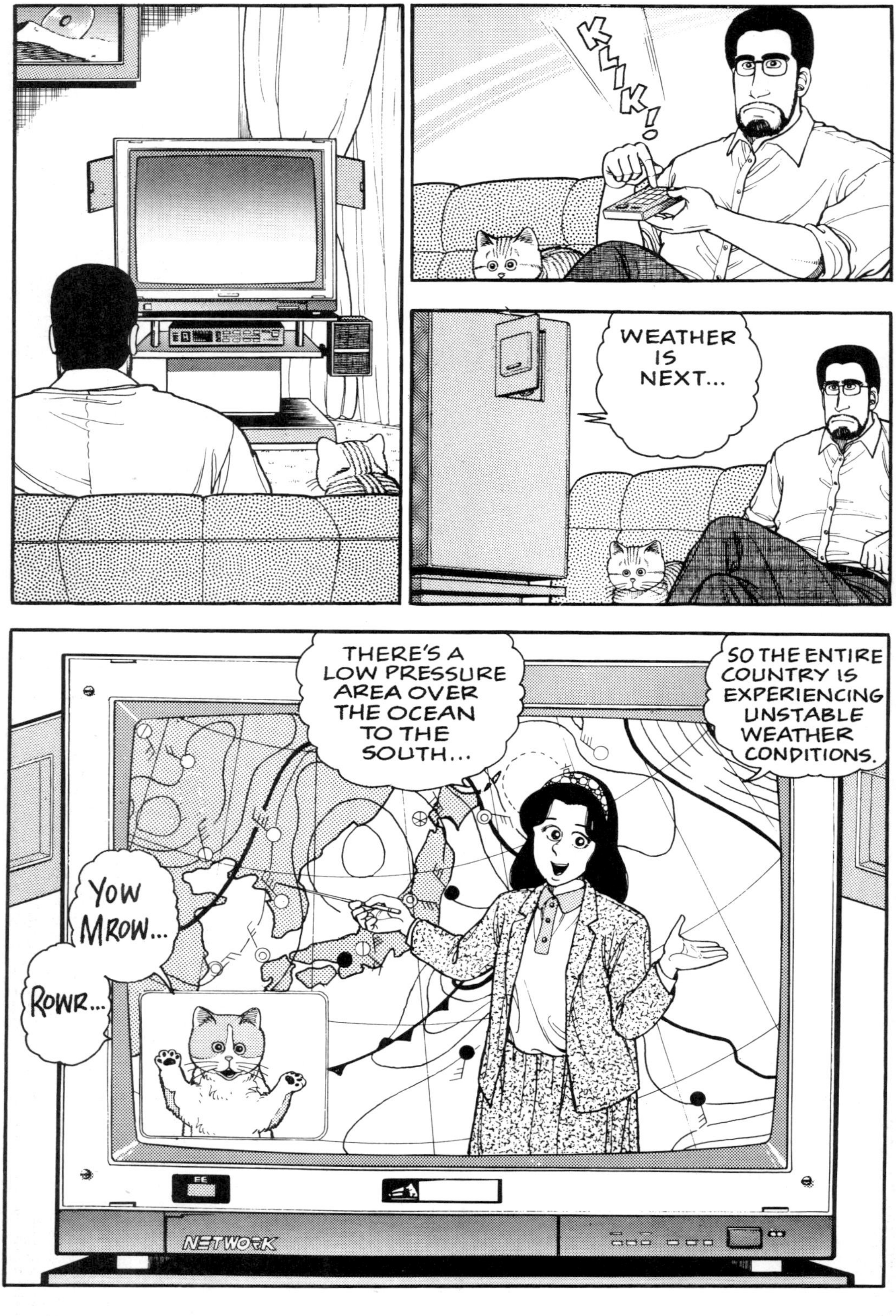
KLIK!
WEATHER IS NEXT...
THERE'S A LOW PRESSURE AREA OVER THE OCEAN TO THE SOUTH...
SO THE ENTIRE COUNTRY IS EXPERIENCING UNSTABLE WEATHER CONDITIONS.
YOW MROW...
ROWR...
NETWORK

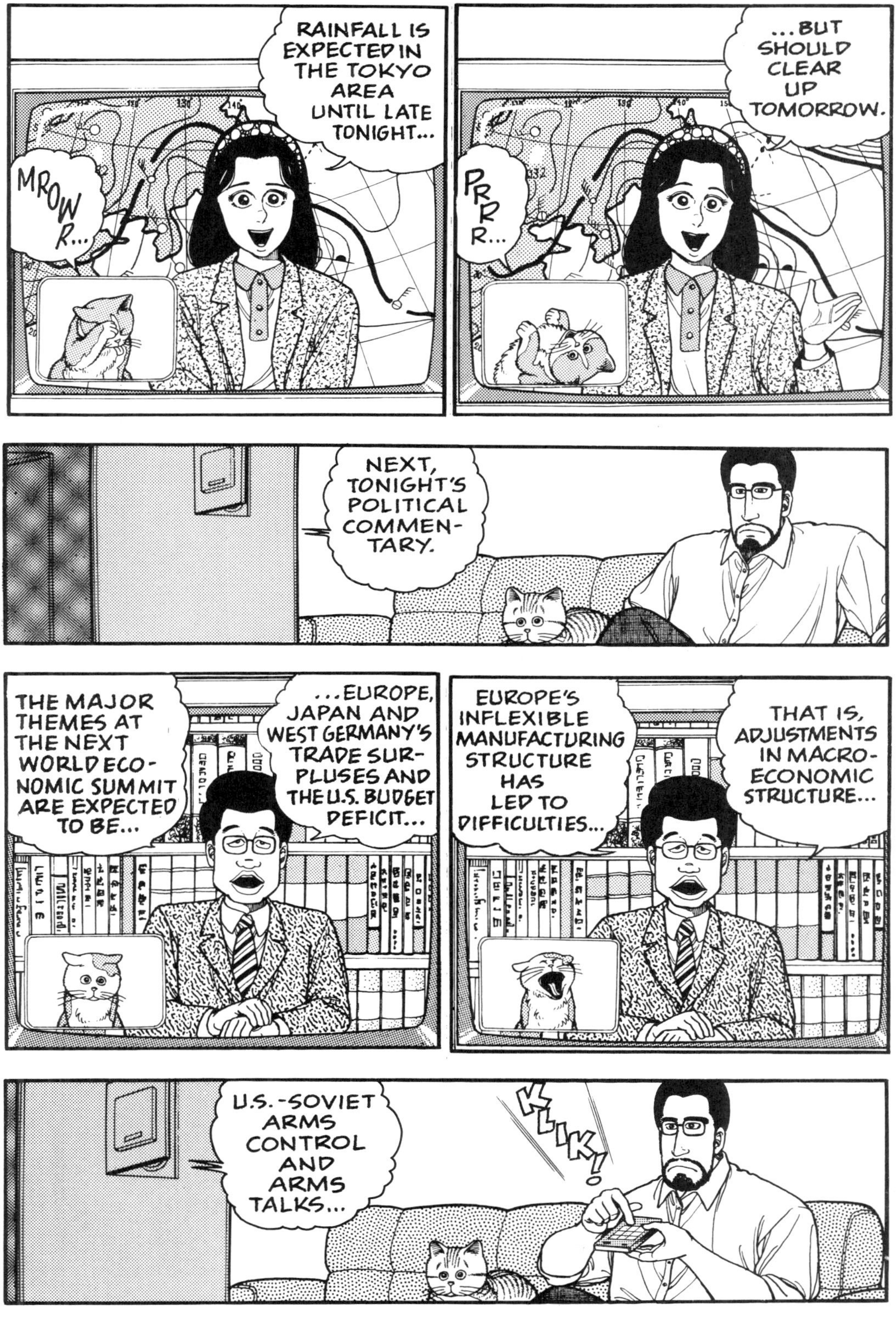
RAINFALL IS EXPECTED IN THE TOKYO AREA UNTIL LATE TONIGHT...
MROWR...
...BUT SHOULD CLEAR UP TOMORROW.
PRRR...
NEXT, TONIGHT'S POLITICAL COMMENTARY.
THE MAJOR THEMES AT THE NEXT WORLD ECONOMIC SUMMIT ARE EXPECTED TO BE...
...EUROPE, JAPAN AND WEST GERMANY'S TRADE SURPLUSES AND THE U.S. BUDGET DEFICIT...
EUROPE'S INFLEXIBLE MANUFACTURING STRUCTURE HAS LED TO DIFFICULTIES...
THAT IS, ADJUSTMENTS IN MACROECONOMIC STRUCTURE...
U.S.-SOVIET ARMS CONTROL AND ARMS TALKS...
KLIK!

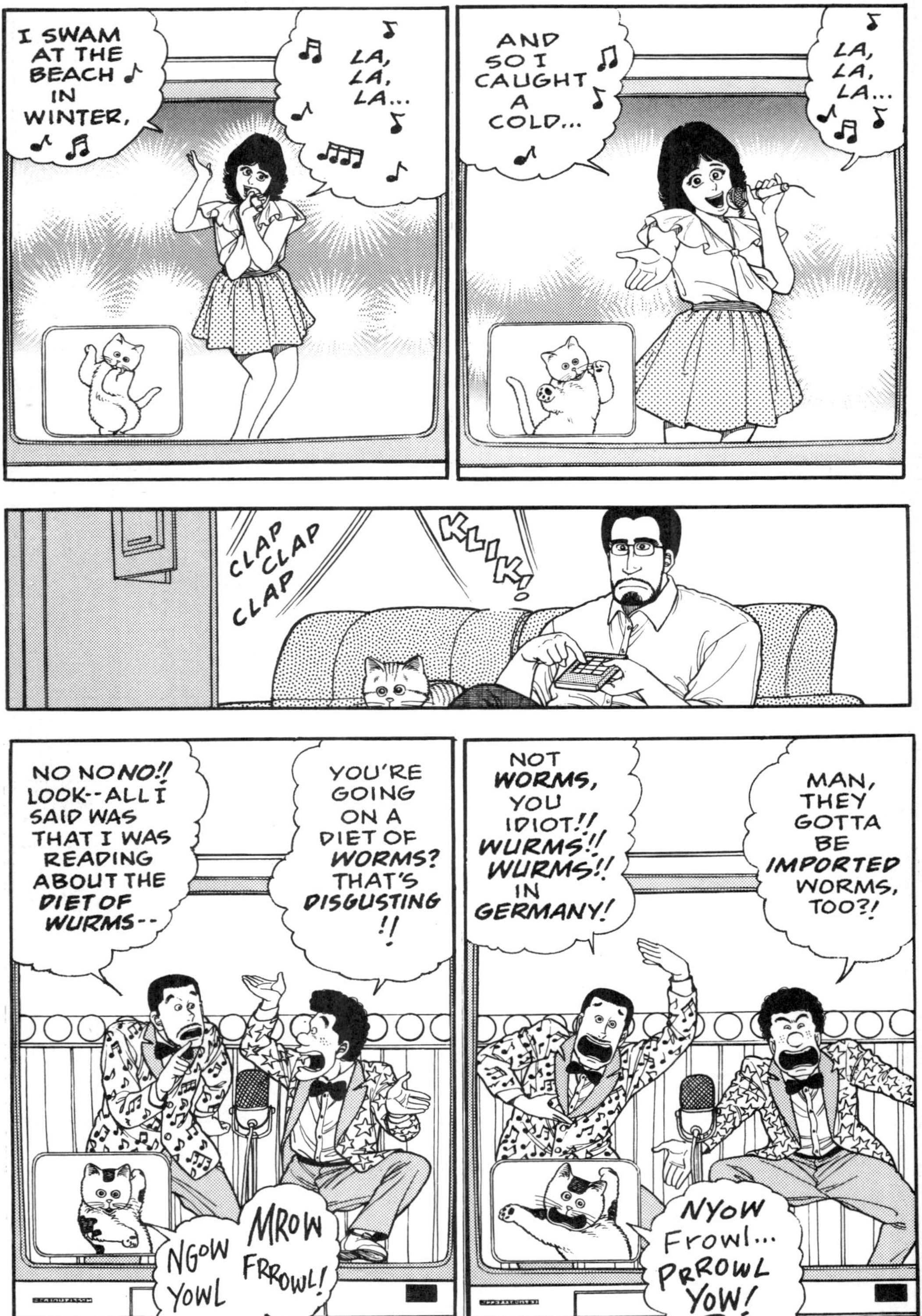
I SWAM AT THE BEACH IN WINTER,
LA, LA, LA...
AND SO I CAUGHT A COLD...
LA, LA, LA...
CLAP CLAP CLAP
KLIK!
NO NO NO!! LOOK--ALL I SAID WAS THAT I WAS READING ABOUT THE DIET OF WURMS--
YOU'RE GOING ON A DIET OF WORMS? THAT'S DISGUSTING!!
NGOW YOWL
MROW FRROWL!
NOT WORMS, YOU IDIOT!! WURMS!! WURMS!! IN GERMANY!
MAN, THEY GOTTA BE IMPORTED WORMS, TOO?!
NYOW Frowl... PRROWL YOW!

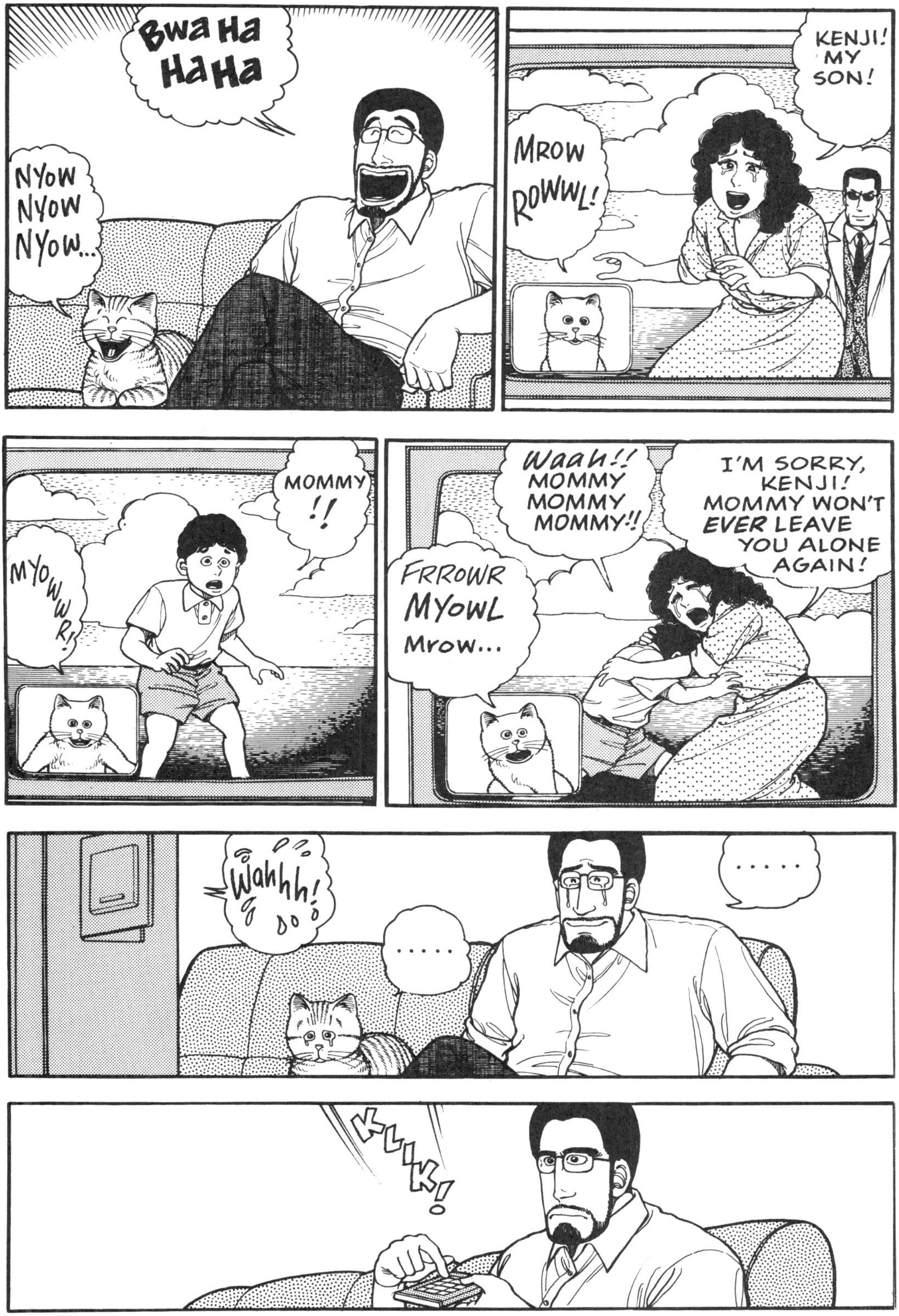
Bwa Ha Ha Ha
NYow NYow NYow...
KENJI! MY SON!
MROW ROWWL!
MOMMY !!
MYOWWR!
Waah!! MOMMY MOMMY MOMMY!!
I'M SORRY, KENJI! MOMMY WON'T EVER LEAVE YOU ALONE AGAIN!
FRROWR MYOWL Mrow...
Wahhh!
.....
.....
KLIK!

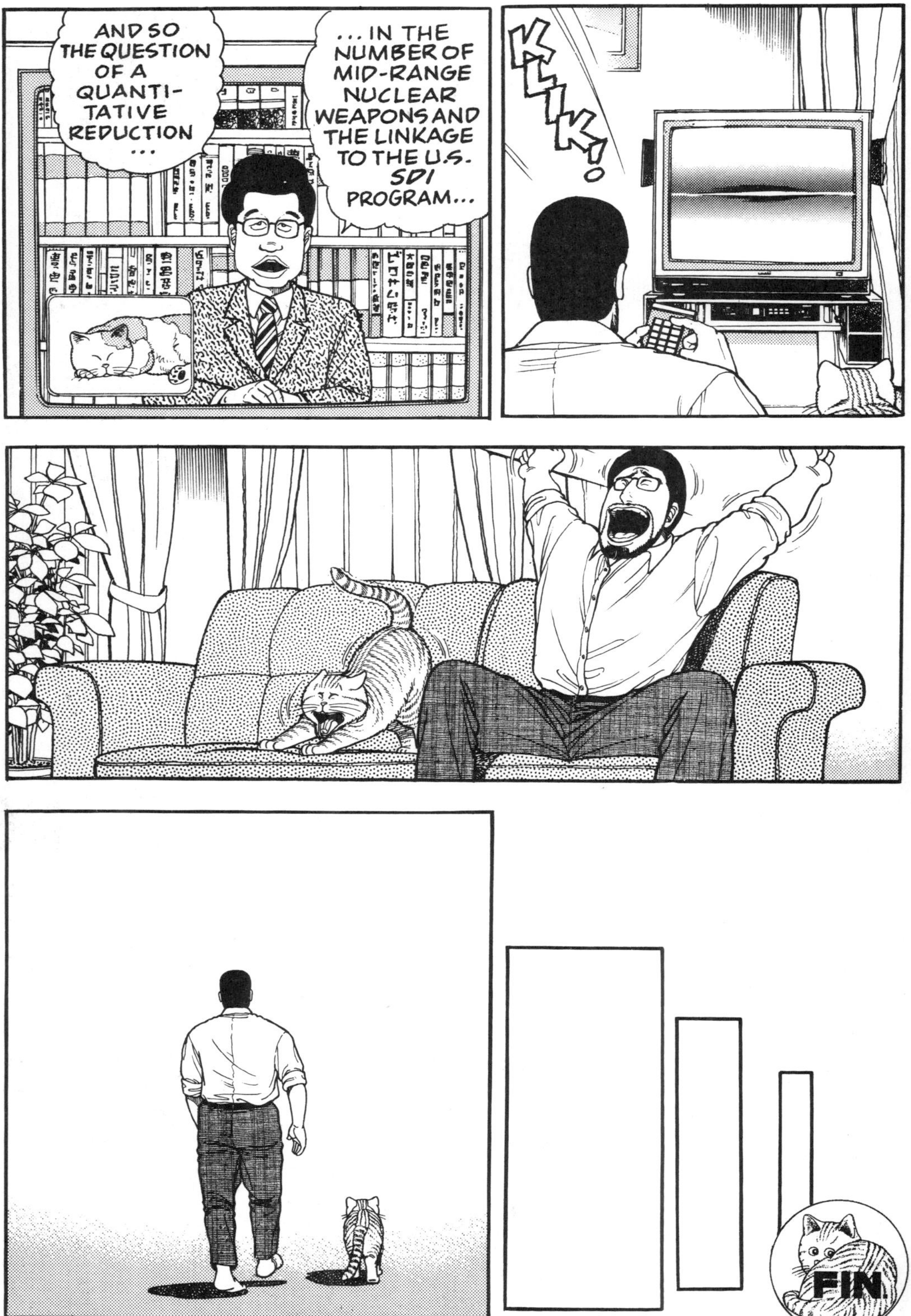
AND SO THE QUESTION OF A QUANTITATIVE REDUCTION ...
... IN THE NUMBER OF MID-RANGE NUCLEAR WEAPONS AND THE LINKAGE TO THE U.S. SDI PROGRAM...
KLIK!
FIN.

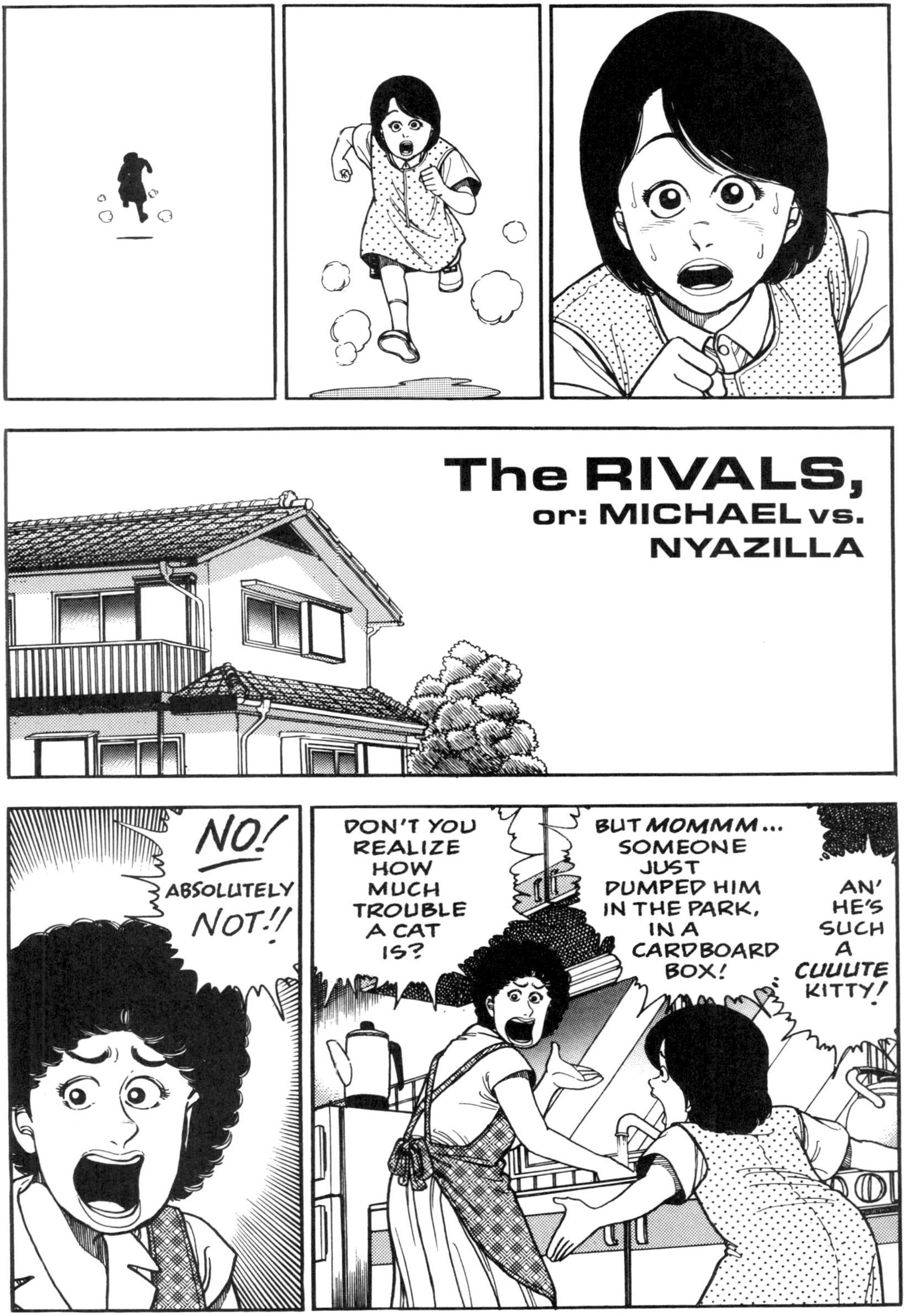
The RIVALS,
or: MICHAEL vs. NYAZILLA
NO! ABSOLUTELY NOT!!
DON'T YOU REALIZE HOW MUCH TROUBLE A CAT IS?
BUT MOMMM... SOMEONE JUST DUMPED HIM IN THE PARK, IN A CARDBOARD BOX!
AN' HE'S SUCH A CUUUTE KITTY!

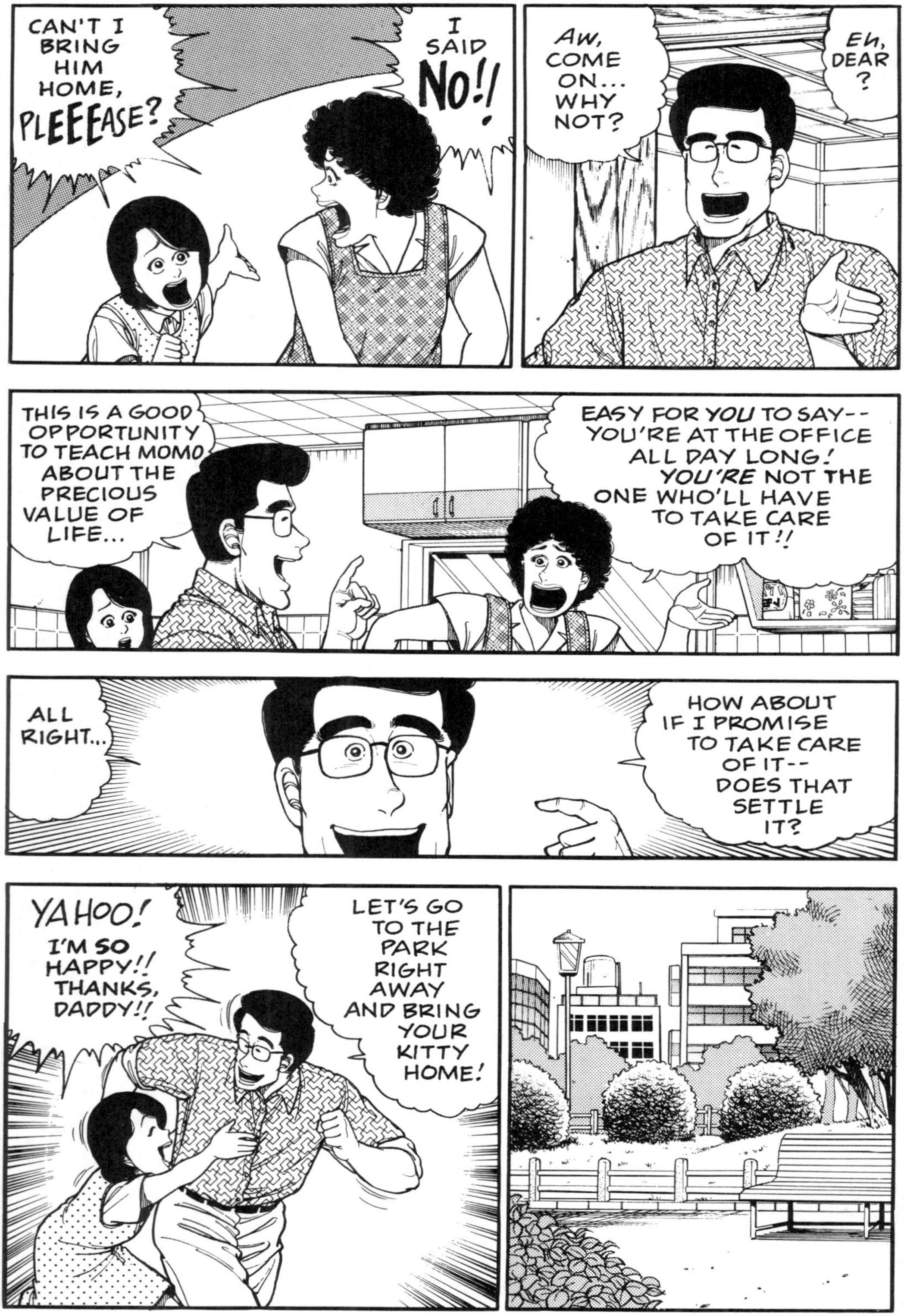
CAN'T I BRING HIM HOME, PLEEEASE?
I SAID NO!!
AW, COME ON... WHY NOT?
EH, DEAR?
THIS IS A GOOD OPPORTUNITY TO TEACH MOMO ABOUT THE PRECIOUS VALUE OF LIFE...
EASY FOR YOU TO SAY-- YOU'RE AT THE OFFICE ALL DAY LONG! YOU'RE NOT THE ONE WHO'LL HAVE TO TAKE CARE OF IT!!
ALL RIGHT...
HOW ABOUT IF I PROMISE TO TAKE CARE OF IT-- DOES THAT SETTLE IT?
YAHOO! I'M SO HAPPY!! THANKS, DADDY!!
LET'S GO TO THE PARK RIGHT AWAY AND BRING YOUR KITTY HOME!

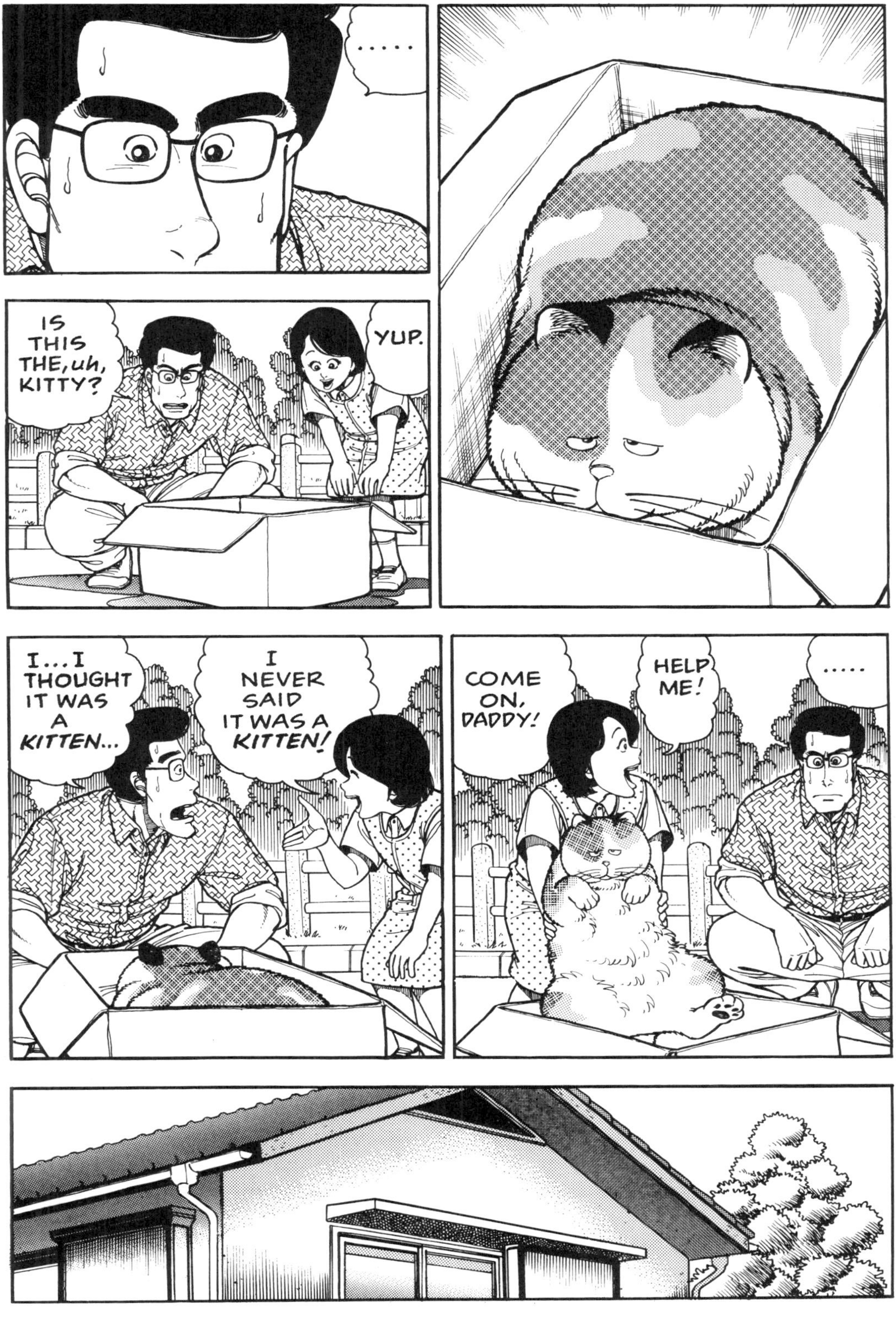
......
IS THIS THE, uh, KITTY?
YUP.
I... I THOUGHT IT WAS A KITTEN...
I NEVER SAID IT WAS A KITTEN!
COME ON, DADDY!
HELP ME!
.....

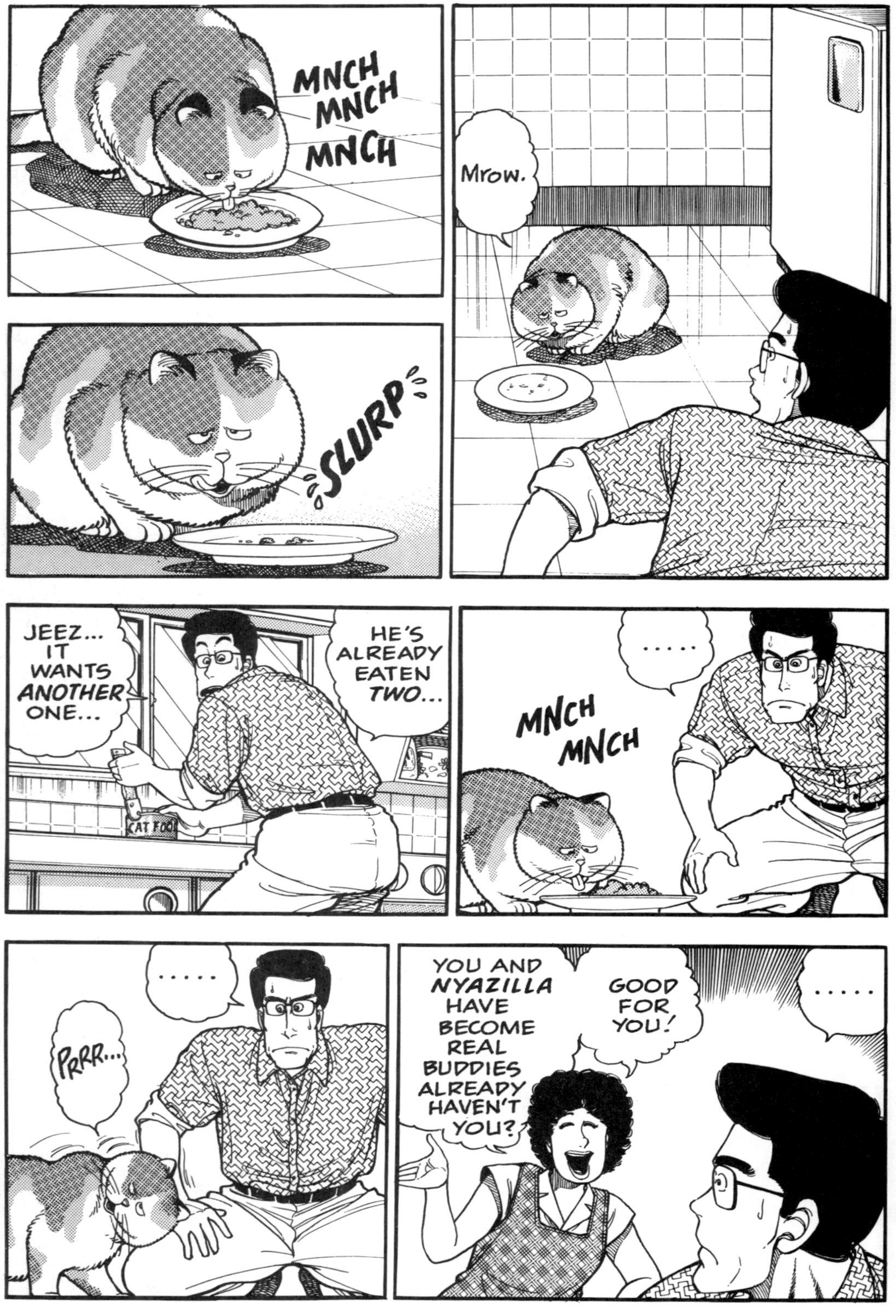
MNCH MNCH MNCH
Mrow.
SLURP
JEEZ... IT WANTS ANOTHER ONE...
HE'S ALREADY EATEN TWO...
CAT FOOD
.....
MNCH MNCH
.....
PRRR...
YOU AND NYAZILLA HAVE BECOME REAL BUDDIES ALREADY HAVEN'T YOU?
GOOD FOR YOU!
.....

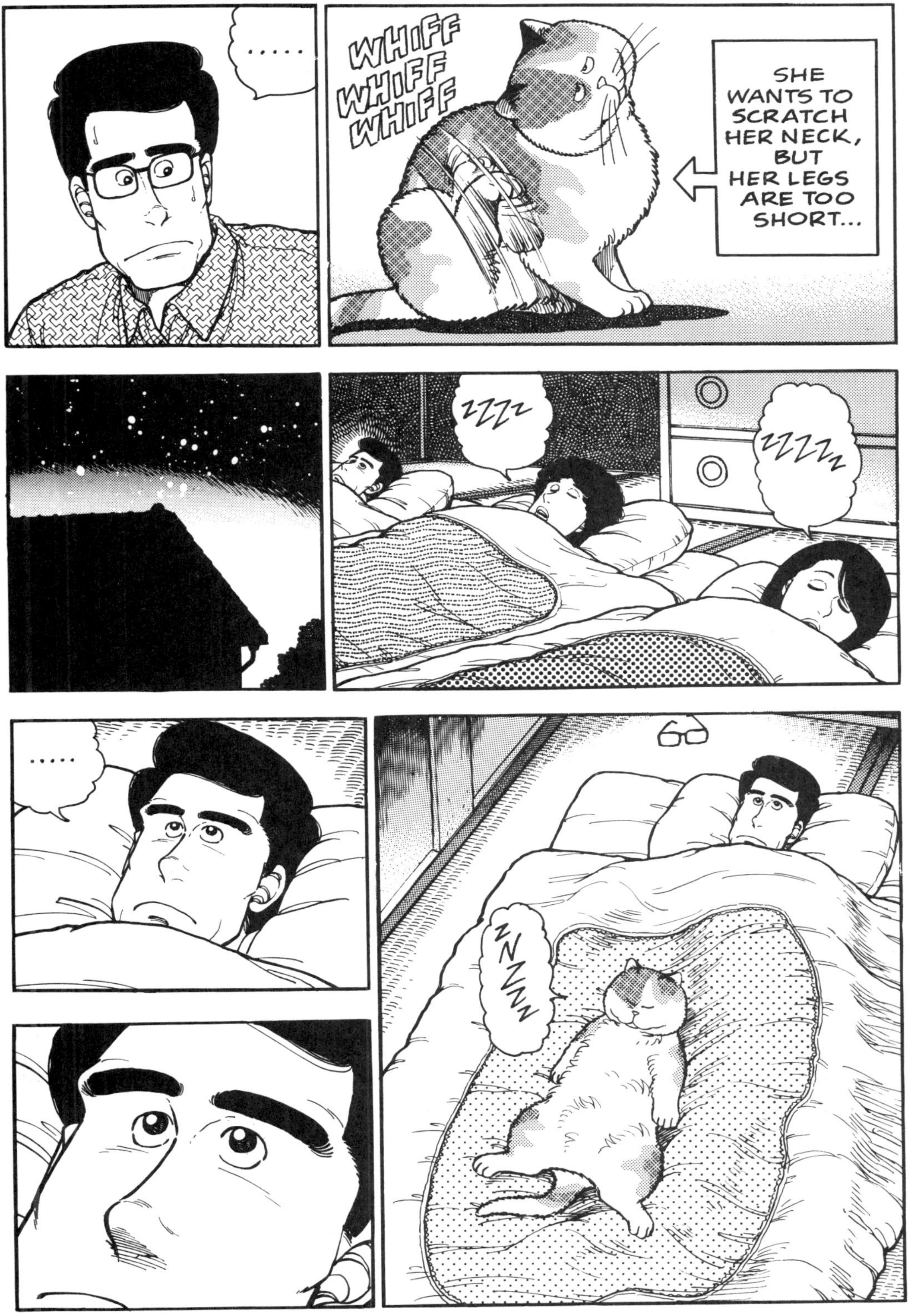
......
WHIFF WHIFF WHIFF
SHE WANTS TO SCRATCH HER NECK, BUT HER LEGS ARE TOO SHORT...
ZZZz
ZZZZz
......
ZZZZZ

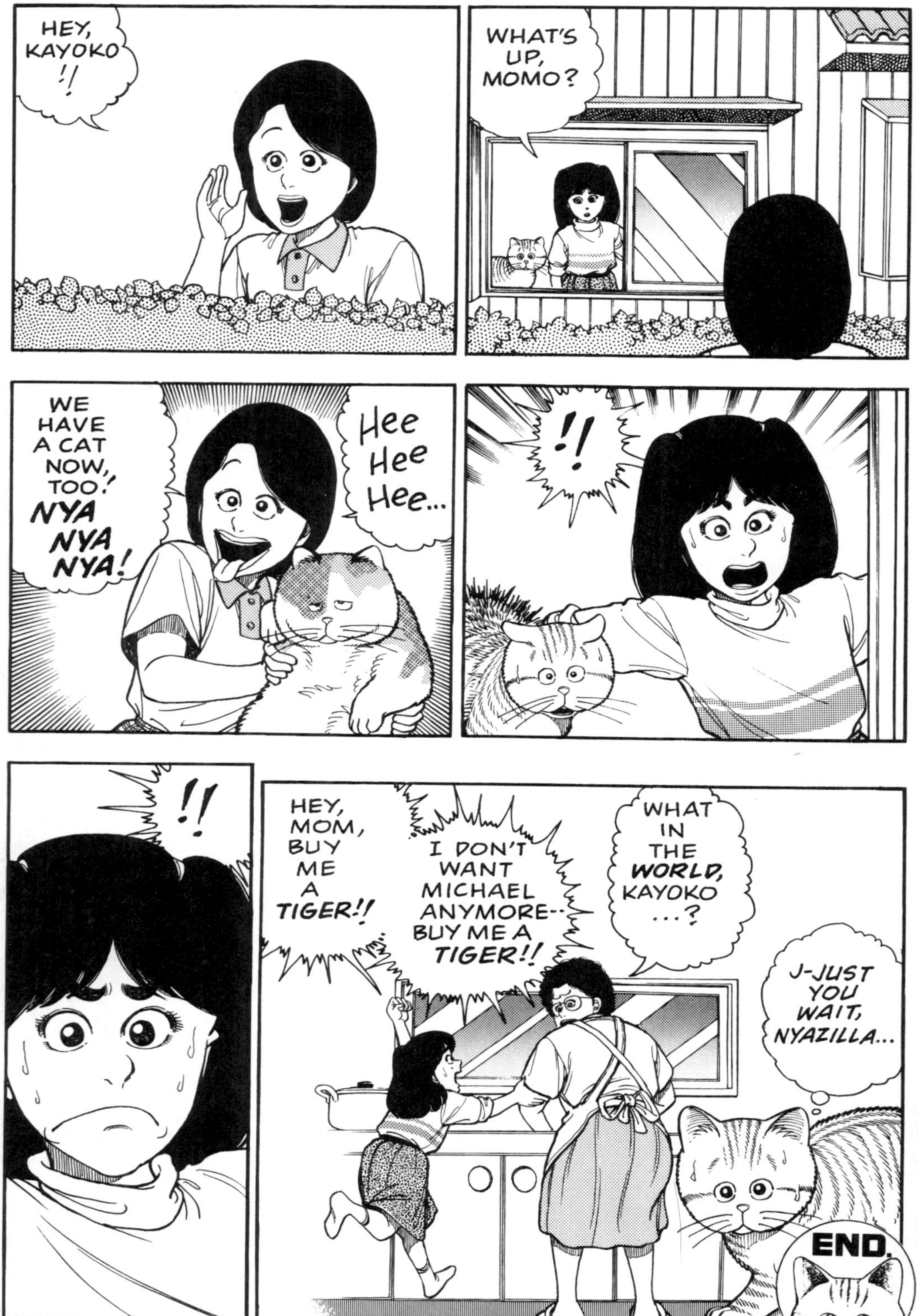

HEY, KAYOKO!!
WHAT'S UP, MOMO?
WE HAVE A CAT NOW, TOO! NYA NYA NYA!
Hee Hee Hee...
!!
!!
HEY, MOM, BUY ME A TIGER!!
I DON'T WANT MICHAEL ANYMORE-- BUY ME A TIGER!!
WHAT IN THE WORLD, KAYOKO...?
J-JUST YOU WAIT, NYAZILLA...
END.

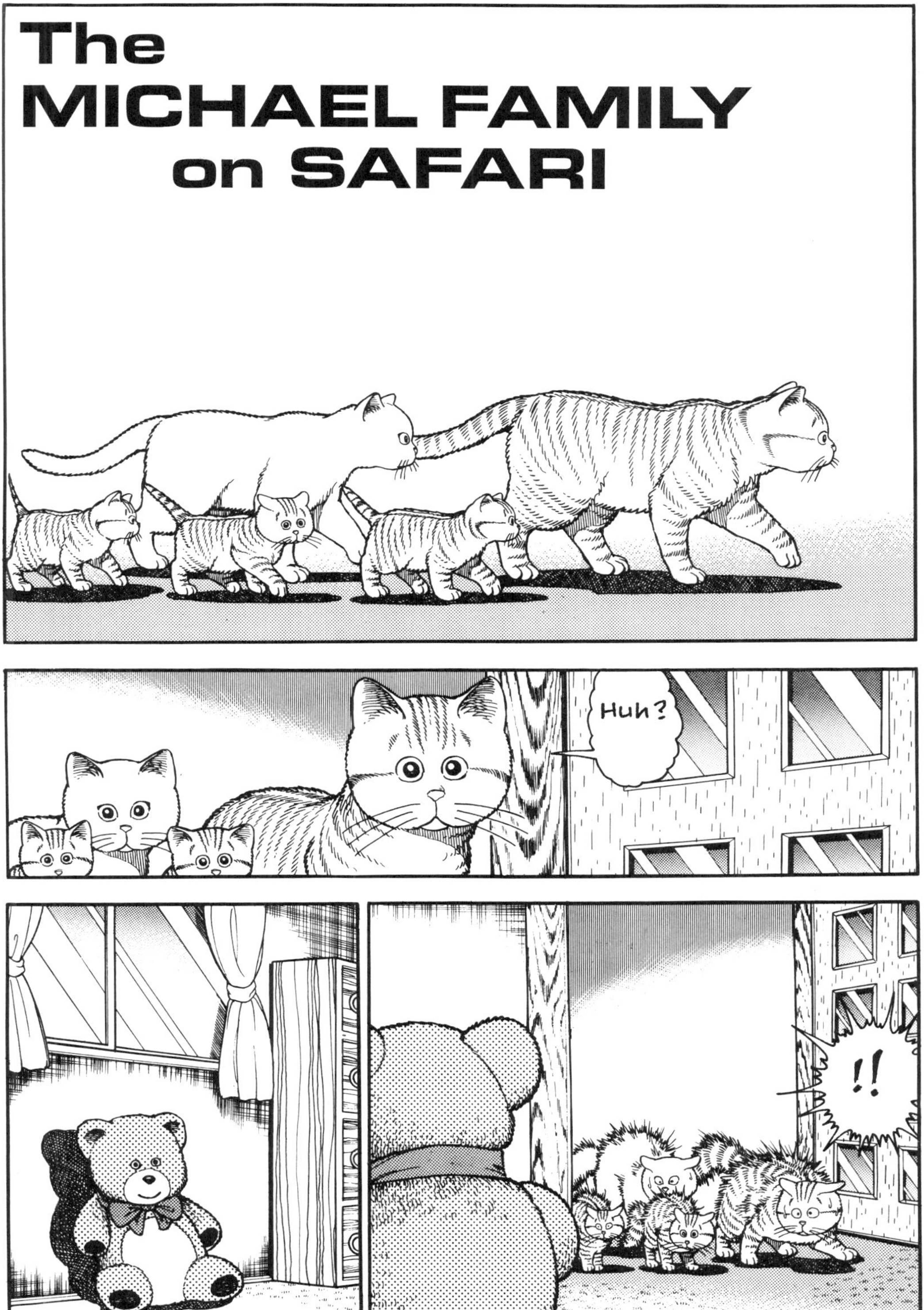
The MICHAEL FAMILY on SAFARI
Huh?
!!

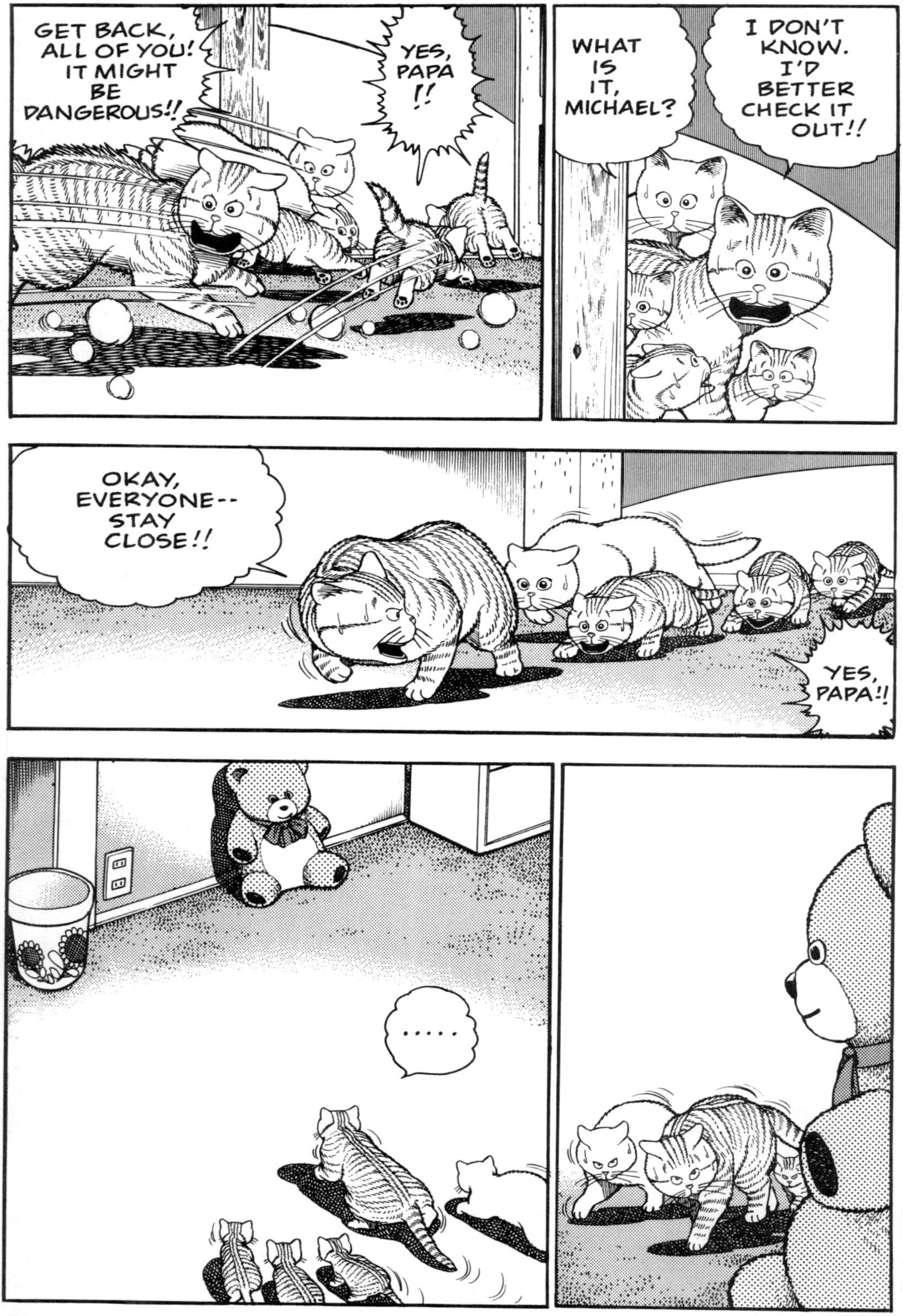
GET BACK, ALL OF YOU! IT MIGHT BE DANGEROUS!!
YES, PAPA!!
WHAT IS IT, MICHAEL?
I DON'T KNOW. I'D BETTER CHECK IT OUT!!
OKAY, EVERYONE-- STAY CLOSE!!
YES, PAPA!!
.....

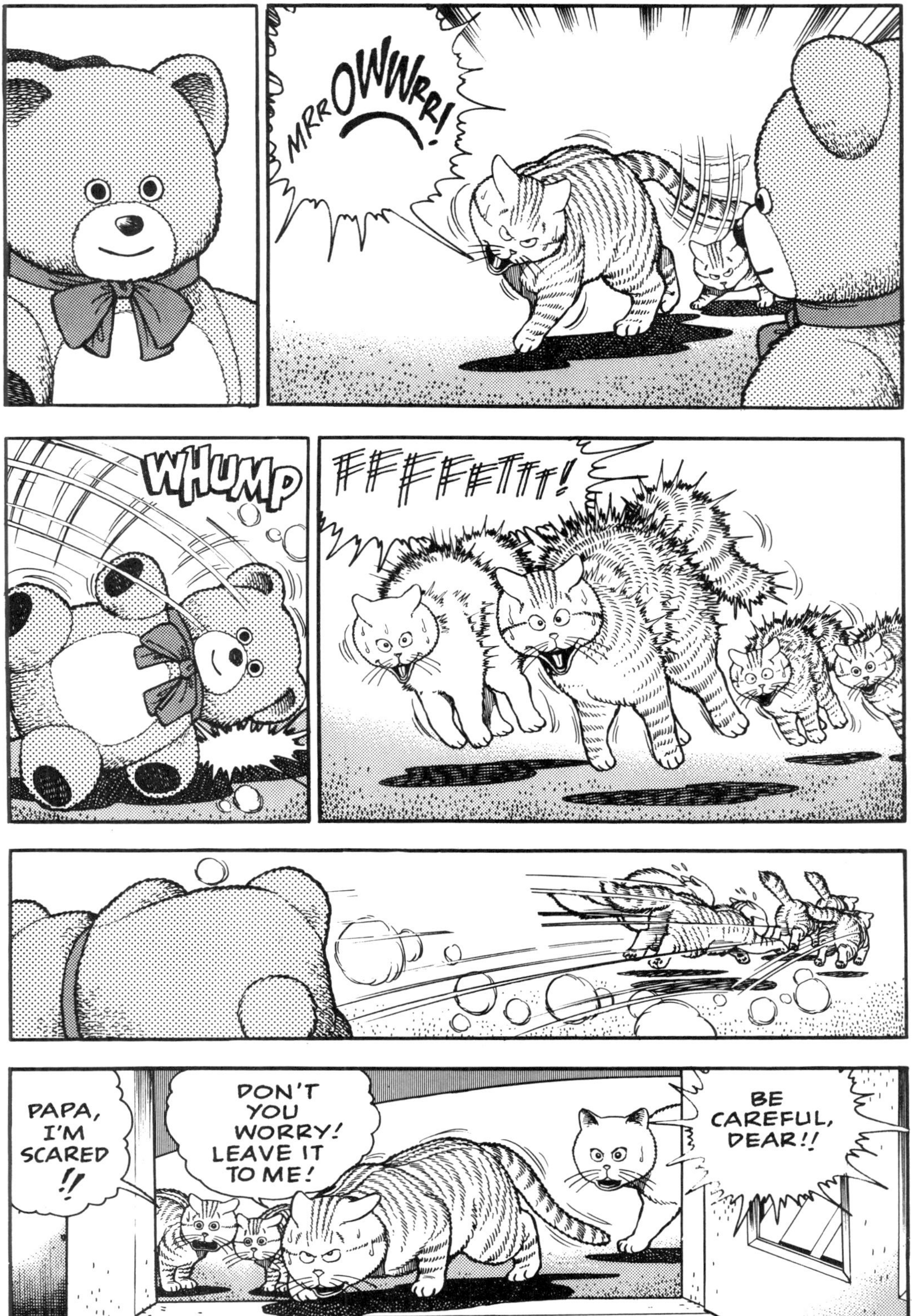
MRROWWRR!
WHUMP
FFFFFTTTT!
PAPA, I'M SCARED !!
DON'T YOU WORRY! LEAVE IT TO ME!
BE CAREFUL, DEAR!!

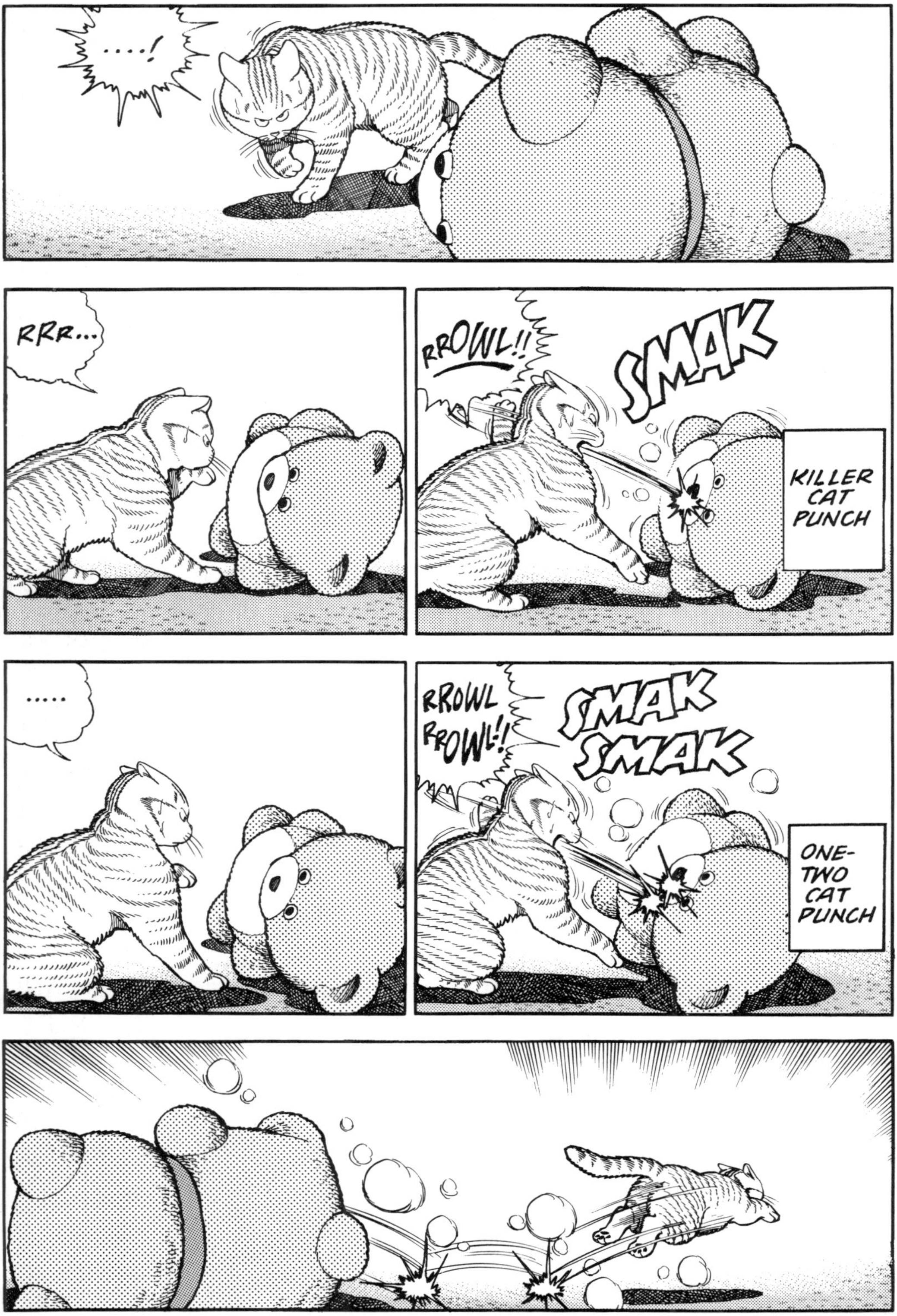
....!
RRR...
RROWL!!
SMAK
KILLER CAT PUNCH
.....
RROWL RROWL!!
SMAK SMAK
ONE-TWO CAT PUNCH

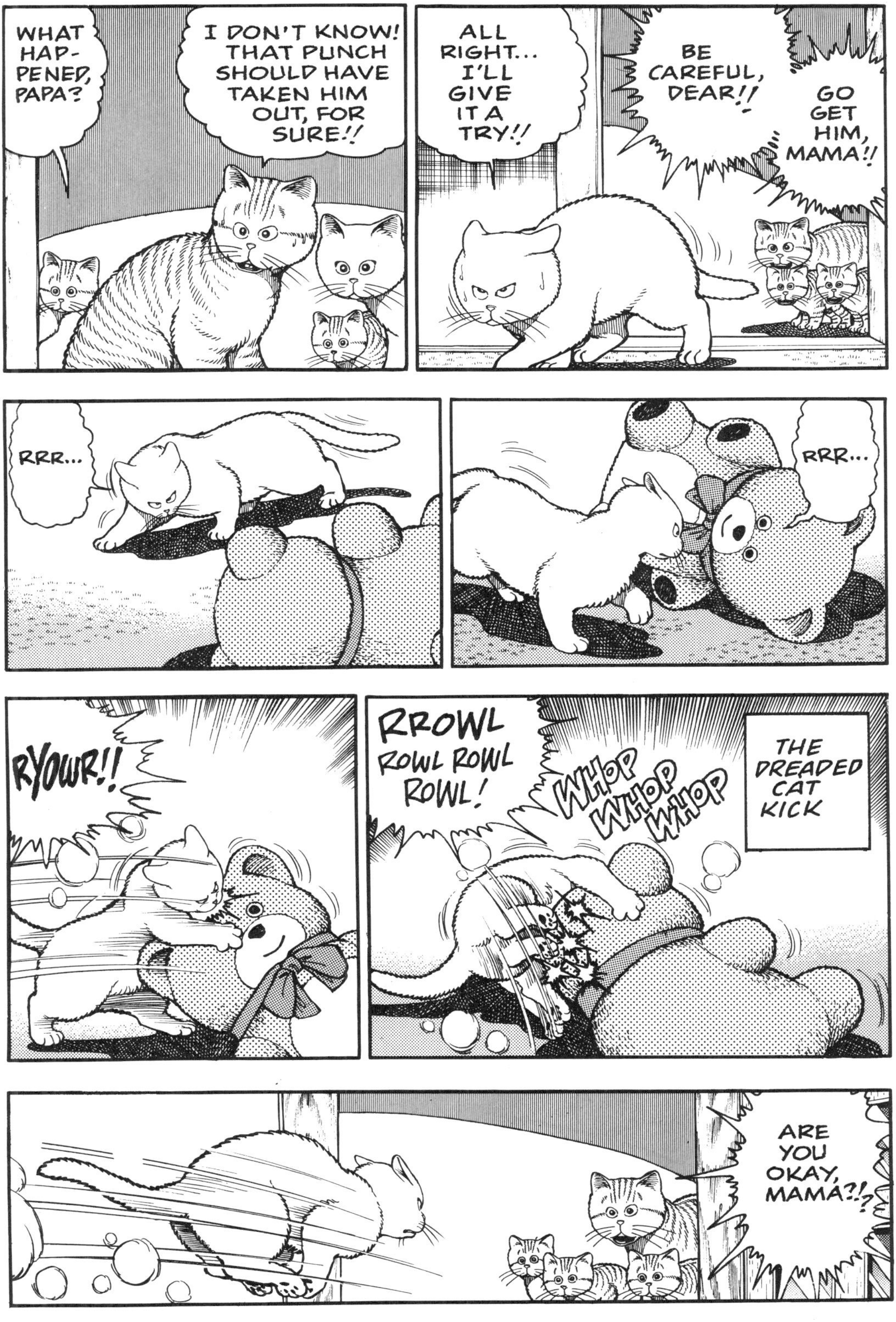
WHAT HAP-PENED, PAPA?
I DON'T KNOW! THAT PUNCH SHOULD HAVE TAKEN HIM OUT, FOR SURE!!
ALL RIGHT... I'LL GIVE IT A TRY!!
BE CAREFUL, DEAR!!
GO GET HIM, MAMA!!
RRR...
RRR...
RYOWR!!
RROWL ROWL ROWL ROWL!
WHOP WHOP WHOP
THE DREADED CAT KICK
ARE YOU OKAY, MAMA?!?

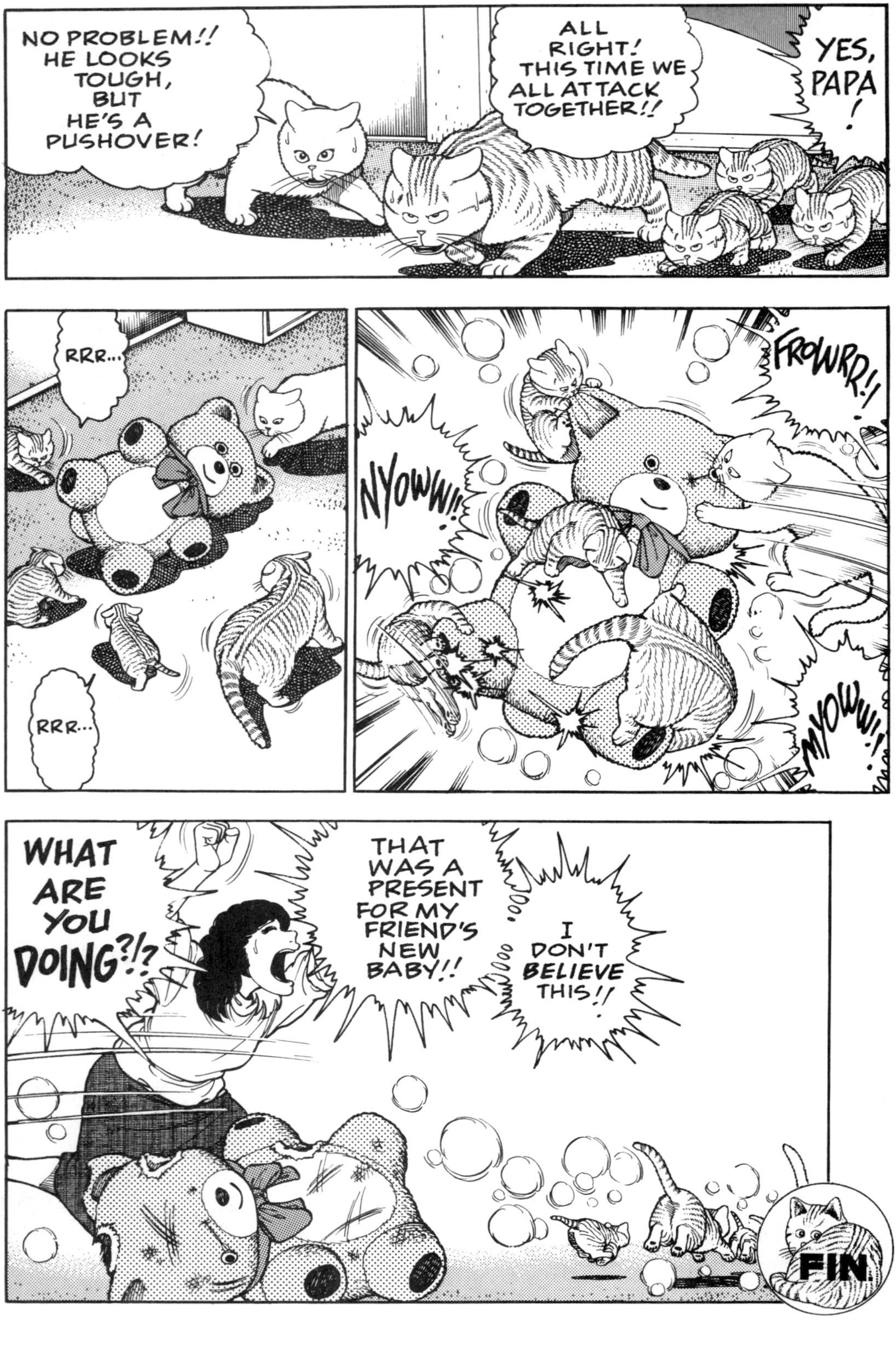
NO PROBLEM!! HE LOOKS TOUGH, BUT HE'S A PUSHOVER!
ALL RIGHT! THIS TIME WE ALL ATTACK TOGETHER!!
YES, PAPA!
RRR...
RRR...
FROWRR!!
NYOWW!!
MYOWW!!
WHAT ARE YOU DOING?!?
THAT WAS A PRESENT FOR MY FRIEND'S NEW BABY!!
I DON'T BELIEVE THIS!!
FIN

WHAT'S NYAZILLA?

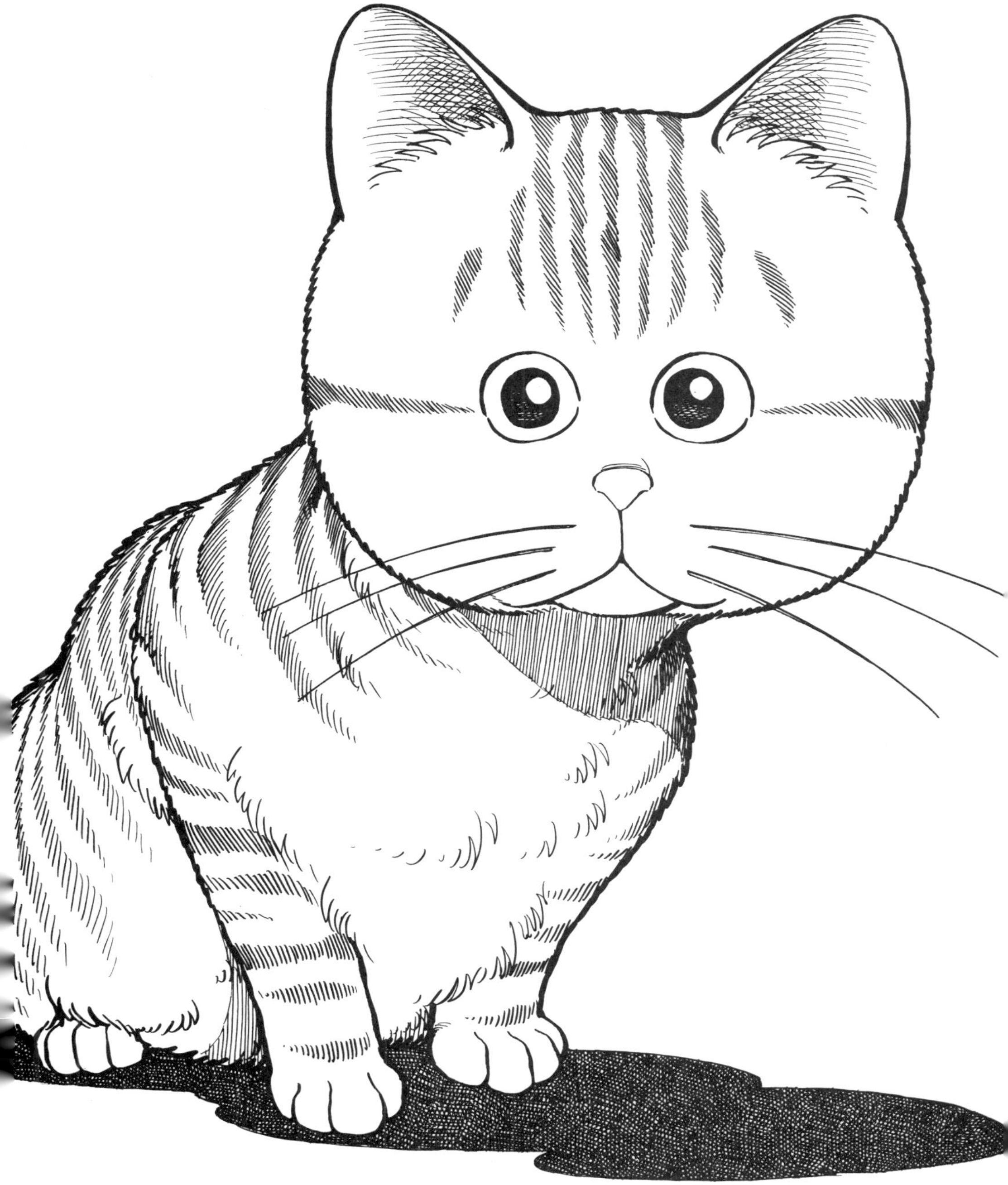

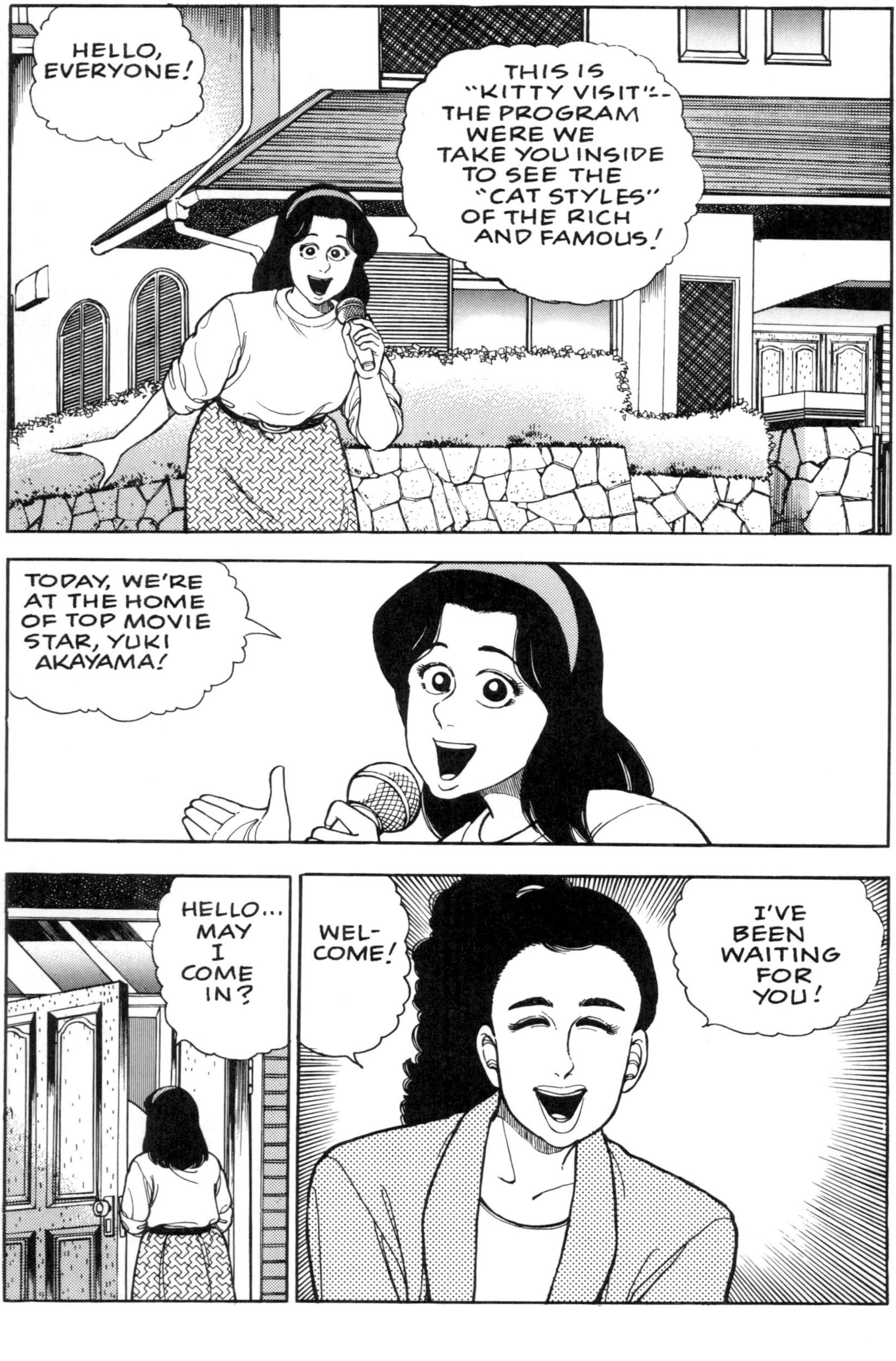
HELLO, EVERYONE!
THIS IS "KITTY VISIT"-- THE PROGRAM WERE WE TAKE YOU INSIDE TO SEE THE "CAT STYLES" OF THE RICH AND FAMOUS!
TODAY, WE'RE AT THE HOME OF TOP MOVIE STAR, YUKI AKAYAMA!
HELLO... MAY I COME IN?
WEL-COME!
I'VE BEEN WAITING FOR YOU!

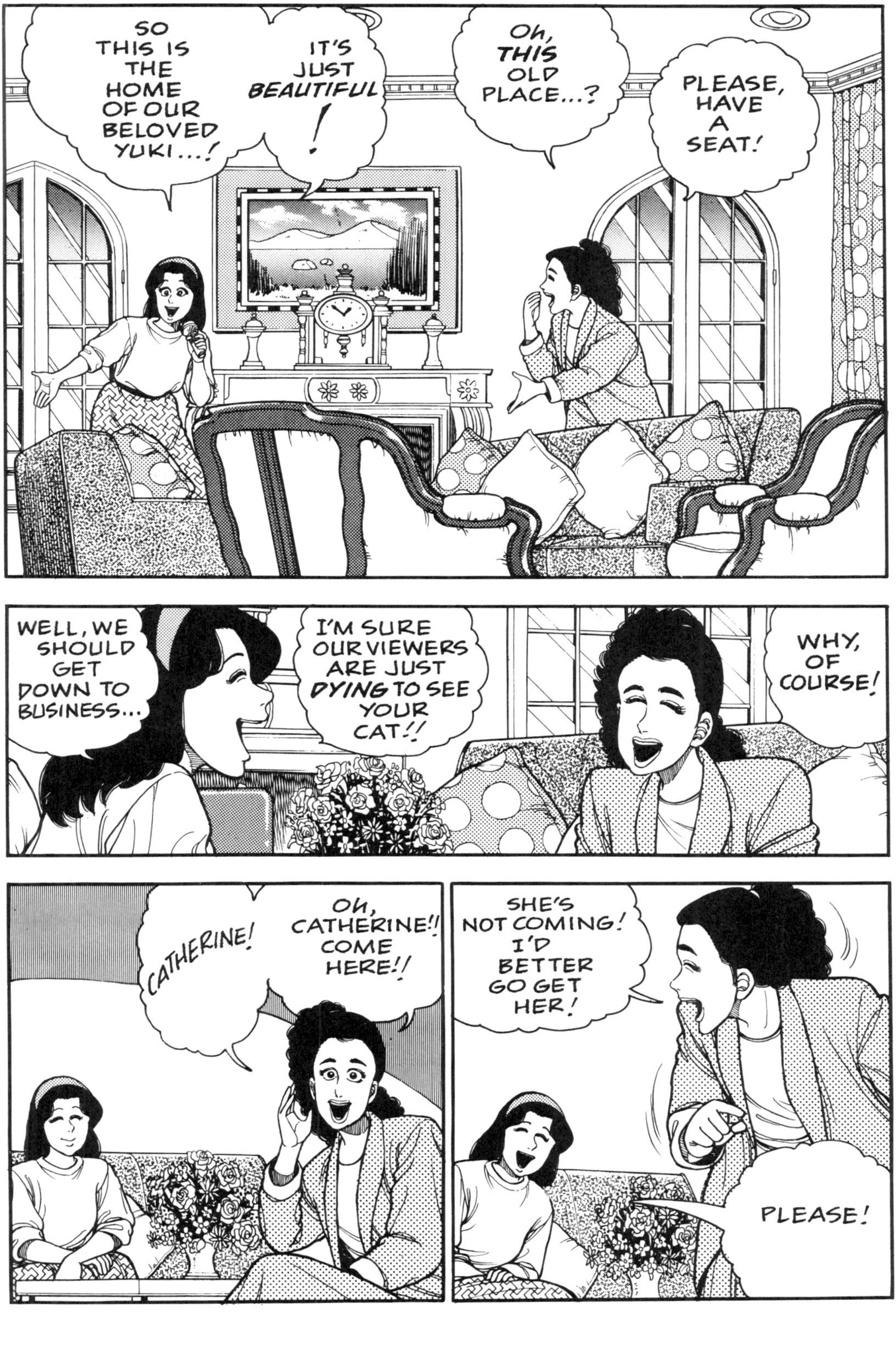
SO THIS IS THE HOME OF OUR BELOVED YUKI...!
IT'S JUST BEAUTIFUL!
Oh, THIS OLD PLACE...?
PLEASE, HAVE A SEAT!
WELL, WE SHOULD GET DOWN TO BUSINESS...
I'M SURE OUR VIEWERS ARE JUST DYING TO SEE YOUR CAT!!
WHY, OF COURSE!
Oh, CATHERINE!! COME HERE!!
CATHERINE!
SHE'S NOT COMING! I'D BETTER GO GET HER!
PLEASE!

CATHERINE! ARE YOU NAPPING, YOU NAUGHTY CAT?
I WANT TO INTRODUCE YOU TO OUR GUEST!
SORRY ABOUT THAT!
I'D LIKE YOU TO MEET CATHERINE!!
!
Ah... er... uhmm...
Eheh...so... WHAT KIND OF CAT IS SHE?
SHE'S A NYAZILLA!

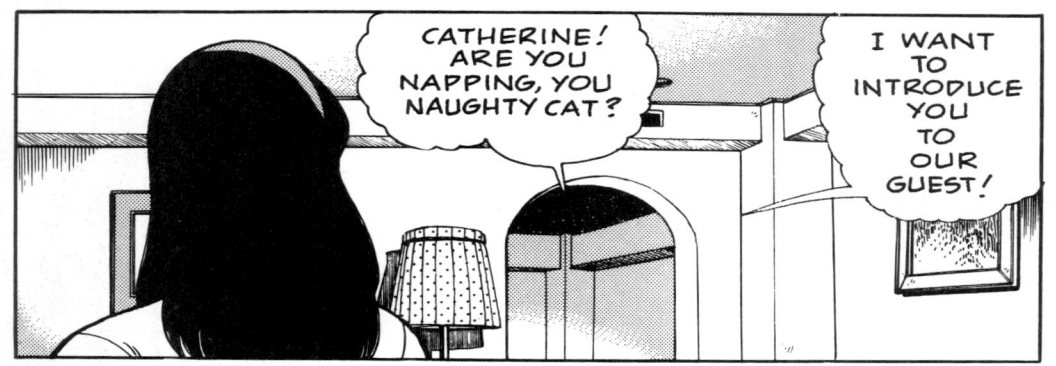

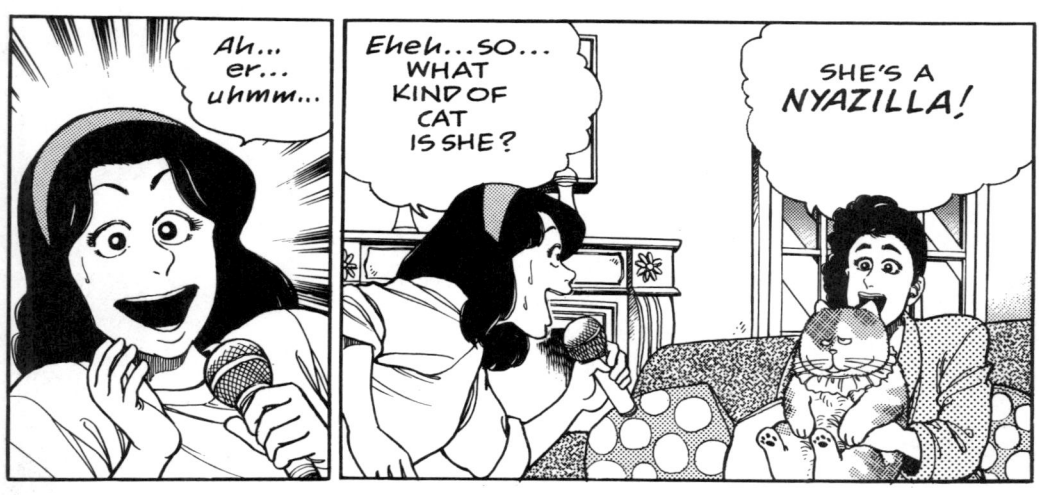

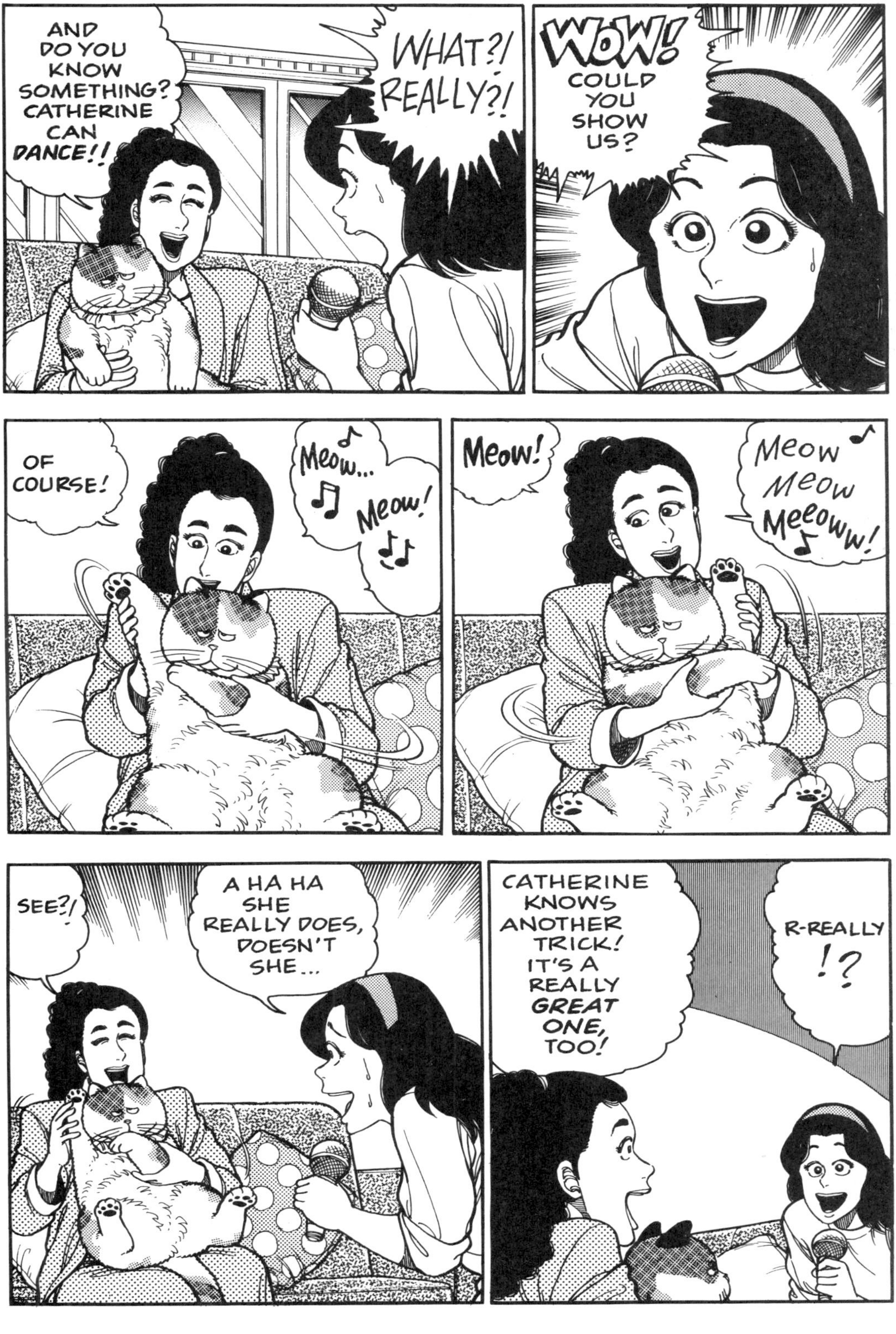
AND DO YOU KNOW SOMETHING? CATHERINE CAN DANCE!!
WHAT?! REALLY?!
WOW! COULD YOU SHOW US?
OF COURSE!
Meow... Meow!
Meow!
Meow Meow Meeoww!
SEE?!
A HA HA SHE REALLY DOES, DOESN'T SHE...
CATHERINE KNOWS ANOTHER TRICK! IT'S A REALLY GREAT ONE, TOO!
R-REALLY !?

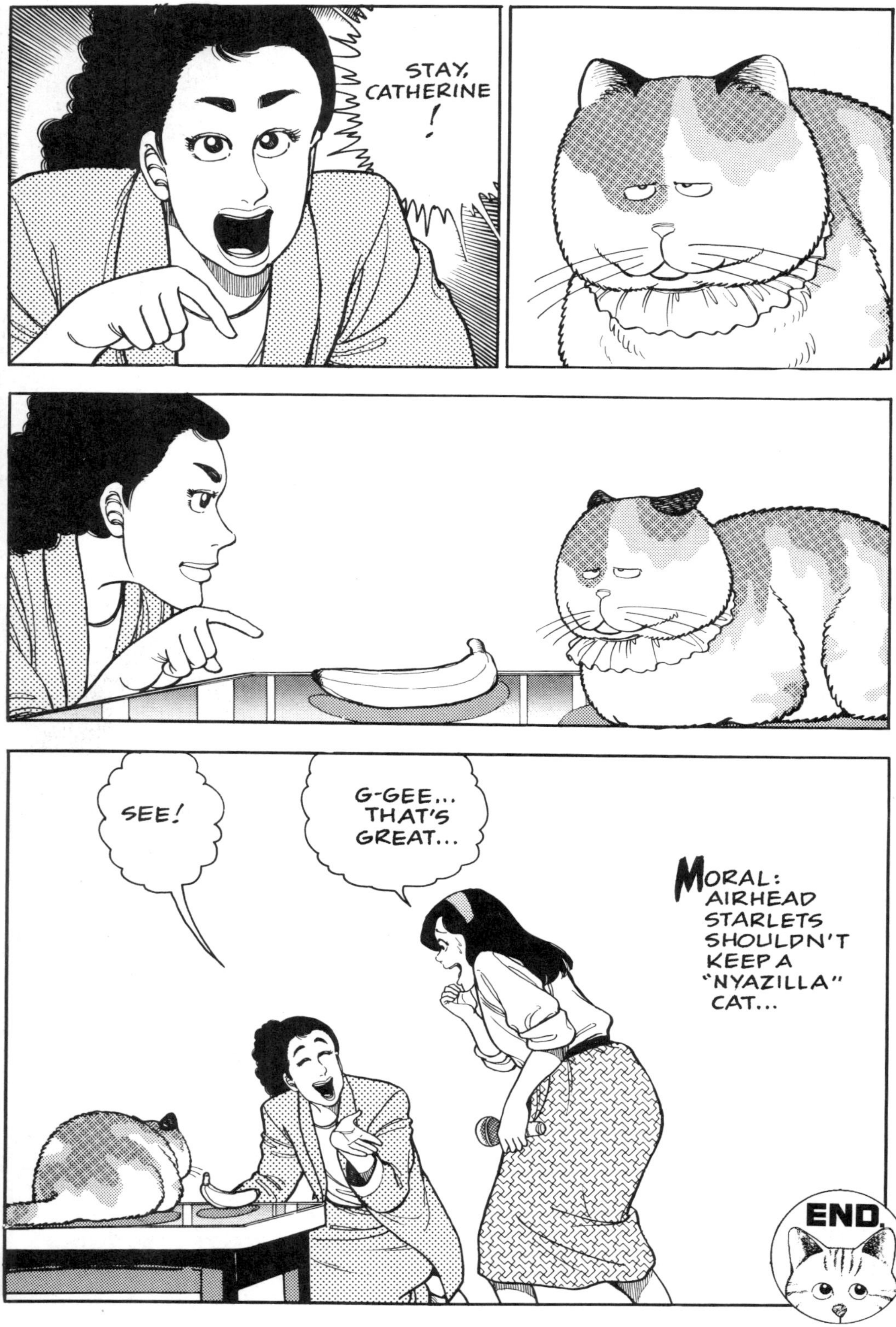
STAY, CATHERINE!
SEE!
G-GEE... THAT'S GREAT...
MORAL: AIRHEAD STARLETS SHOULDN'T KEEP A "NYAZILLA" CAT...
END.

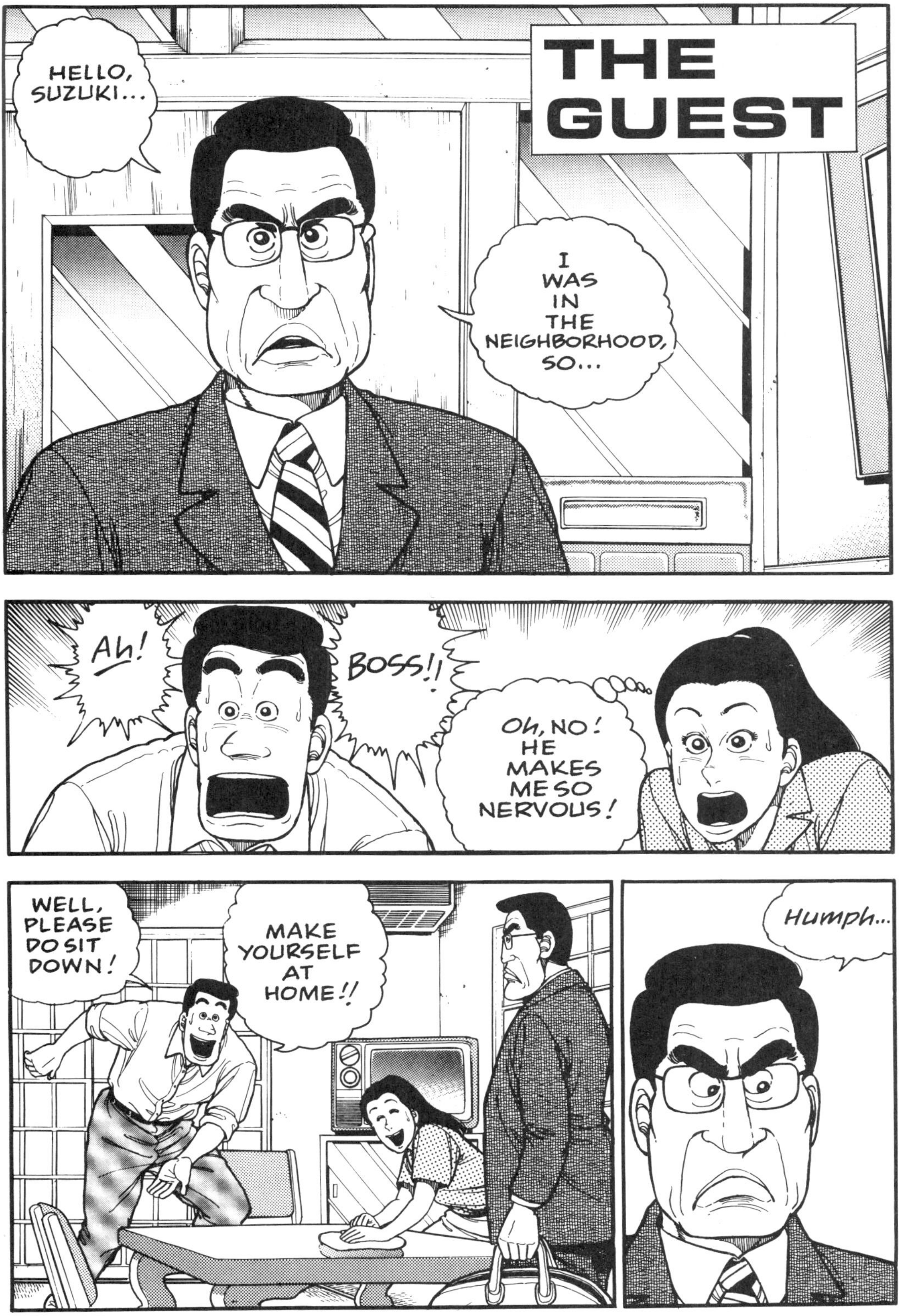
THE GUEST
HELLO, SUZUKI...
I WAS IN THE NEIGHBORHOOD, SO...
Ah!
BOSS!!
Oh, NO! HE MAKES ME SO NERVOUS!
WELL, PLEASE DO SIT DOWN!
MAKE YOURSELF AT HOME!!
Humph...

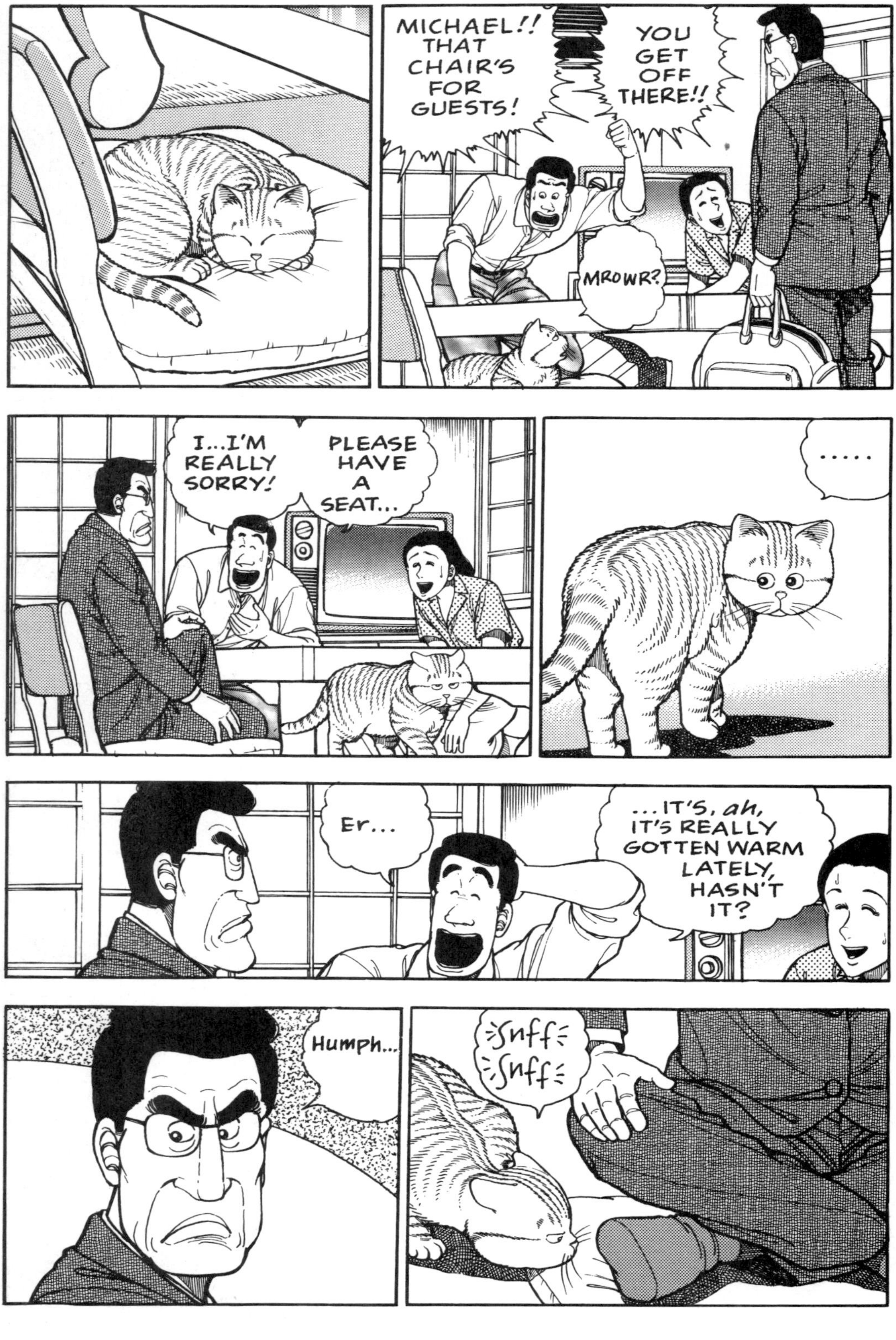

MICHAEL!! THAT CHAIR'S FOR GUESTS!
YOU GET OFF THERE!!
MROWR?
I...I'M REALLY SORRY!
PLEASE HAVE A SEAT...
.....
Er...
...IT'S, ah, IT'S REALLY GOTTEN WARM LATELY, HASN'T IT?
Humph...
Snff Snff

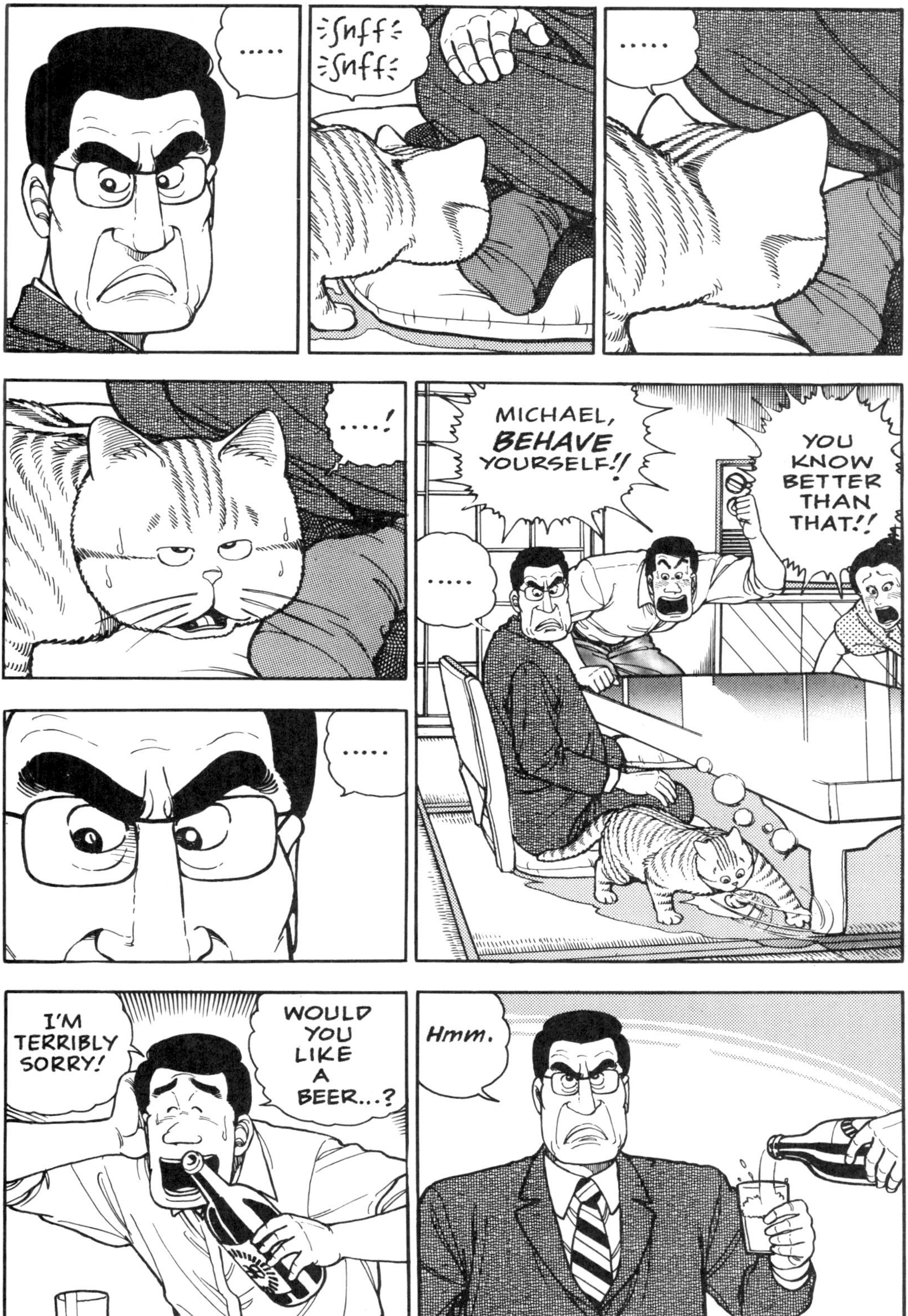
.....
SNFF SNFF
.....
....!
.....
MICHAEL, BEHAVE YOURSELF!!
YOU KNOW BETTER THAN THAT!!
.....
I'M TERRIBLY SORRY!
WOULD YOU LIKE A BEER...?
Hmm.

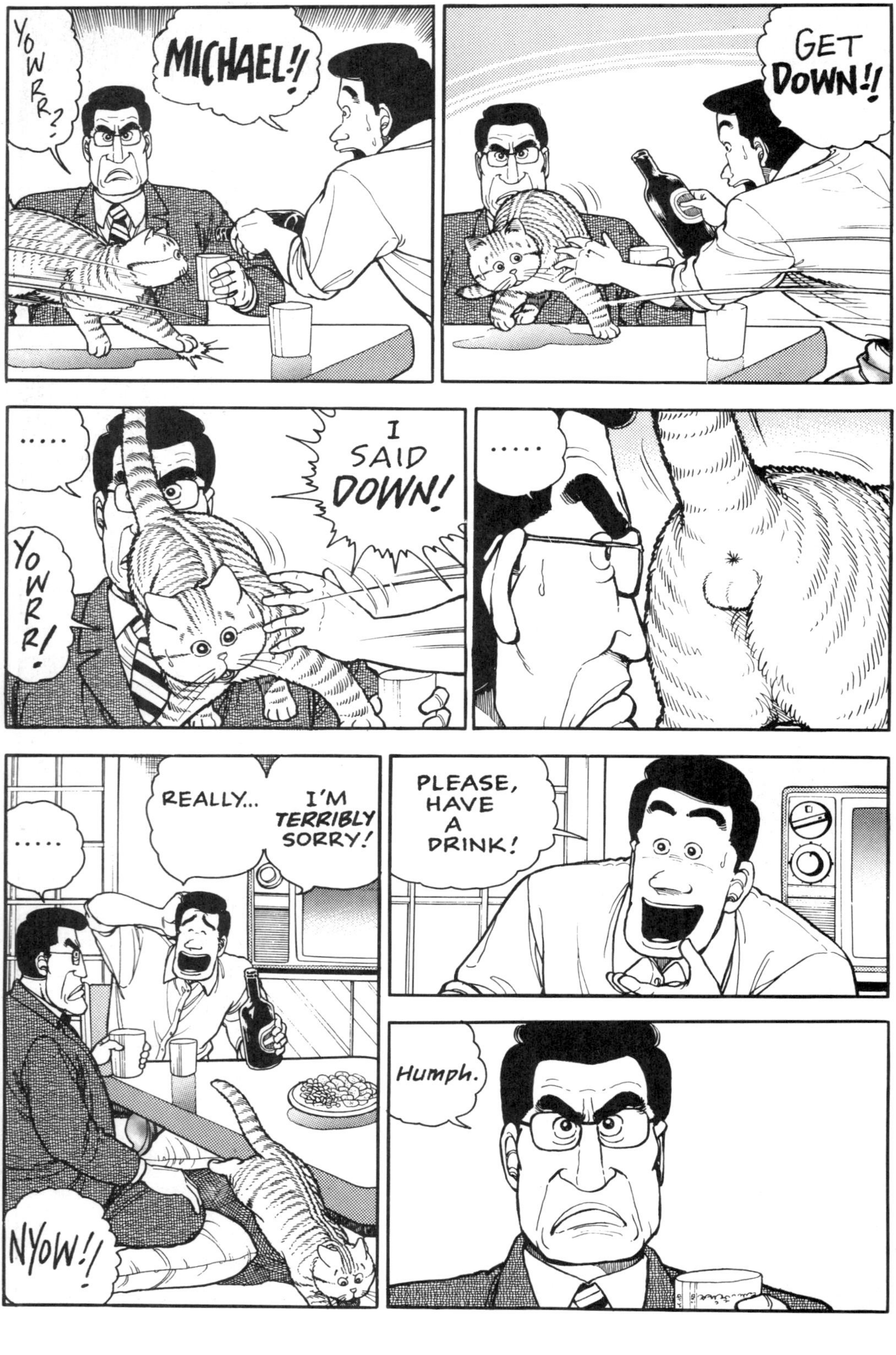

YOWRR?
MICHAEL!!
GET DOWN!!
.....
YOWRR!
I SAID DOWN!
.....
.....
REALLY... I'M TERRIBLY SORRY!
NYOW!!
PLEASE, HAVE A DRINK!
Humph.

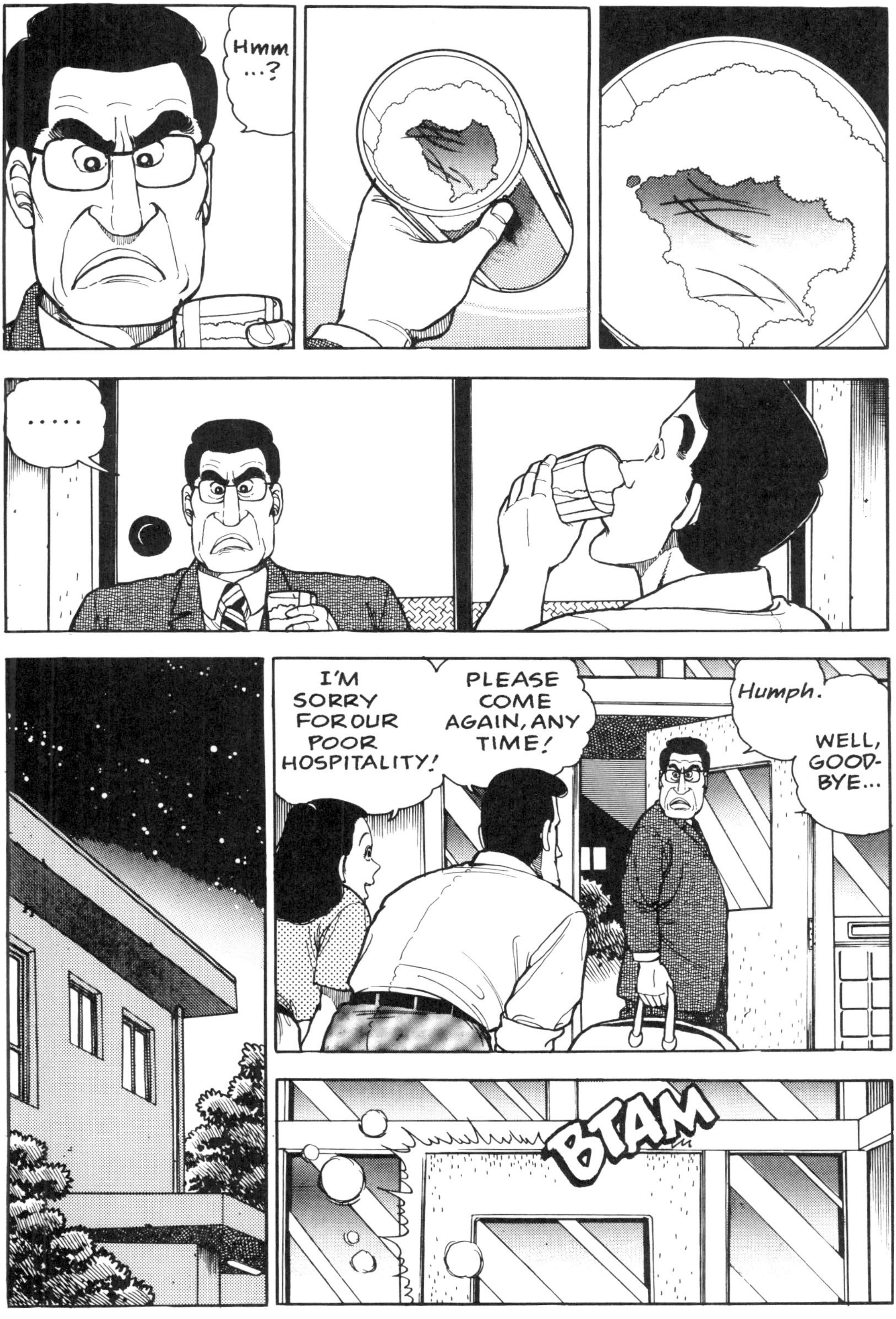
Hmm ...?
.....
I'M SORRY FOR OUR POOR HOSPITALITY!
PLEASE COME AGAIN, ANY TIME!
Humph.
WELL, GOOD-BYE...
BTAM

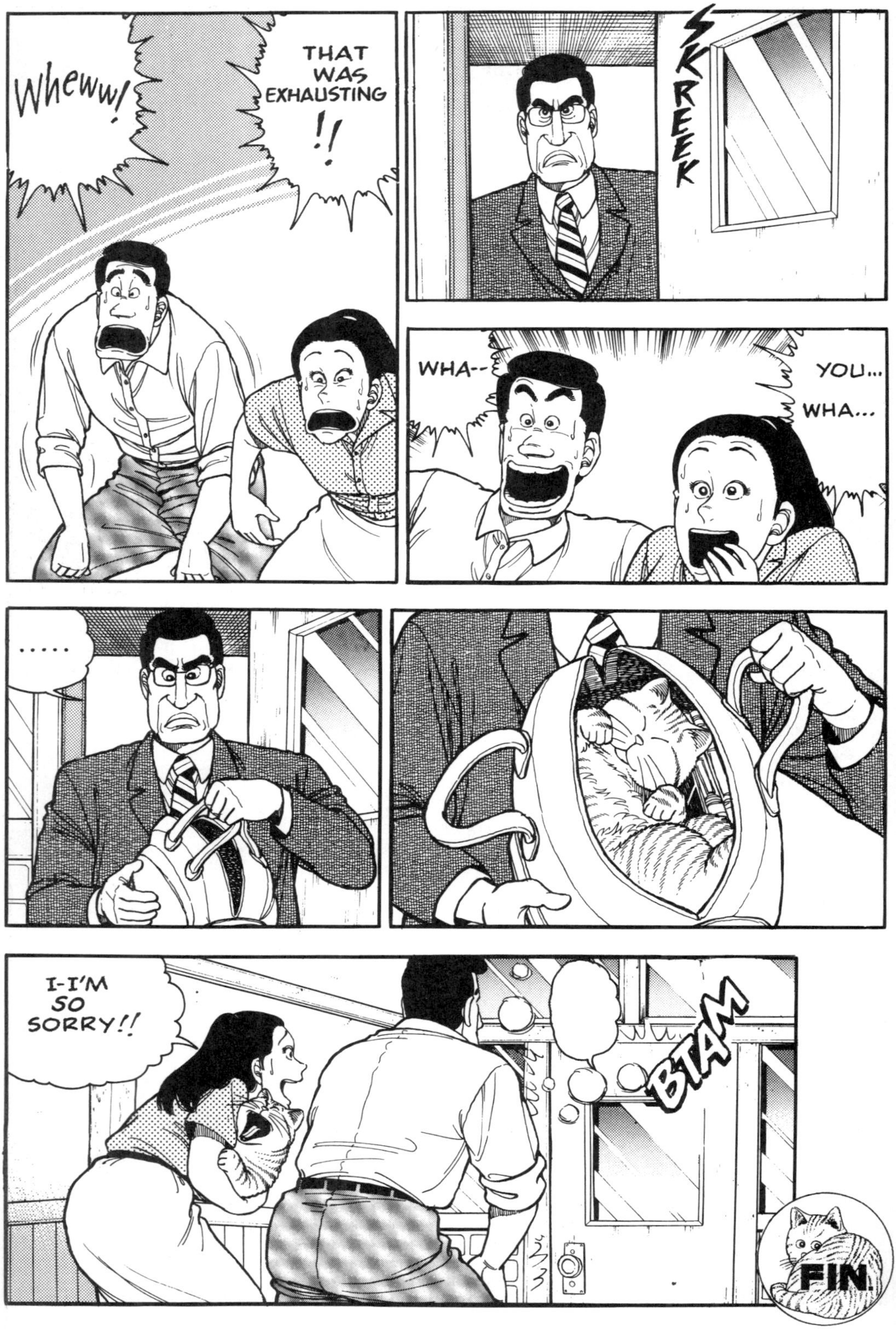
Wheww!
THAT WAS EXHAUSTING !!
SKREEK
WHA--
YOU...
WHA...
.....
I-I'M SO SORRY!!
BTAM
FIN.

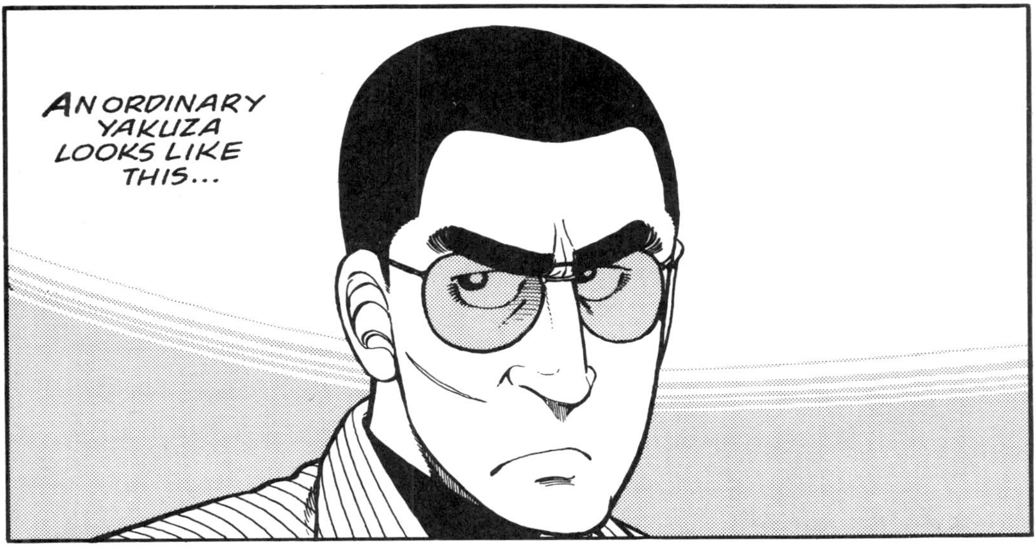
AN ORDINARY YAKUZA LOOKS LIKE THIS...

MACHISMO!

YAKUZA K vs. YAKUZA M!!

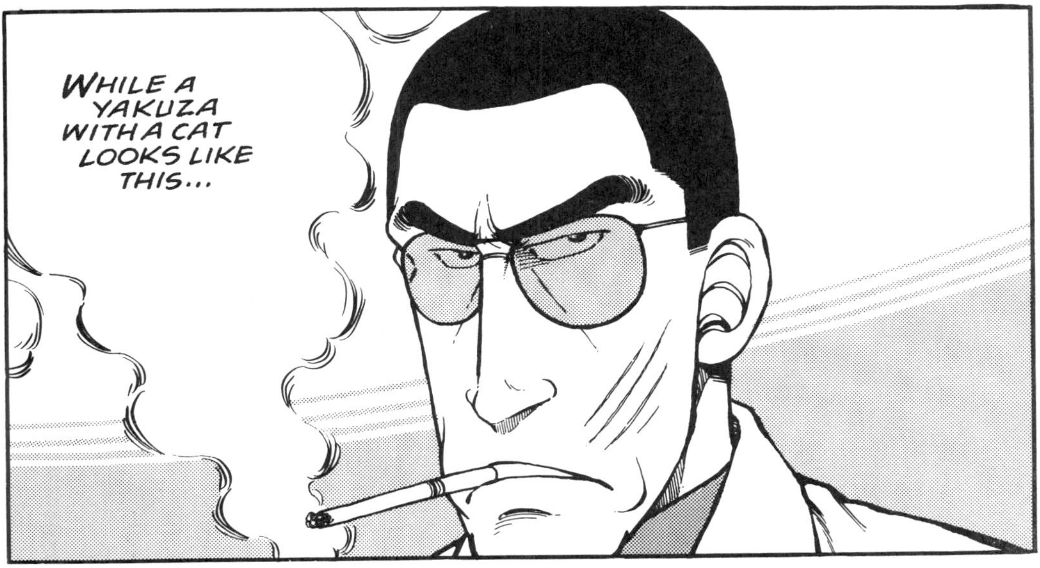
WHILE A YAKUZA WITH A CAT LOOKS LIKE THIS...

Ding Dongg
Hmm ...?
WHO'S THERE?
IT'S ME!! "M" FROM THE KODANSHA GANG!!
Uh-oh...
WAIT A MINUTE!!
....!
NYOW?
MRROWWR!
BTAM

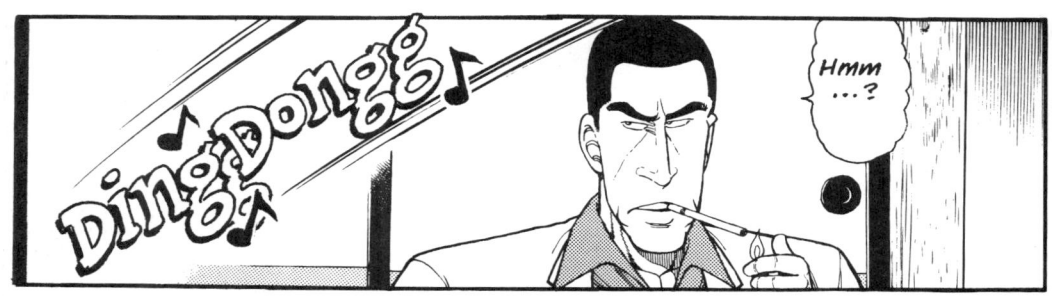

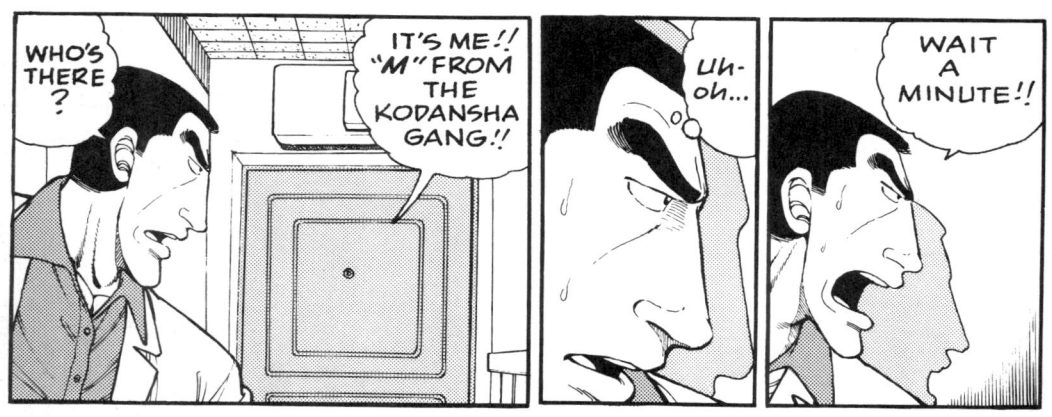

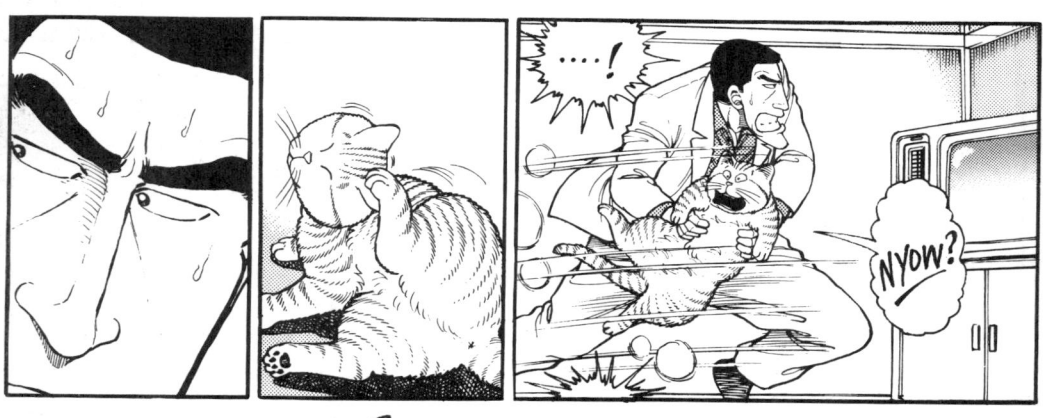

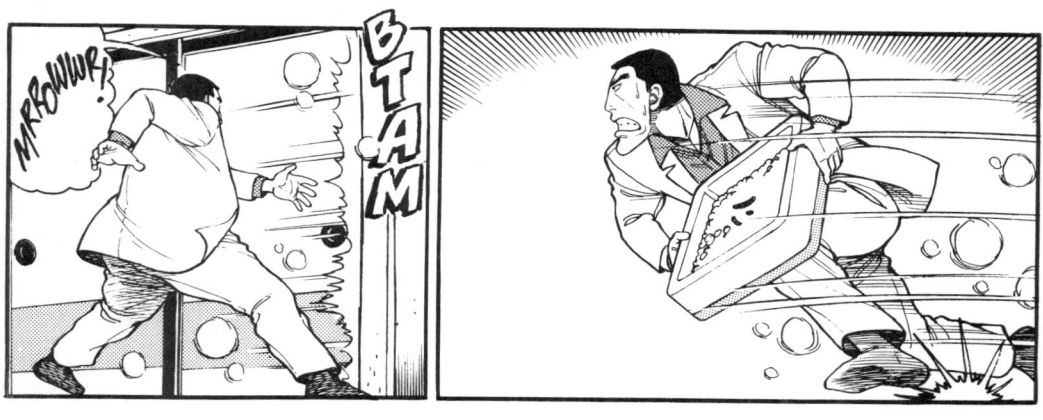

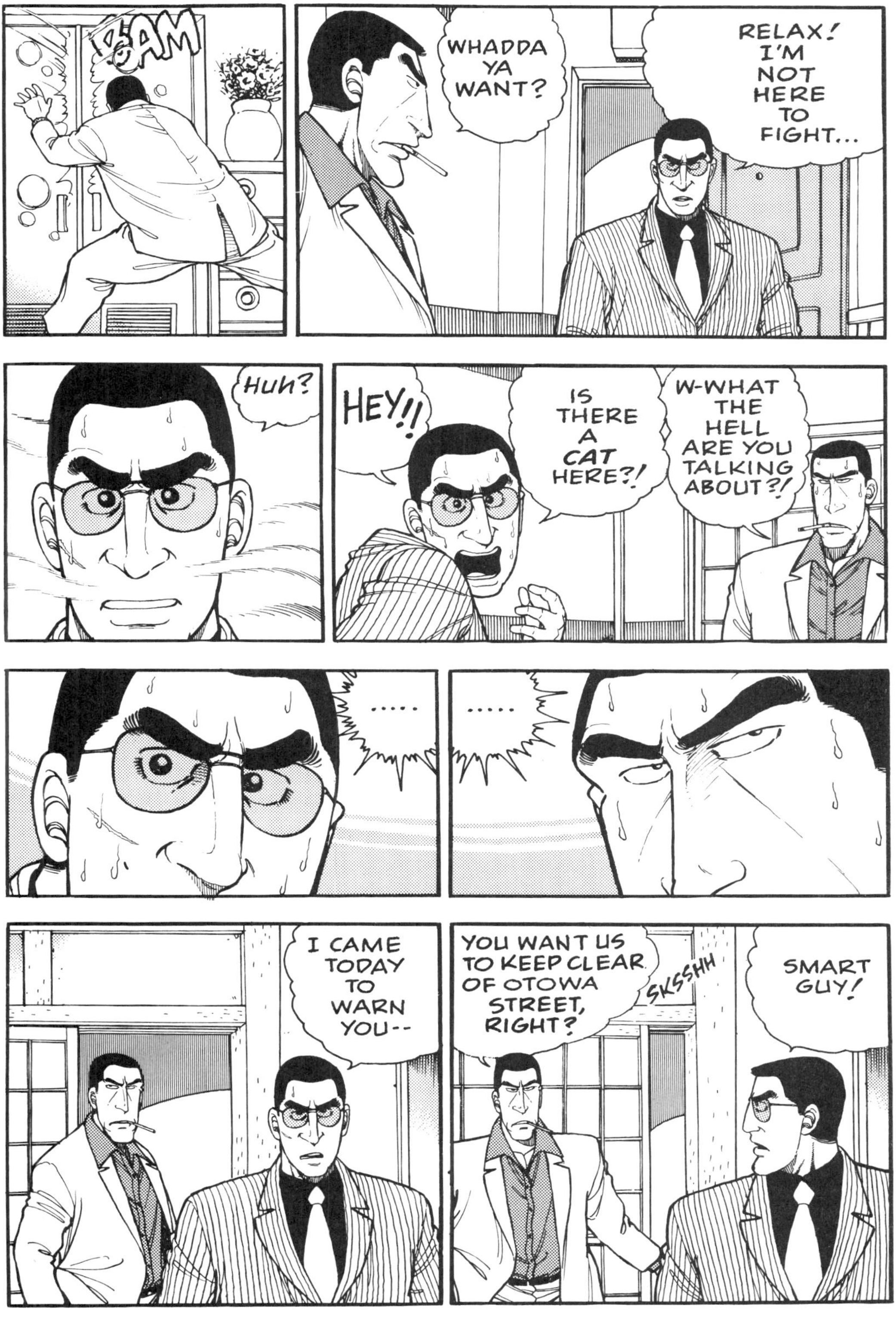
BAM
WHADDA YA WANT?
RELAX! I'M NOT HERE TO FIGHT...
Huh?
HEY!!
IS THERE A CAT HERE?!
W-WHAT THE HELL ARE YOU TALKING ABOUT?!
.....
.....
I CAME TODAY TO WARN YOU--
YOU WANT US TO KEEP CLEAR OF OTOWA STREET, RIGHT?
SKSSHH
SMART GUY!

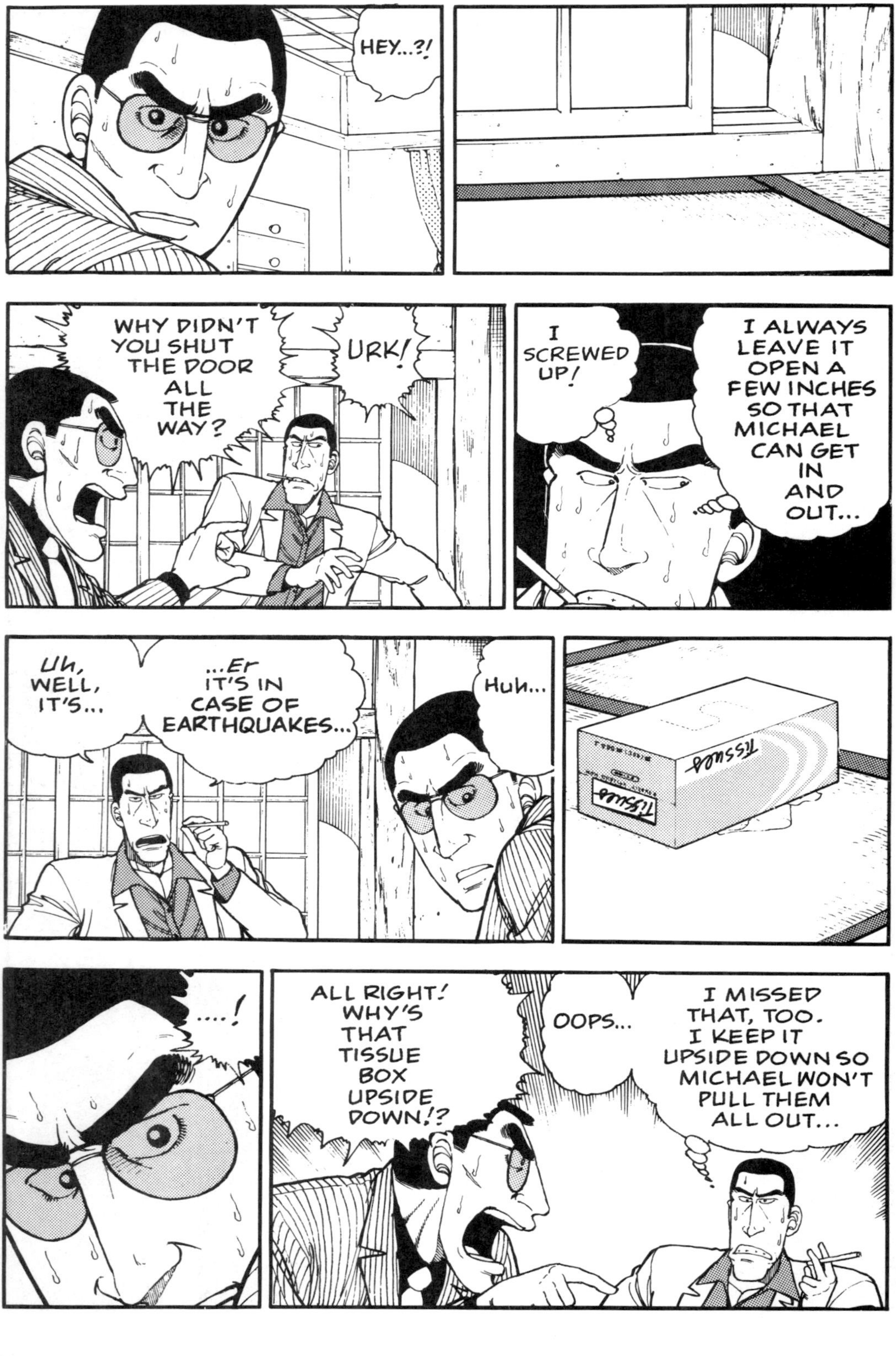
HEY...?!
WHY DIDN'T YOU SHUT THE DOOR ALL THE WAY?
URK!
I SCREWED UP!
I ALWAYS LEAVE IT OPEN A FEW INCHES SO THAT MICHAEL CAN GET IN AND OUT...
Uh, WELL, IT'S...
...Er IT'S IN CASE OF EARTHQUAKES...
Huh...
....!
ALL RIGHT! WHY'S THAT TISSUE BOX UPSIDE DOWN!?
OOPS...
I MISSED THAT, TOO. I KEEP IT UPSIDE DOWN SO MICHAEL WON'T PULL THEM ALL OUT...

Ah, WELL, THAT...
IT'S...ah, BECAUSE I USE IT FOR A TABLE WHEN I EAT!
.....
LET'S GET TO THE POINT ...
NEITHER OF US WANTS ANY BLOOD-SHED...
SO I FIGURE WE OUGHTTA MAKE SOME KINDA DEAL...
NROWR?
WHA-- ?
H-HEY!
DIDN'T YOU HEAR A CAT?
Uh ...
SORRY ABOUT THAT... GOT A BIT OF STOMACH TROUBLE...
SEE?
FRAPPP
.....
Hrmph... ANY-WAY...
I JUST WANT YOU GUYS TO REALIZE SOMETHIN' ...

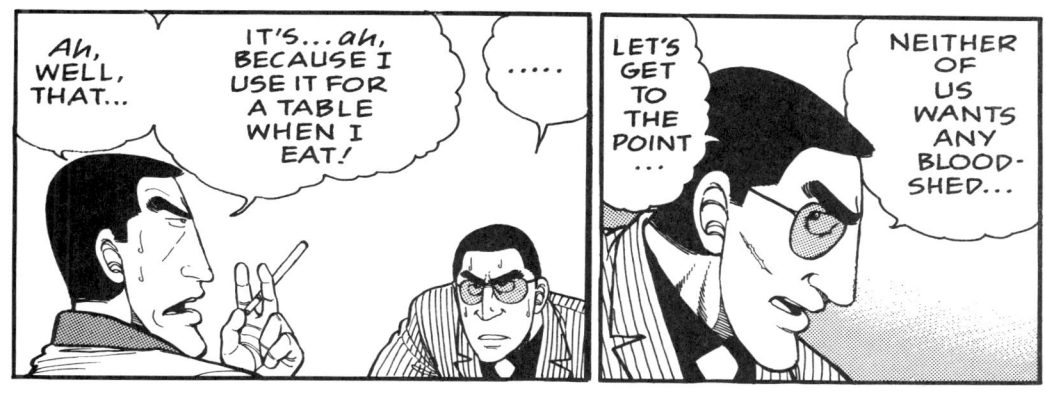

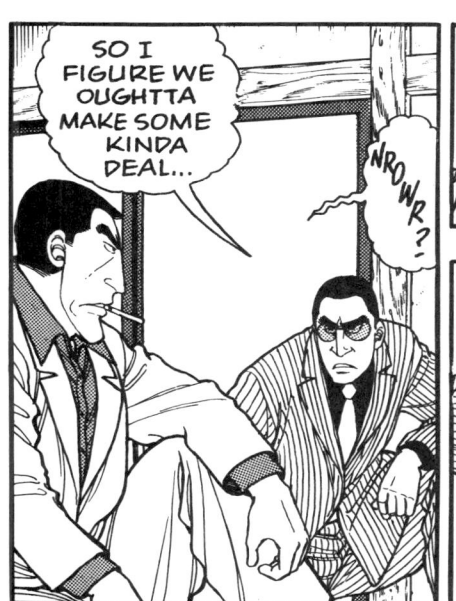

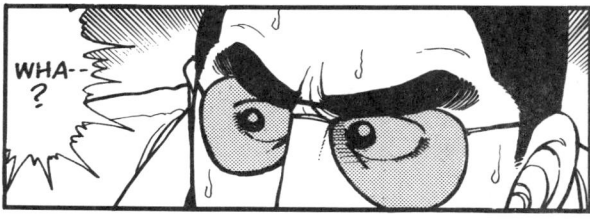

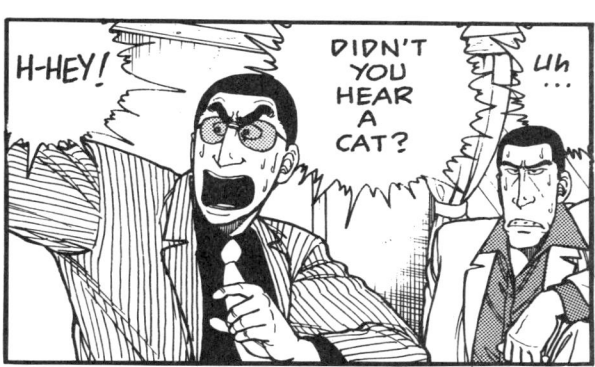

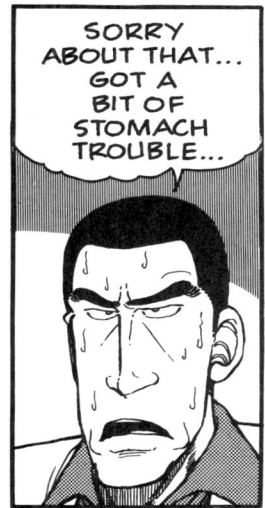

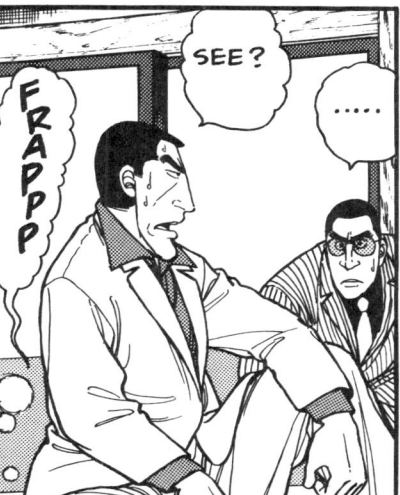

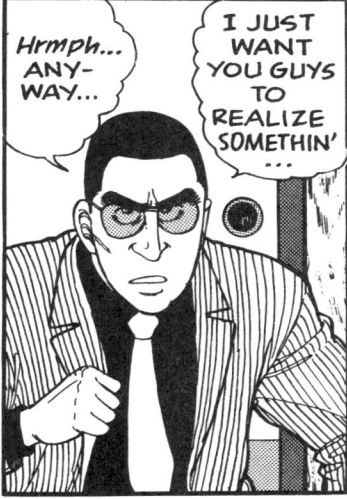

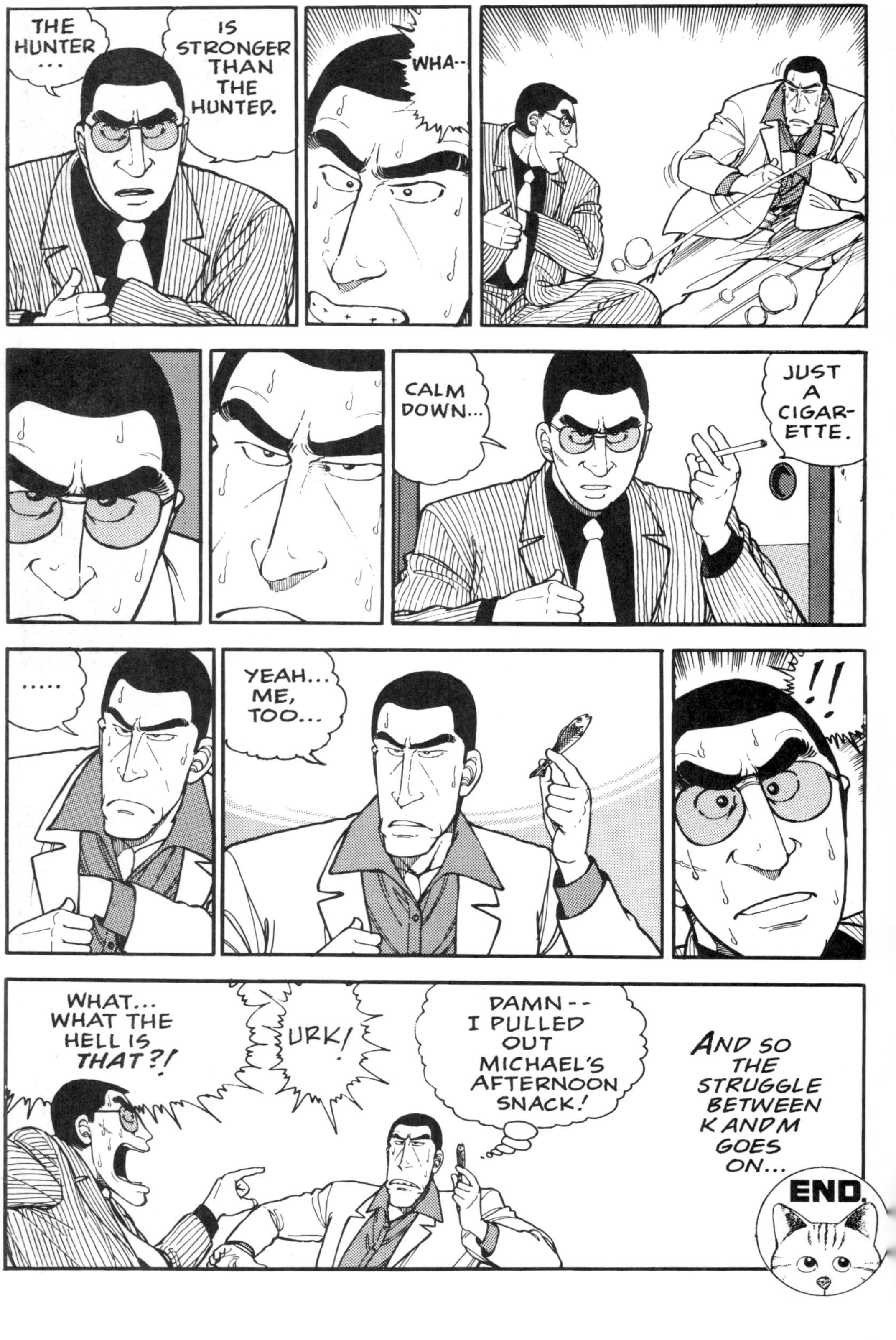
THE HUNTER ...
IS STRONGER THAN THE HUNTED.
WHA--
CALM DOWN...
JUST A CIGAR-ETTE.
.....
YEAH... ME, TOO...
!!
WHAT... WHAT THE HELL IS *THAT*?!
URK!
DAMN -- I PULLED OUT MICHAEL'S AFTERNOON SNACK!
AND SO THE STRUGGLE BETWEEN K AND M GOES ON...
END.

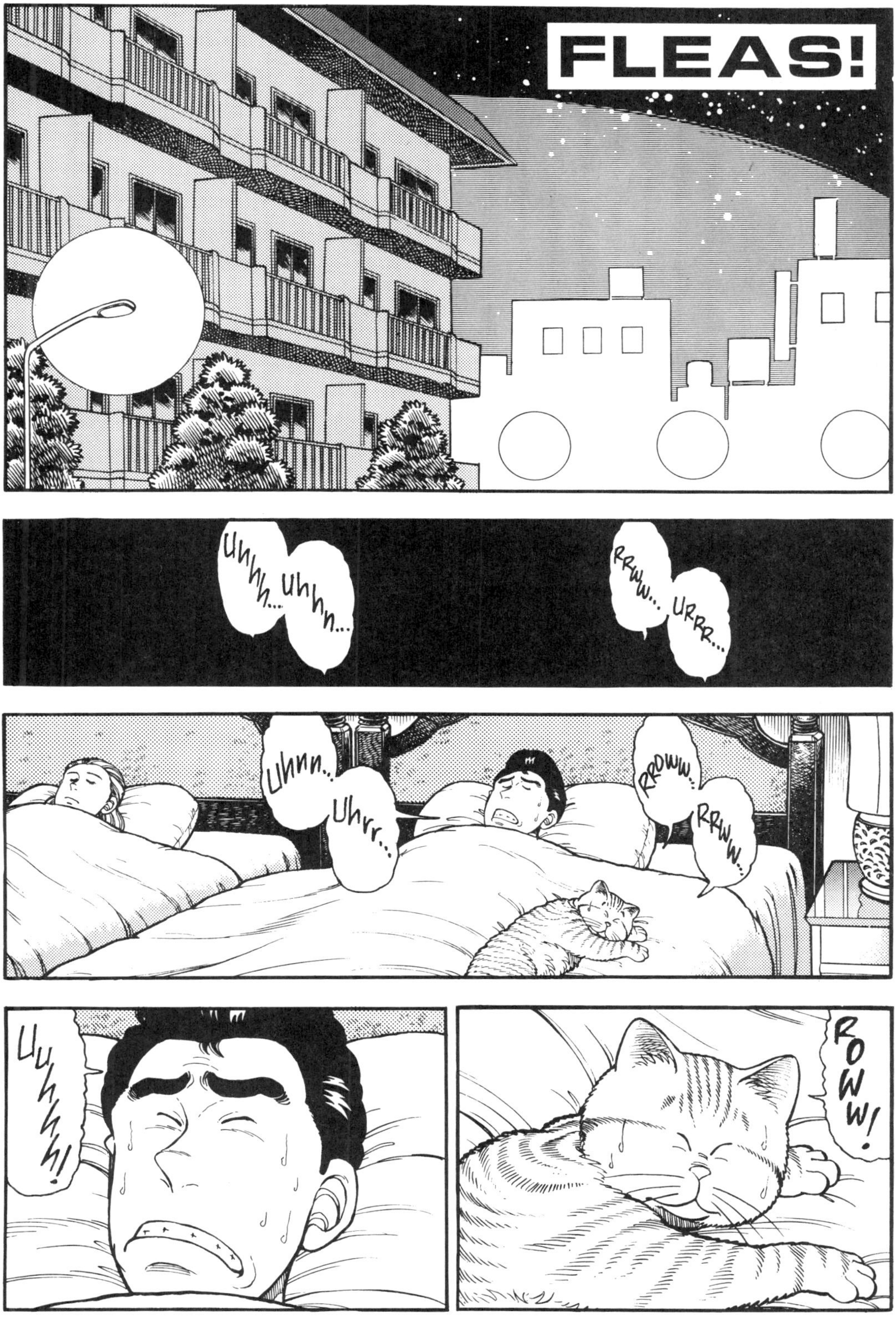
FLEAS!
Uhhh...
uhhn...
Rrww...
Urrr...
Uhnn...
Uhrr...
Rrowww...
Rrww...
Uuhhhh!
Roww!

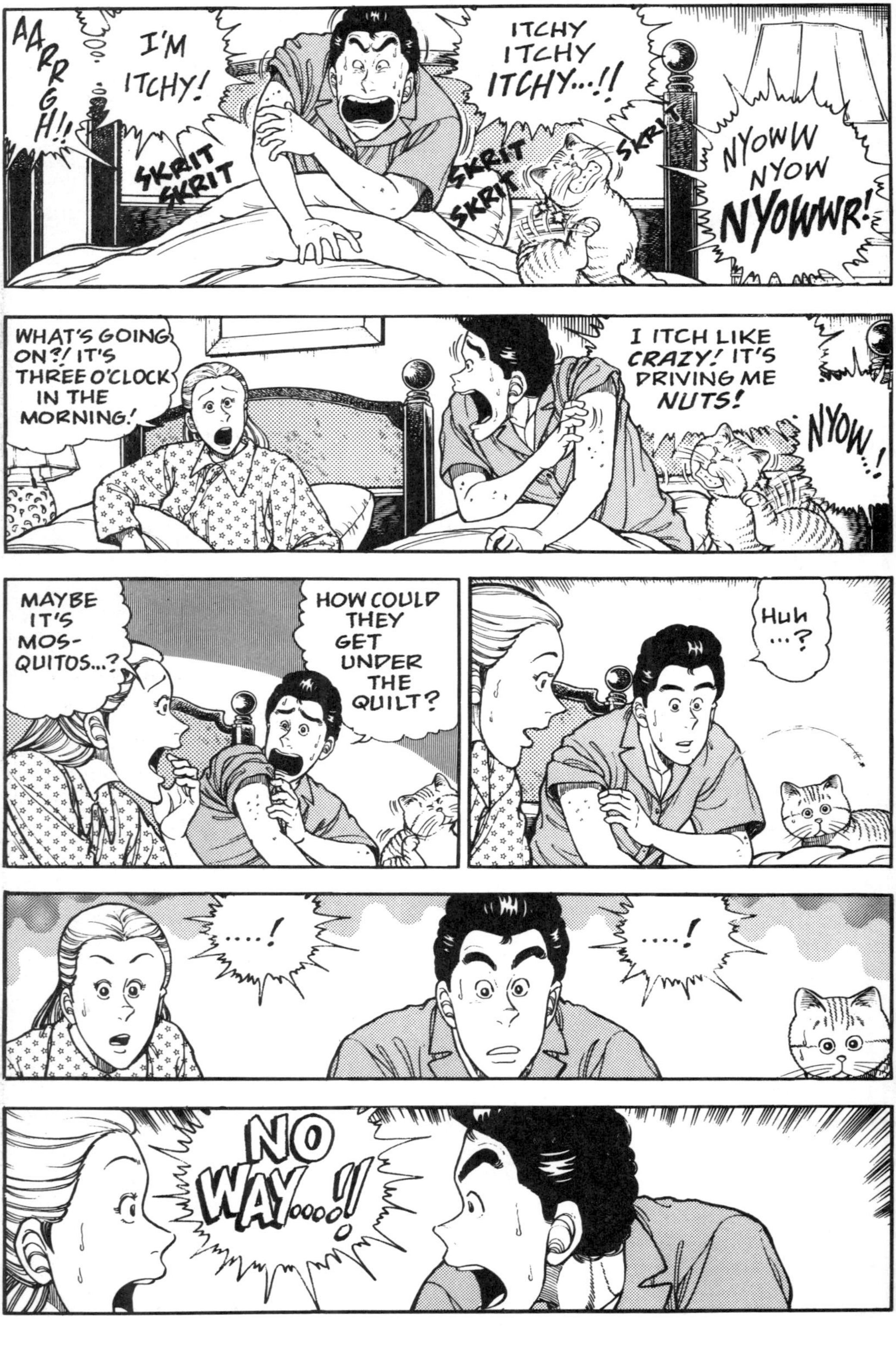
AARRGH!!
I'M ITCHY!
SKRIT SKRIT
ITCHY ITCHY ITCHY...!!
SKRIT SKRIT
SKRIT
NYOWW NYOW NYOWWR!
WHAT'S GOING ON?! IT'S THREE O'CLOCK IN THE MORNING!
I ITCH LIKE CRAZY! IT'S DRIVING ME NUTS!
NYOW...!
MAYBE IT'S MOS-QUITOS...?
HOW COULD THEY GET UNDER THE QUILT?
Huh...?
....!
....!
NO WAYoooo!!

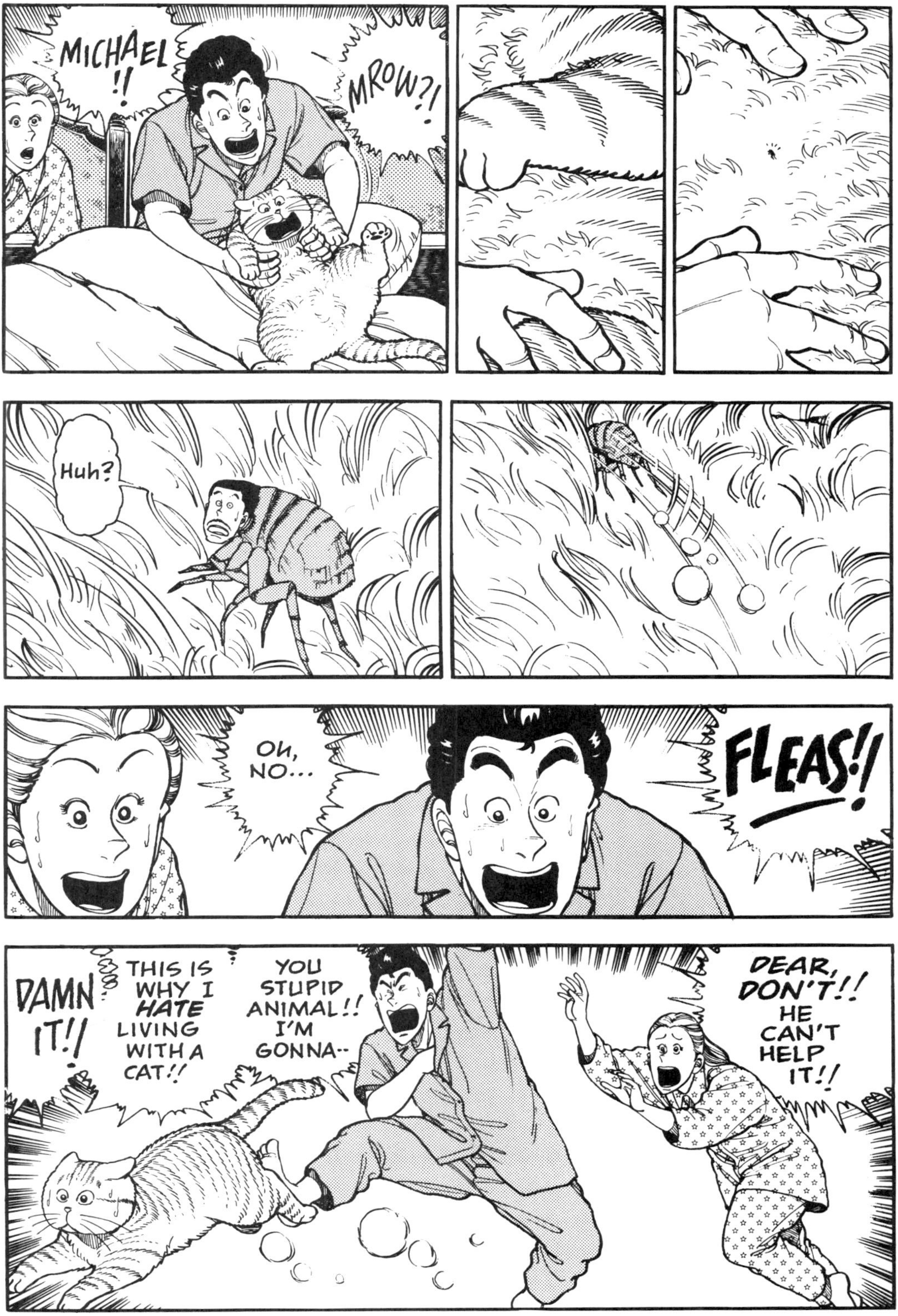
MICHAEL !!
MROW?!
Huh?
OH, NO...
FLEAS!!
DAMN IT!!
THIS IS WHY I HATE LIVING WITH A CAT!!
YOU STUPID ANIMAL!! I'M GONNA--
DEAR, DON'T!! HE CAN'T HELP IT!!

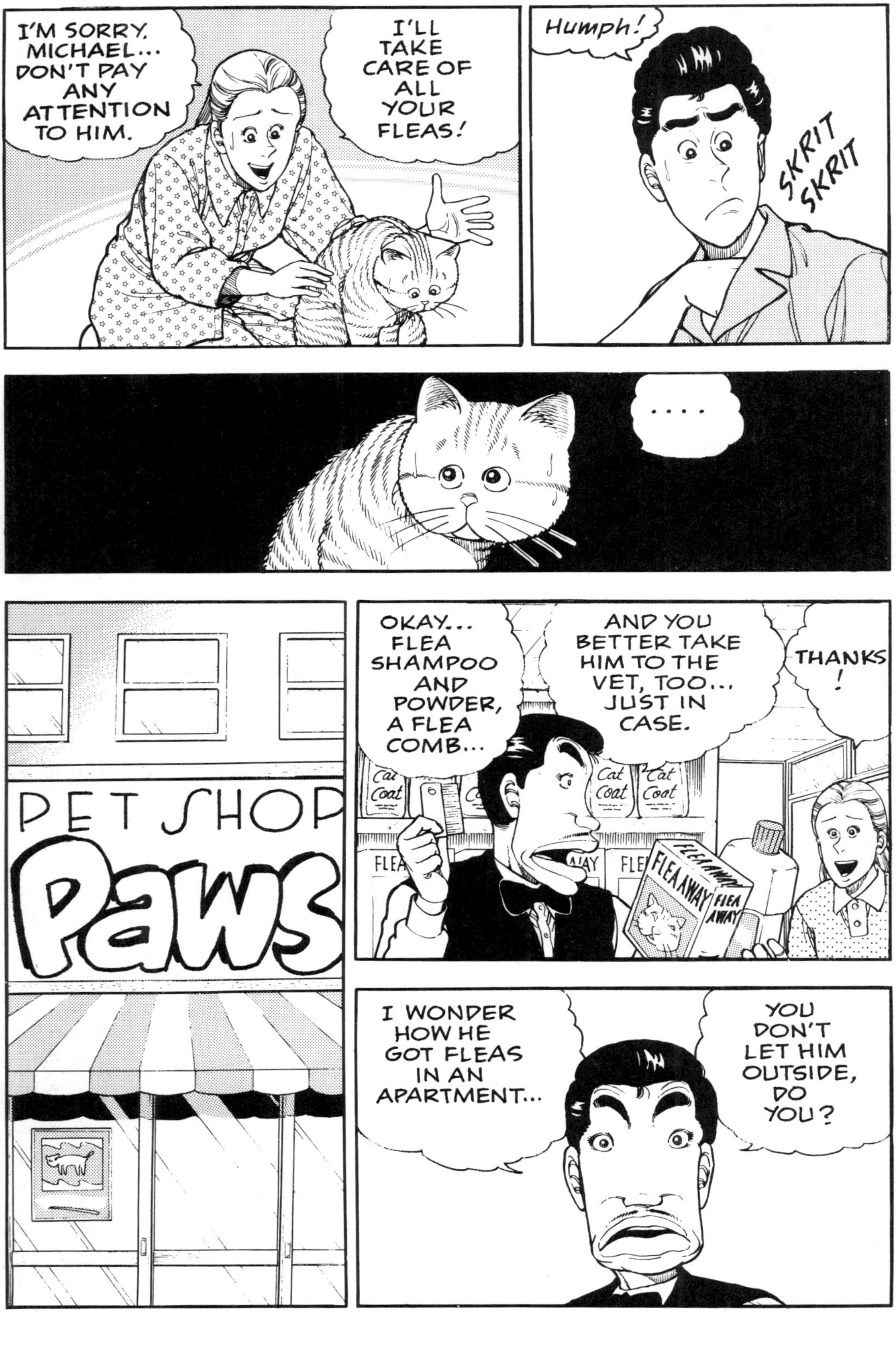

I'M SORRY, MICHAEL... DON'T PAY ANY ATTENTION TO HIM.
I'LL TAKE CARE OF ALL YOUR FLEAS!
Humph!
SKRIT SKRIT
....
PET SHOP
Paws
OKAY... FLEA SHAMPOO AND POWDER, A FLEA COMB...
AND YOU BETTER TAKE HIM TO THE VET, TOO... JUST IN CASE.
THANKS!
Cat Coat
FLEA AWAY
I WONDER HOW HE GOT FLEAS IN AN APARTMENT...
YOU DON'T LET HIM OUTSIDE, DO YOU?

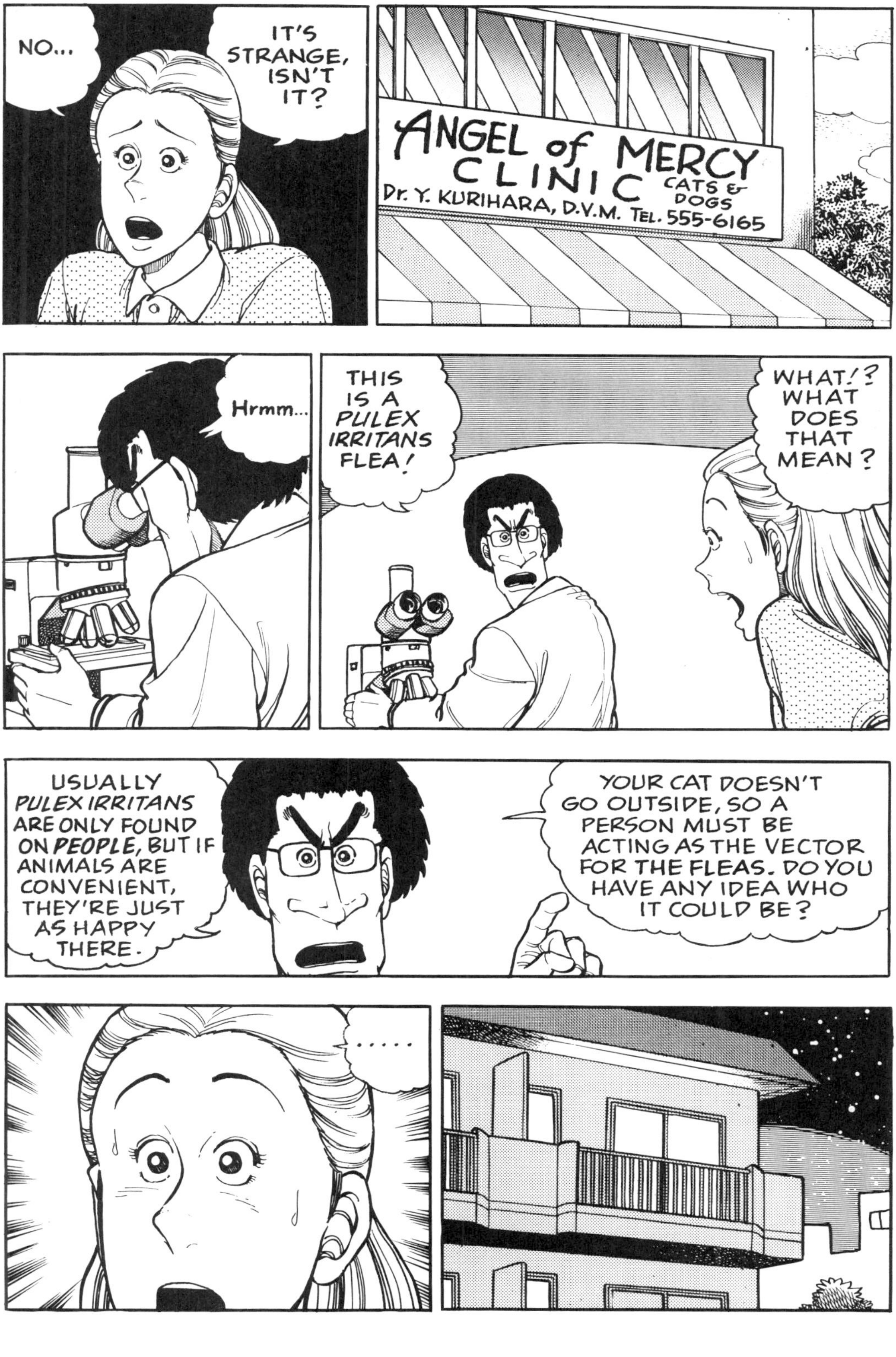
NO...
IT'S STRANGE, ISN'T IT?
ANGEL of MERCY CLINIC CATS & DOGS
Dr. Y. KURIHARA, D.V.M. TEL. 555-6165
Hrmm...
THIS IS A PULEX IRRITANS FLEA!
WHAT!? WHAT DOES THAT MEAN?
USUALLY PULEX IRRITANS ARE ONLY FOUND ON PEOPLE, BUT IF ANIMALS ARE CONVENIENT, THEY'RE JUST AS HAPPY THERE.
YOUR CAT DOESN'T GO OUTSIDE, SO A PERSON MUST BE ACTING AS THE VECTOR FOR THE FLEAS. DO YOU HAVE ANY IDEA WHO IT COULD BE?
.....

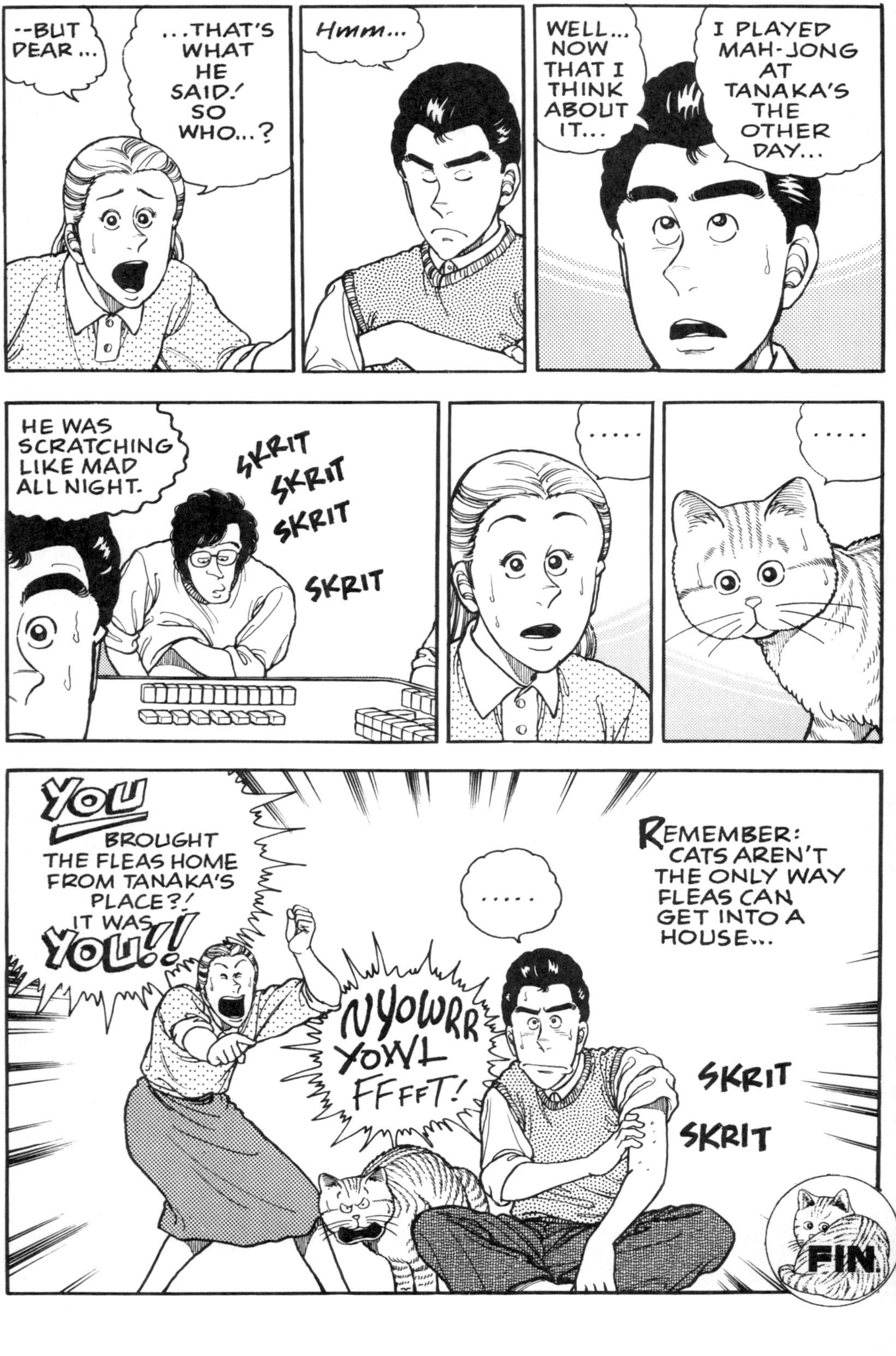

--BUT DEAR...
...THAT'S WHAT HE SAID! SO WHO...?
Hmm...
WELL... NOW THAT I THINK ABOUT IT...
I PLAYED MAH-JONG AT TANAKA'S THE OTHER DAY...
HE WAS SCRATCHING LIKE MAD ALL NIGHT.
SKRIT SKRIT SKRIT SKRIT
.....
.....
YOU BROUGHT THE FLEAS HOME FROM TANAKA'S PLACE?! IT WAS YOU!!
.....
REMEMBER: CATS AREN'T THE ONLY WAY FLEAS CAN GET INTO A HOUSE...
NYOWRR YOWL FFFFT!
SKRIT SKRIT
FIN

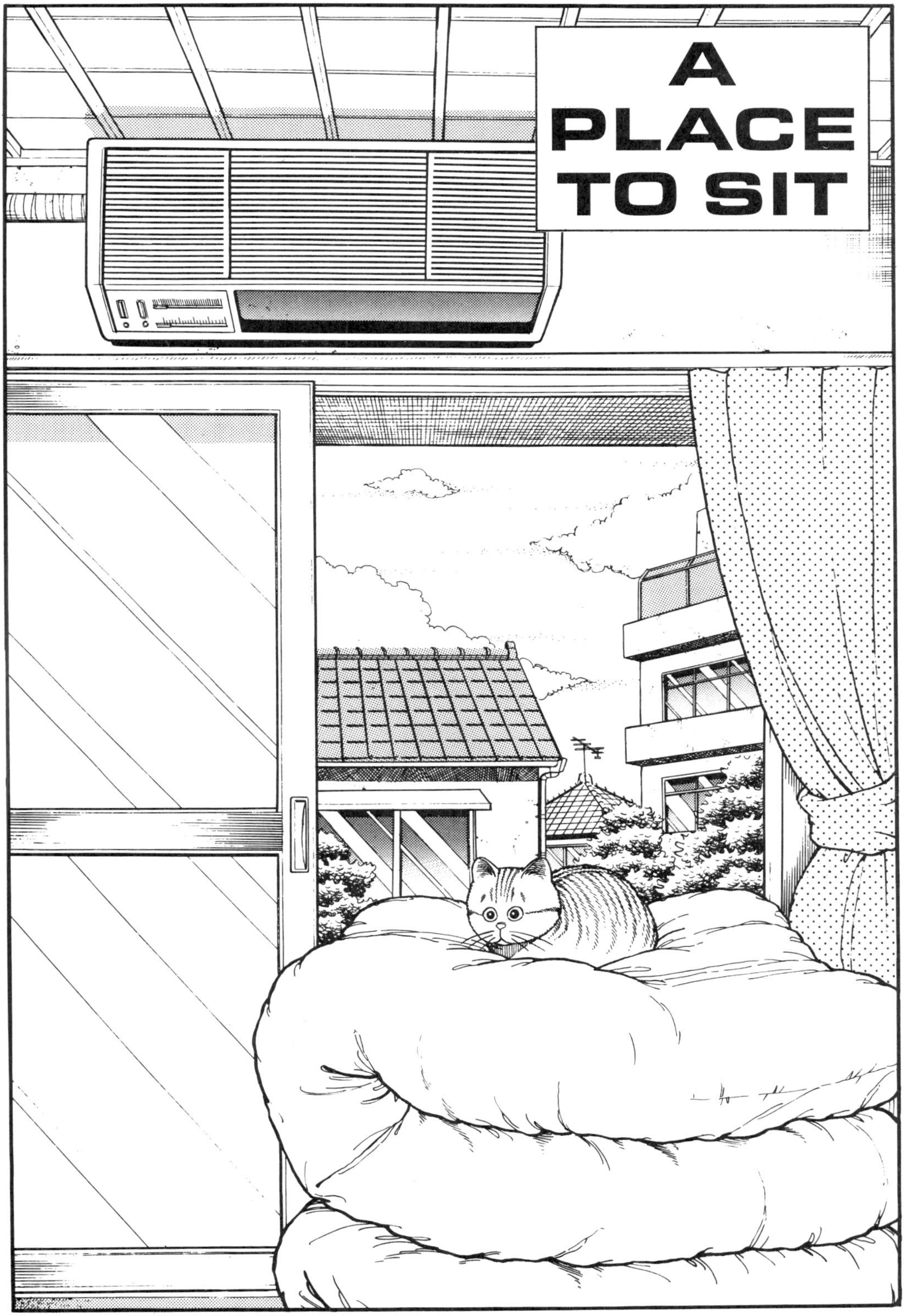
A
PLACE
TO SIT

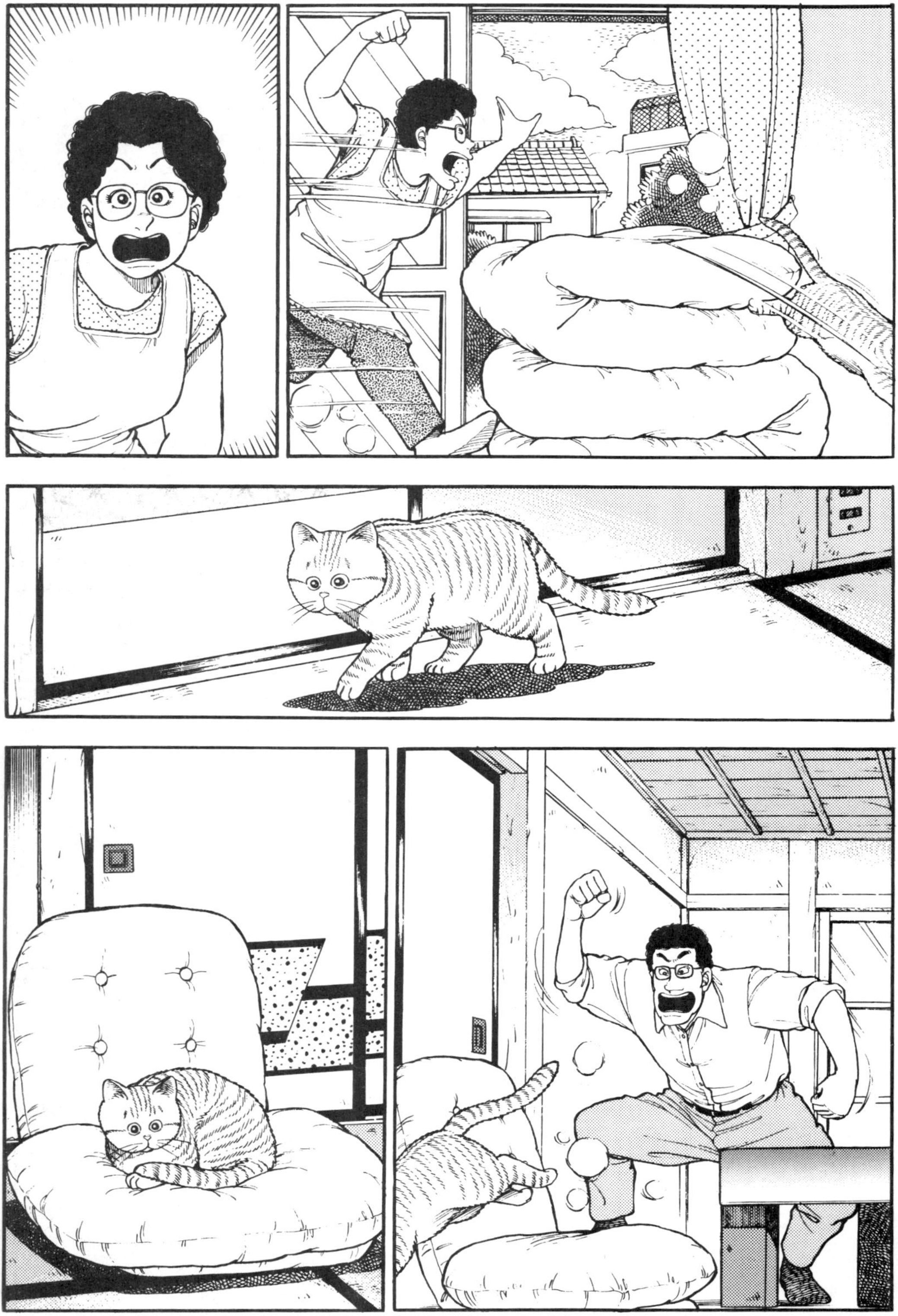

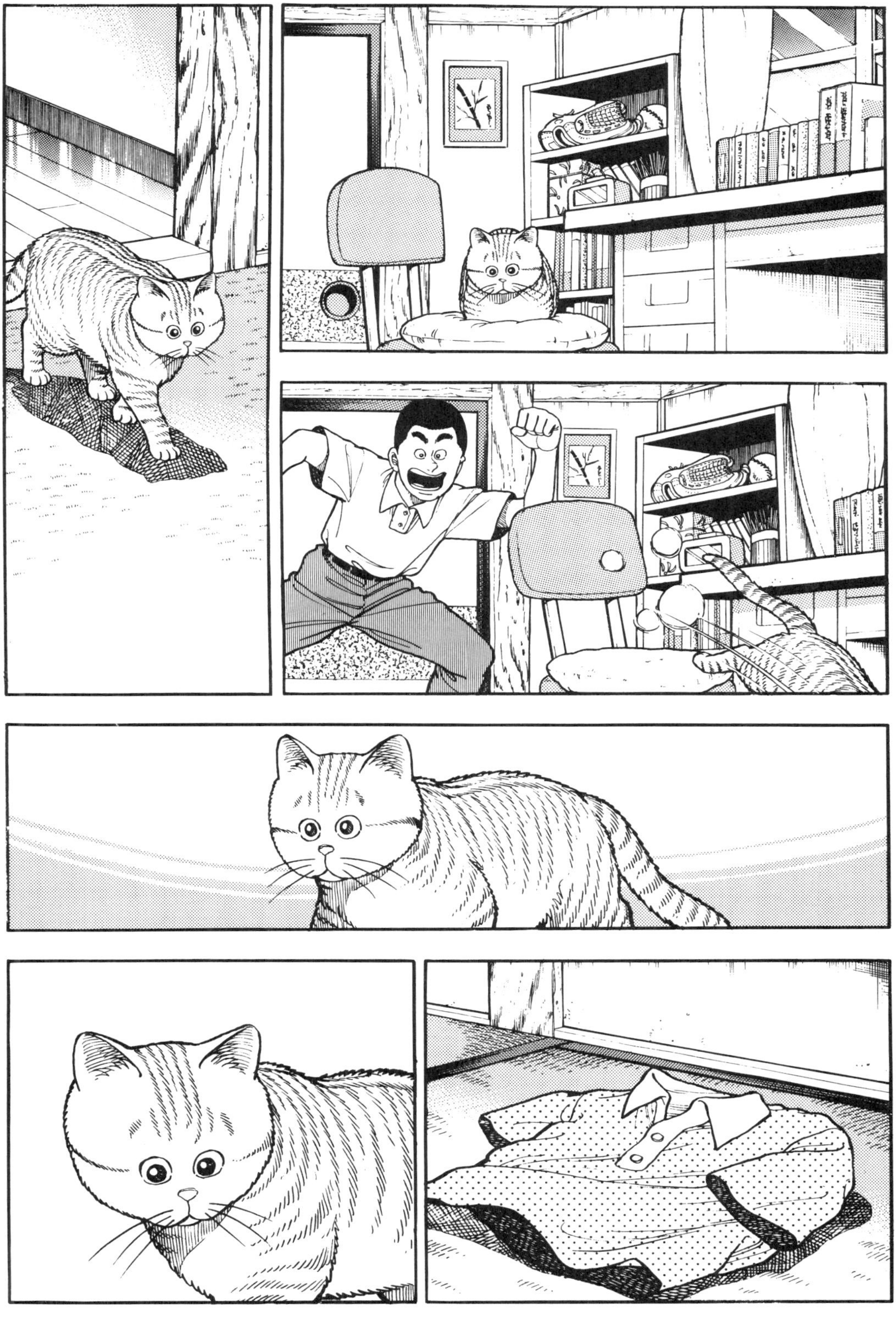

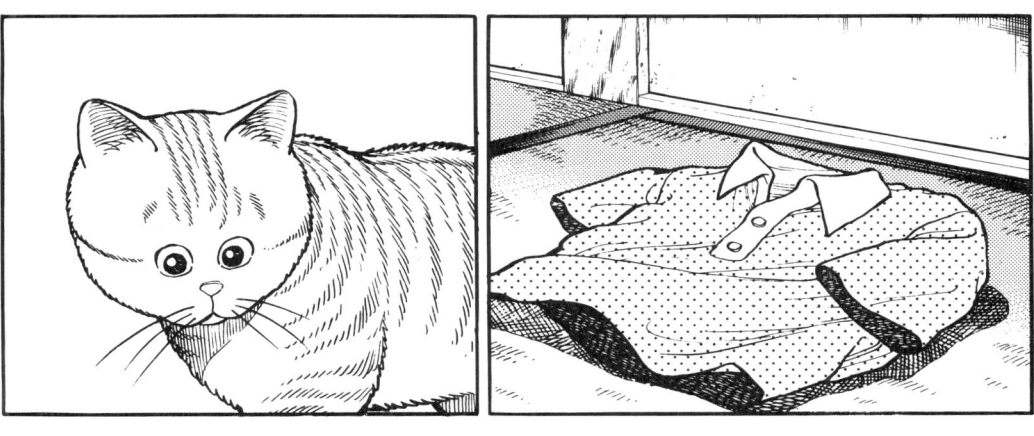

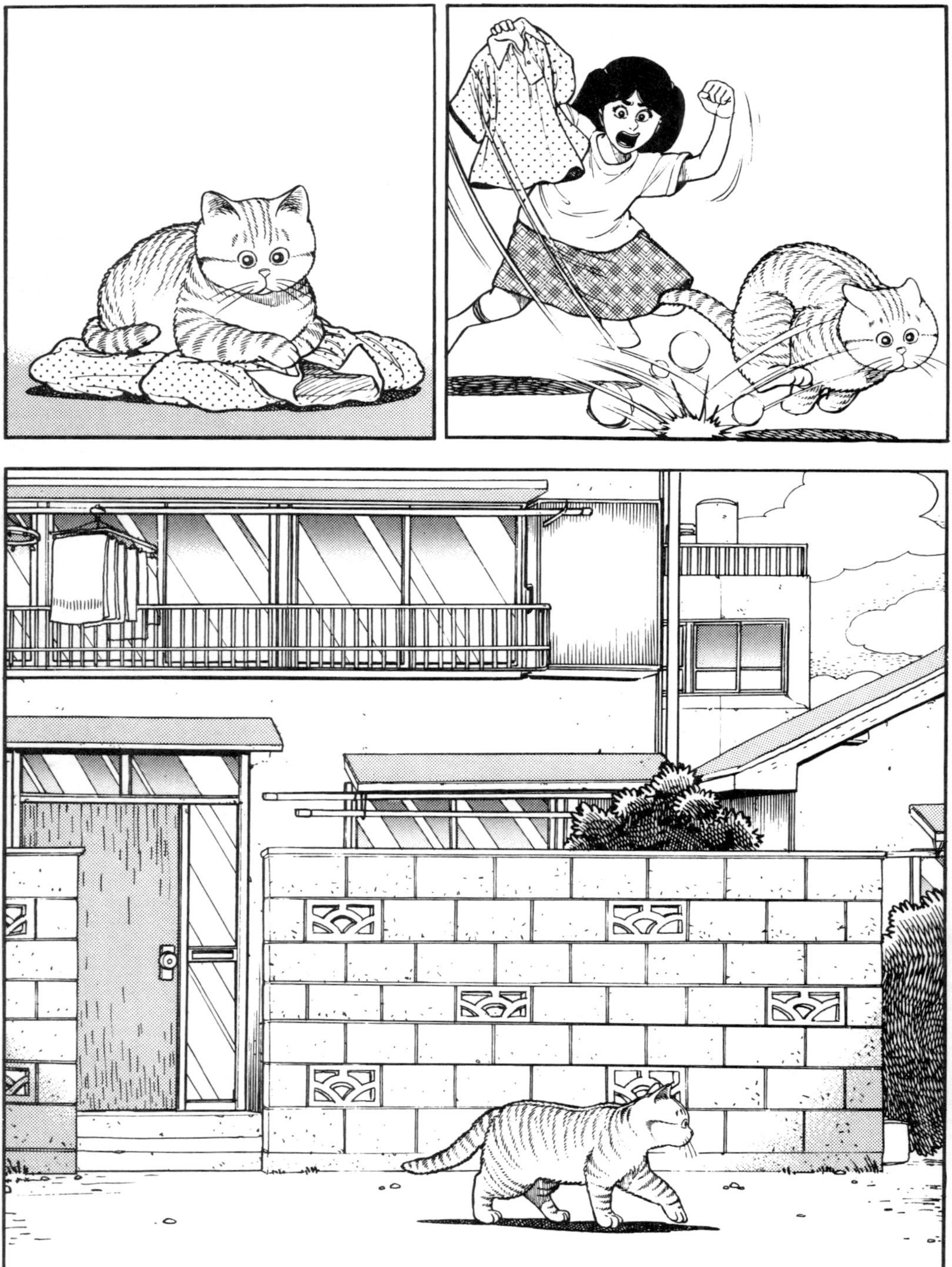

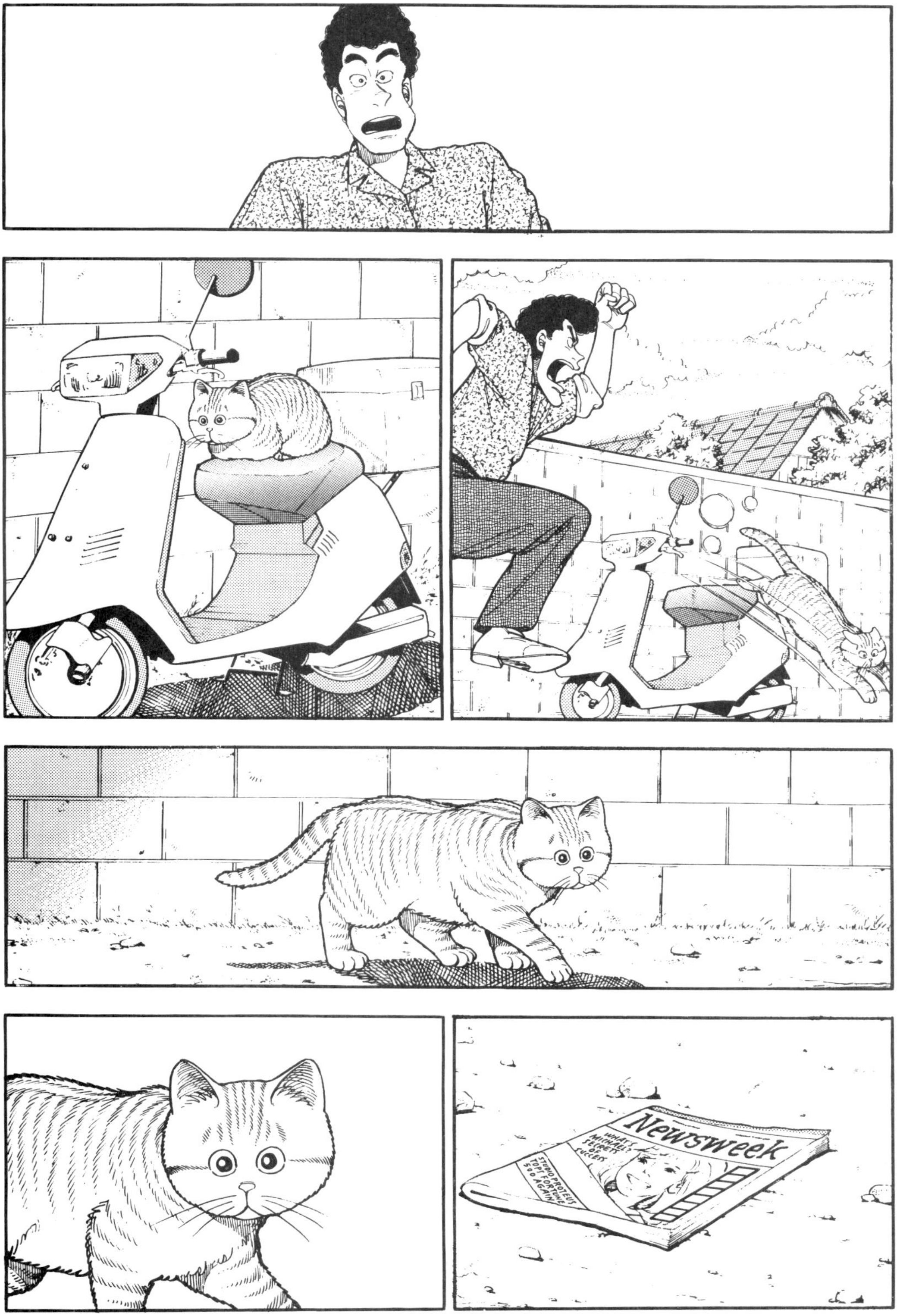
Newsweek
WHAT'S MICHAEL'S SECRETS OF SUCCESS
STUDIO PROTEUS TOPS FORTUNE 500 AGAIN

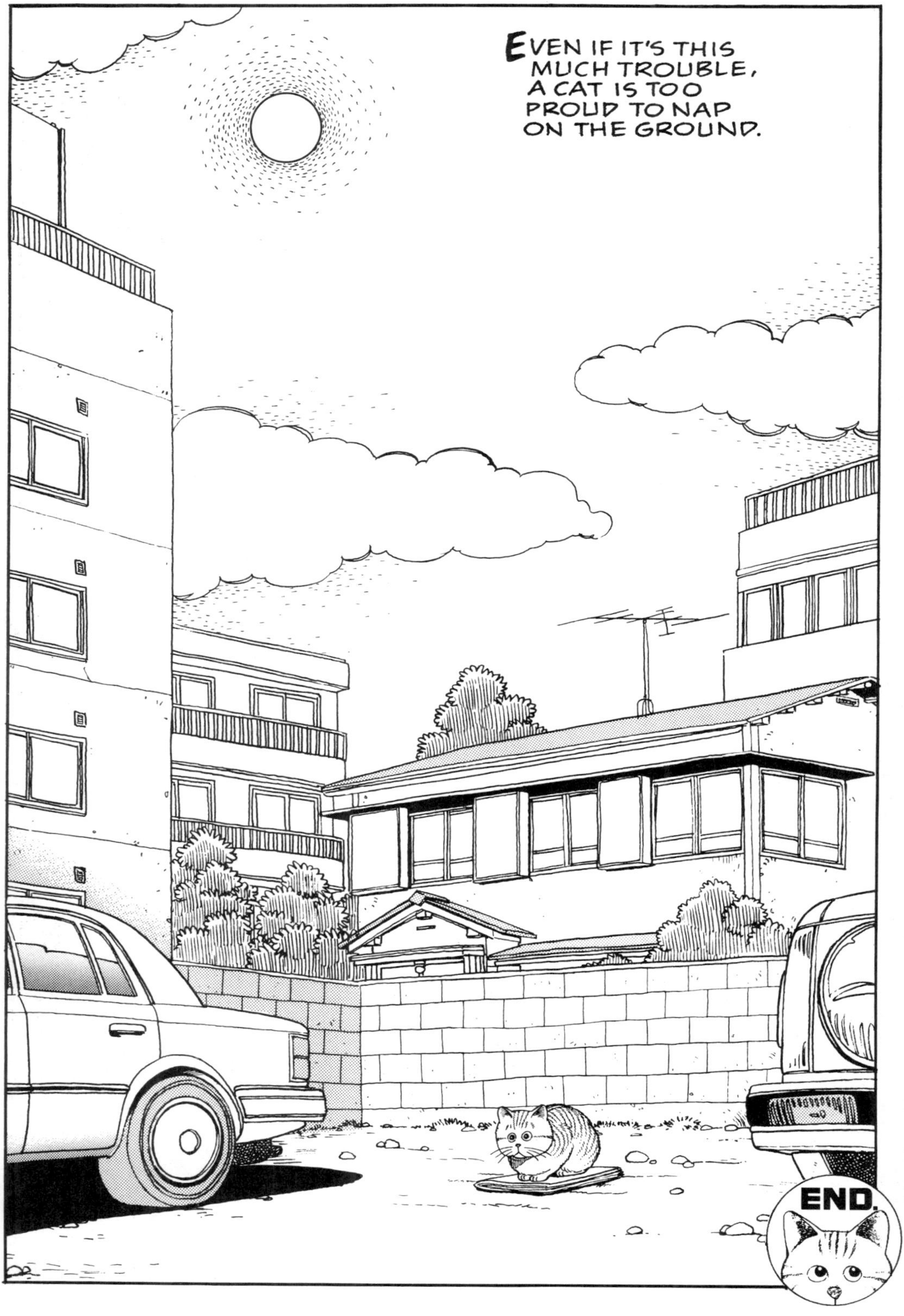
EVEN IF IT'S THIS MUCH TROUBLE, A CAT IS TOO PROUD TO NAP ON THE GROUND.
END.

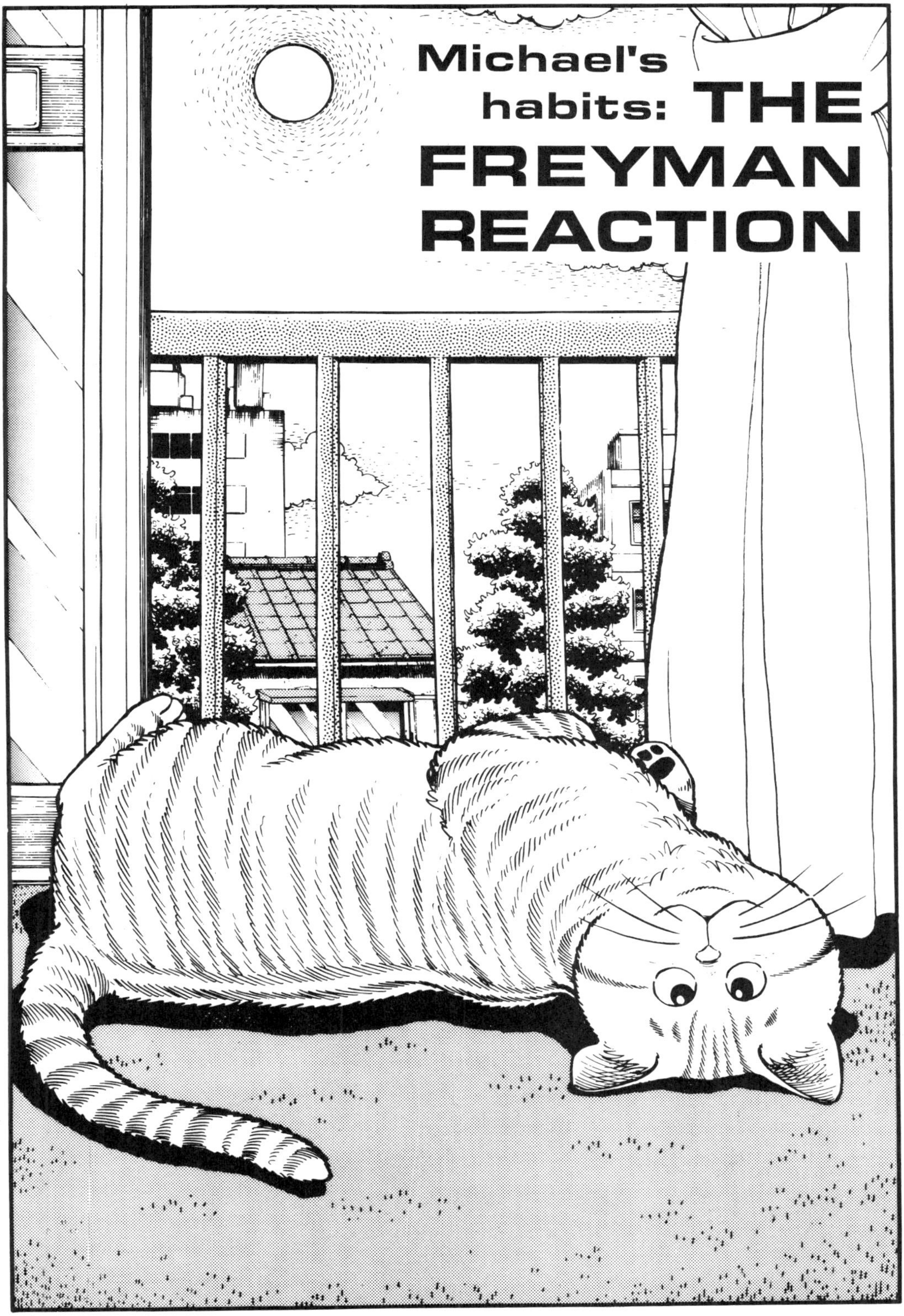
Michael's habits: THE FREYMAN REACTION

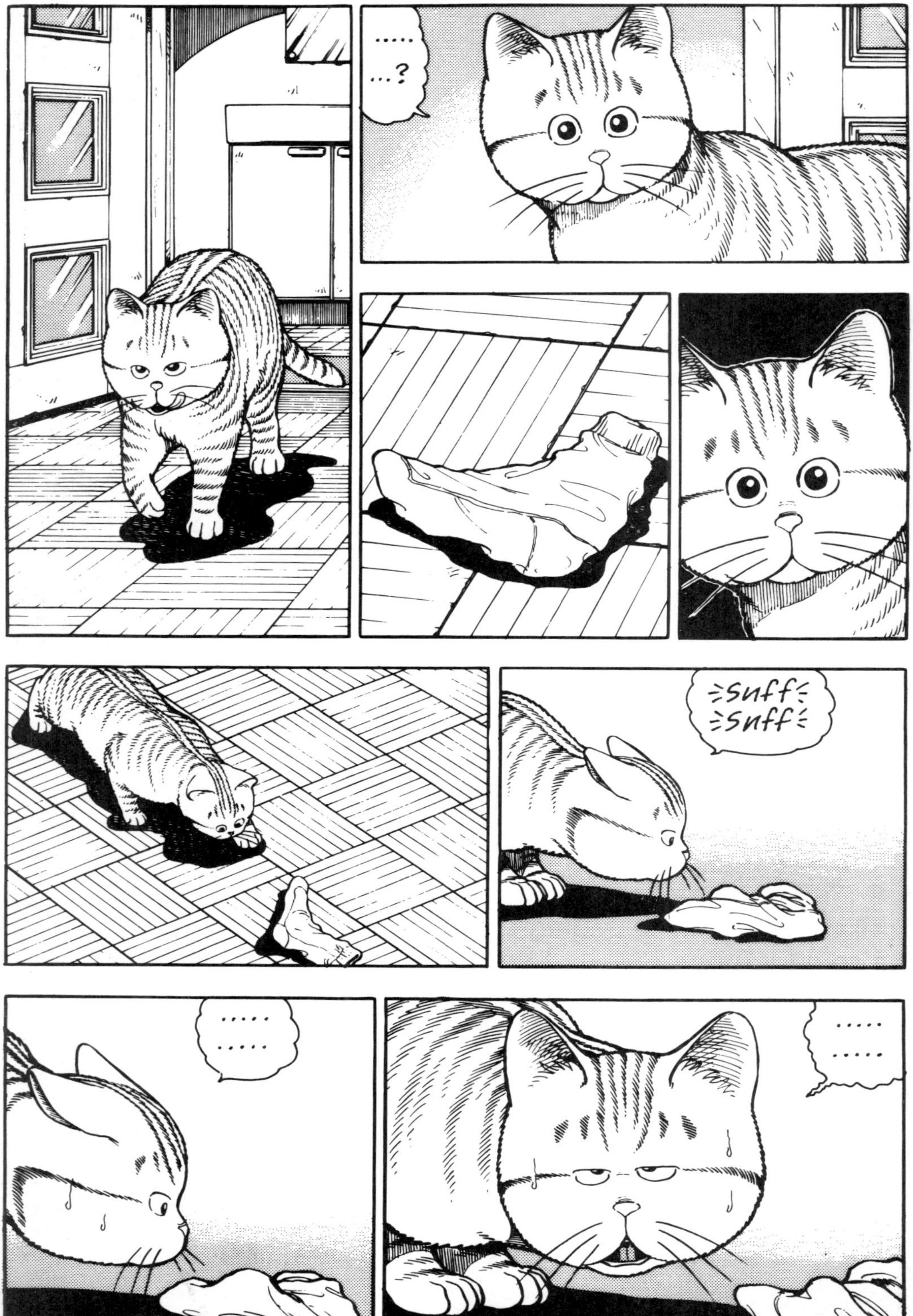
.....
...?
SNFF SNFF
.....
.....
.....
.....

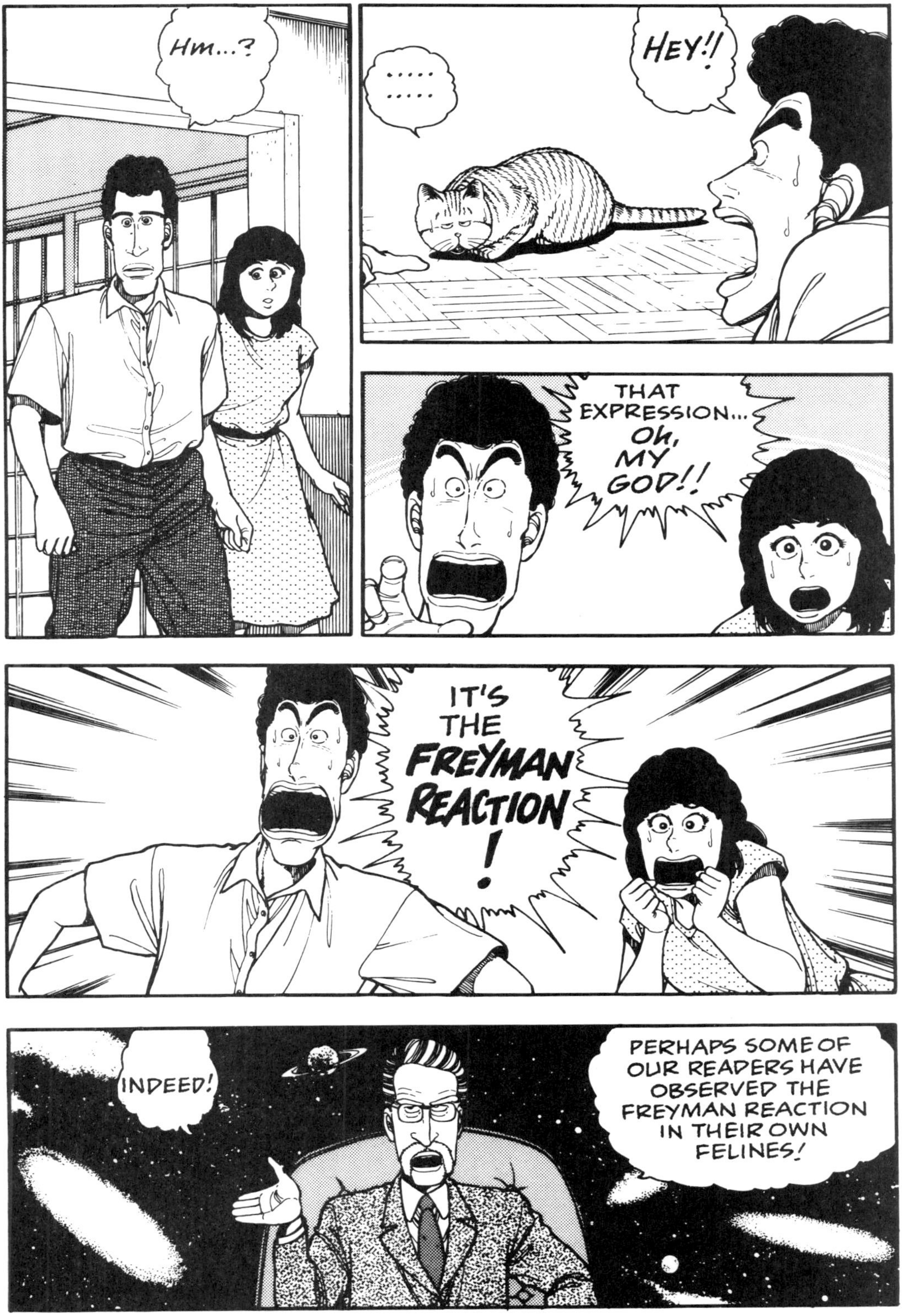
Hm...?
HEY!!
.....
.....
THAT EXPRESSION... Oh, MY GOD!!
IT'S THE FREYMAN REACTION!
INDEED!
PERHAPS SOME OF OUR READERS HAVE OBSERVED THE FREYMAN REACTION IN THEIR OWN FELINES!

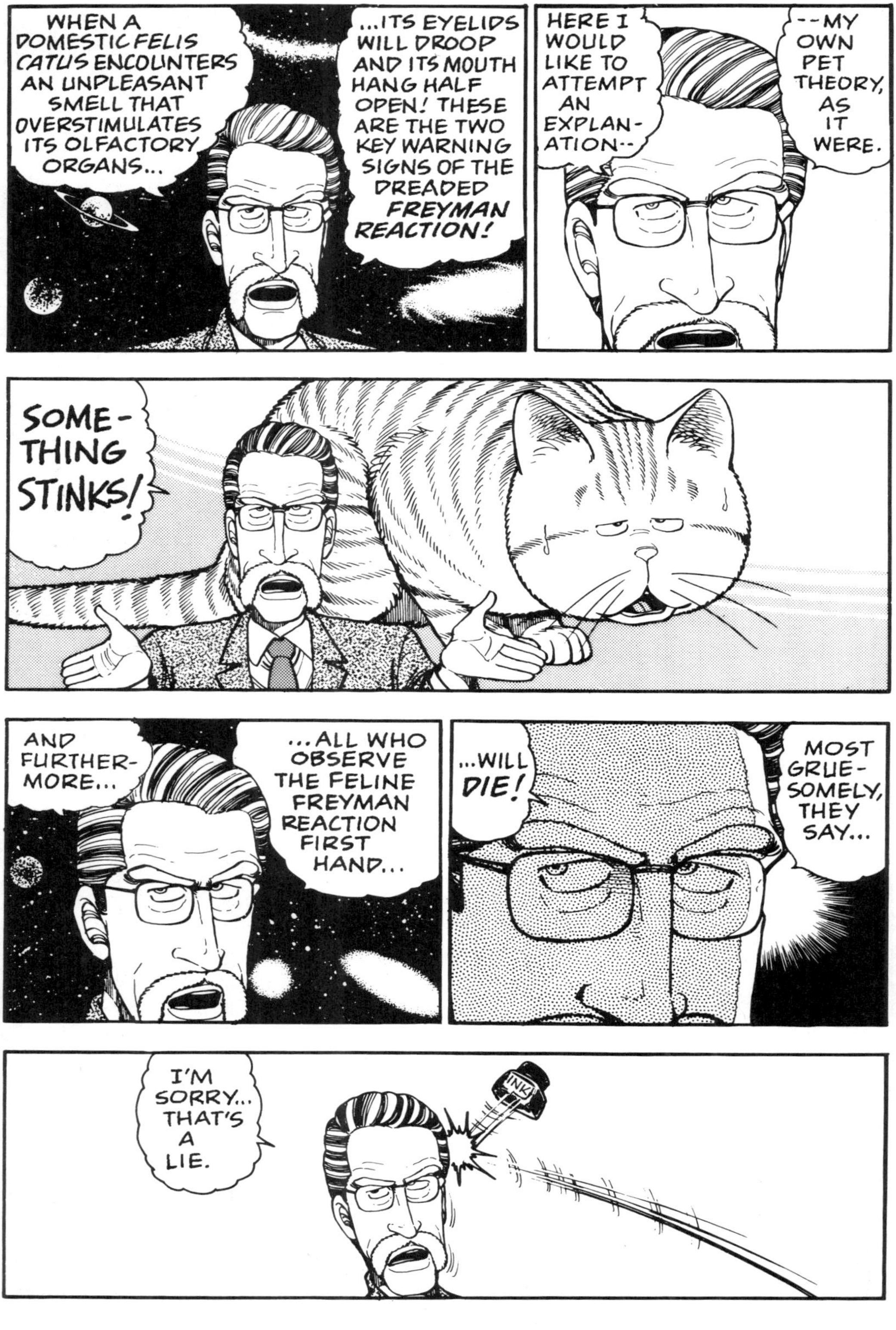

WHEN A DOMESTIC FELIS CATUS ENCOUNTERS AN UNPLEASANT SMELL THAT OVERSTIMULATES ITS OLFACTORY ORGANS...
...ITS EYELIDS WILL DROOP AND ITS MOUTH HANG HALF OPEN! THESE ARE THE TWO KEY WARNING SIGNS OF THE DREADED FREYMAN REACTION!
HERE I WOULD LIKE TO ATTEMPT AN EXPLANATION--
--MY OWN PET THEORY, AS IT WERE.
SOMETHING STINKS!
AND FURTHERMORE...
...ALL WHO OBSERVE THE FELINE FREYMAN REACTION FIRST HAND...
...WILL DIE!
MOST GRUESOMELY, THEY SAY...
I'M SORRY... THAT'S A LIE.
INK

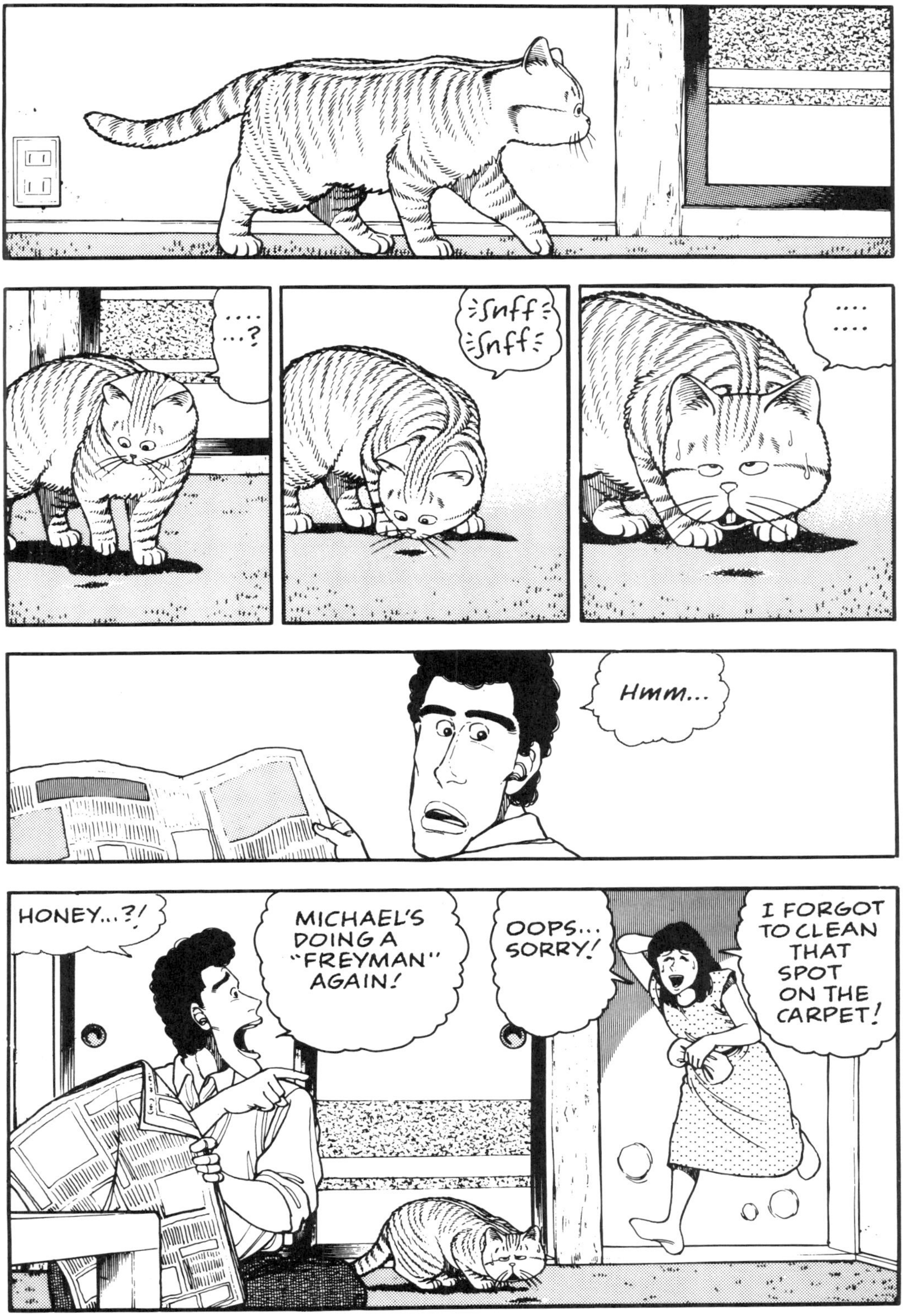
....
...?
Snff
Snff
....
....
Hmm...
HONEY...?!
MICHAEL'S DOING A "FREYMAN" AGAIN!
OOPS... SORRY!
I FORGOT TO CLEAN THAT SPOT ON THE CARPET!

IN THIS FASHION, THE FREYMAN REACTION HAS BEEN USED SINCE ANCIENT TIMES TO FIND OFFENSIVE STAINS ON WALL-TO-WALL-CARPET-- URK
PFRRT
Snff
Snff
....
...?
Snff
Snff
....
...?
SORRY!
MUST HAVE BEEN SOMETHING I HAD FOR LUNCH.
AW, C'MON, GUYS! DON'T "FREYMAN" AT ME!
....
....
FIN

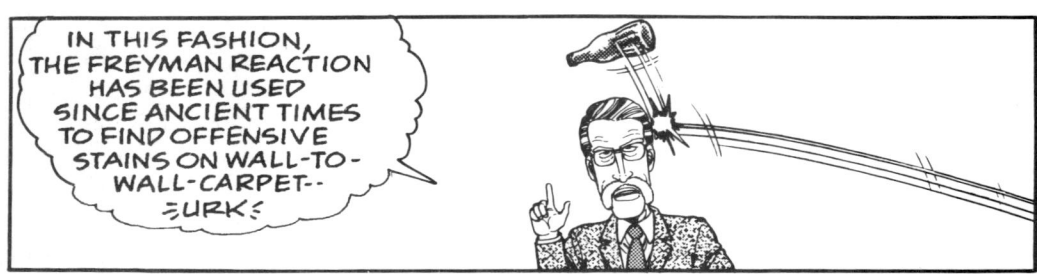

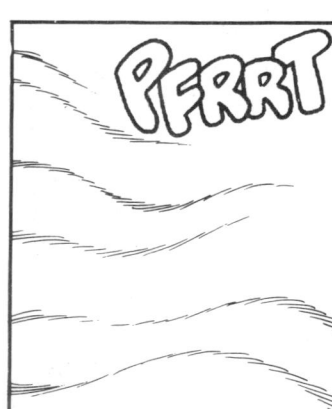

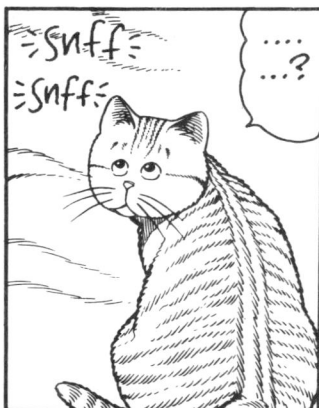

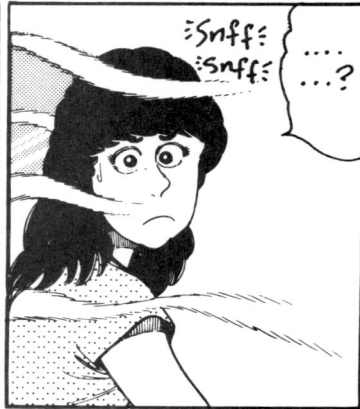

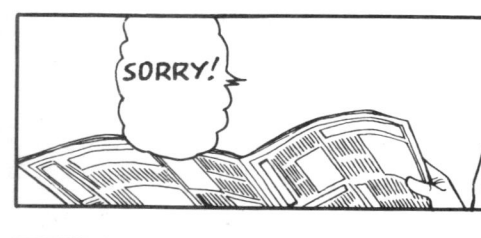

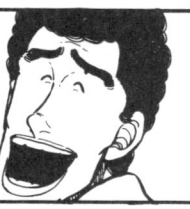

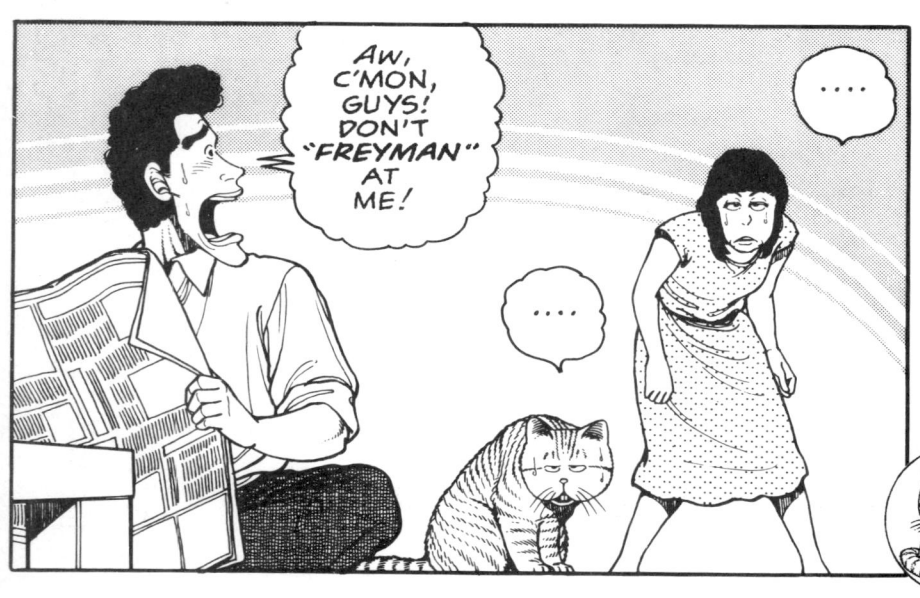

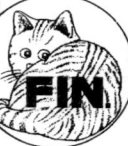

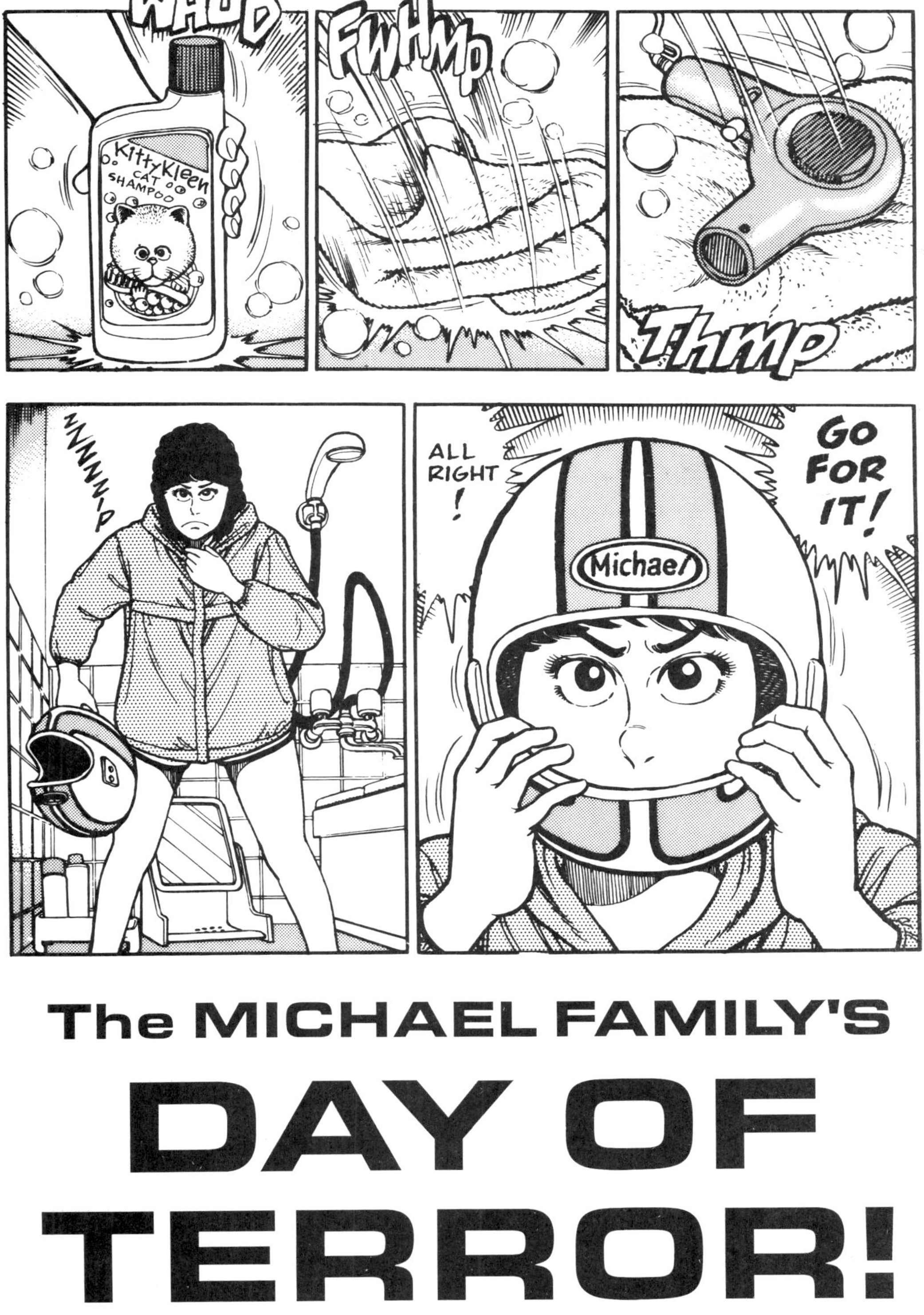
WHUD
Kitty Kleen
CAT
SHAMPOO
FWHMP
THMP
ZZZZZZIP
ALL RIGHT!
GO FOR IT!
Michael

The MICHAEL FAMILY'S

DAY OF TERROR!

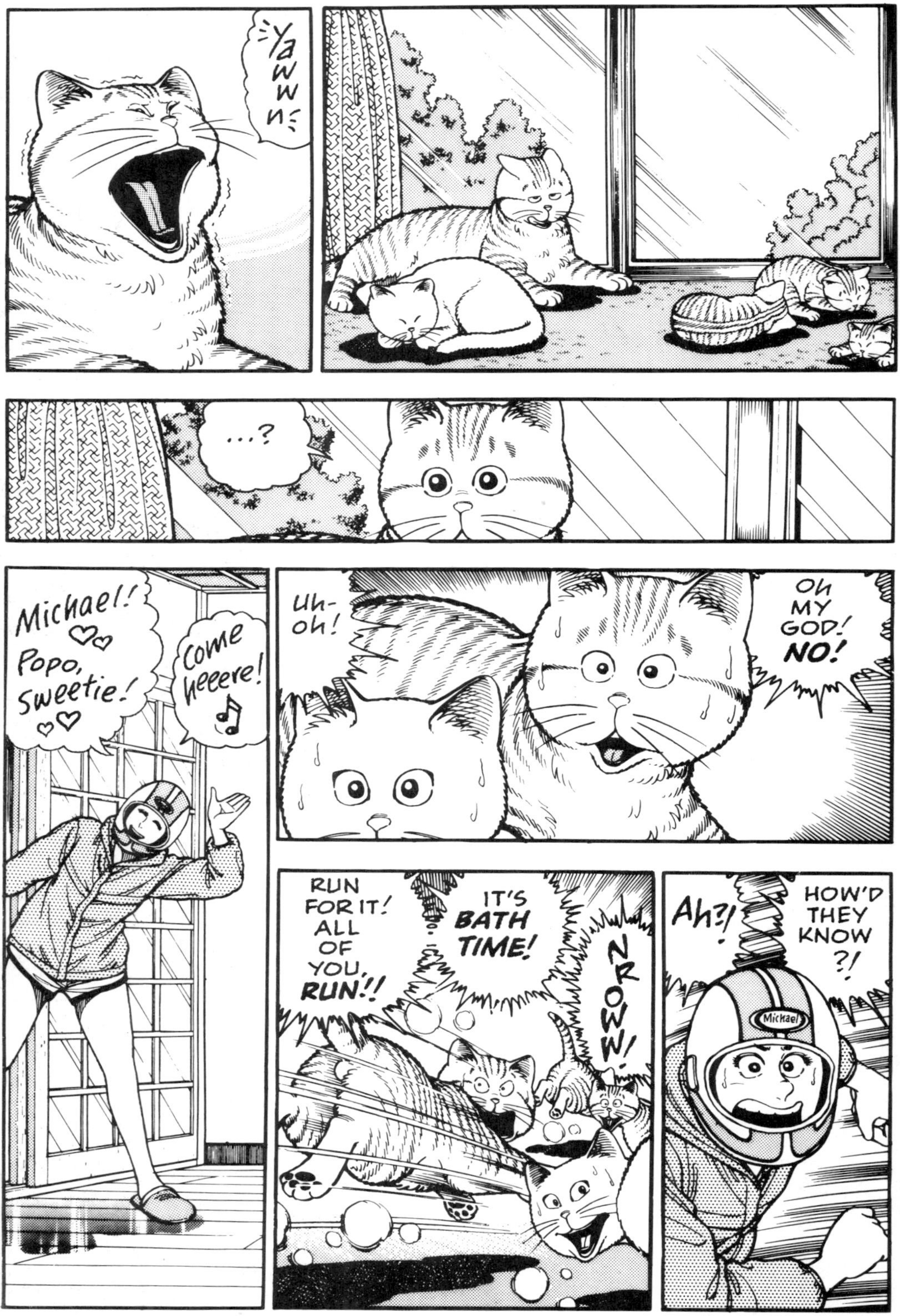
Yawwn
...?
Michael! Popo, sweetie!
Come heeere!
Uh-oh!
Oh my God! NO!
RUN FOR IT! ALL OF YOU, RUN!!
IT'S BATH TIME!
NROWW!
Ah?!
HOW'D THEY KNOW?!
Michael

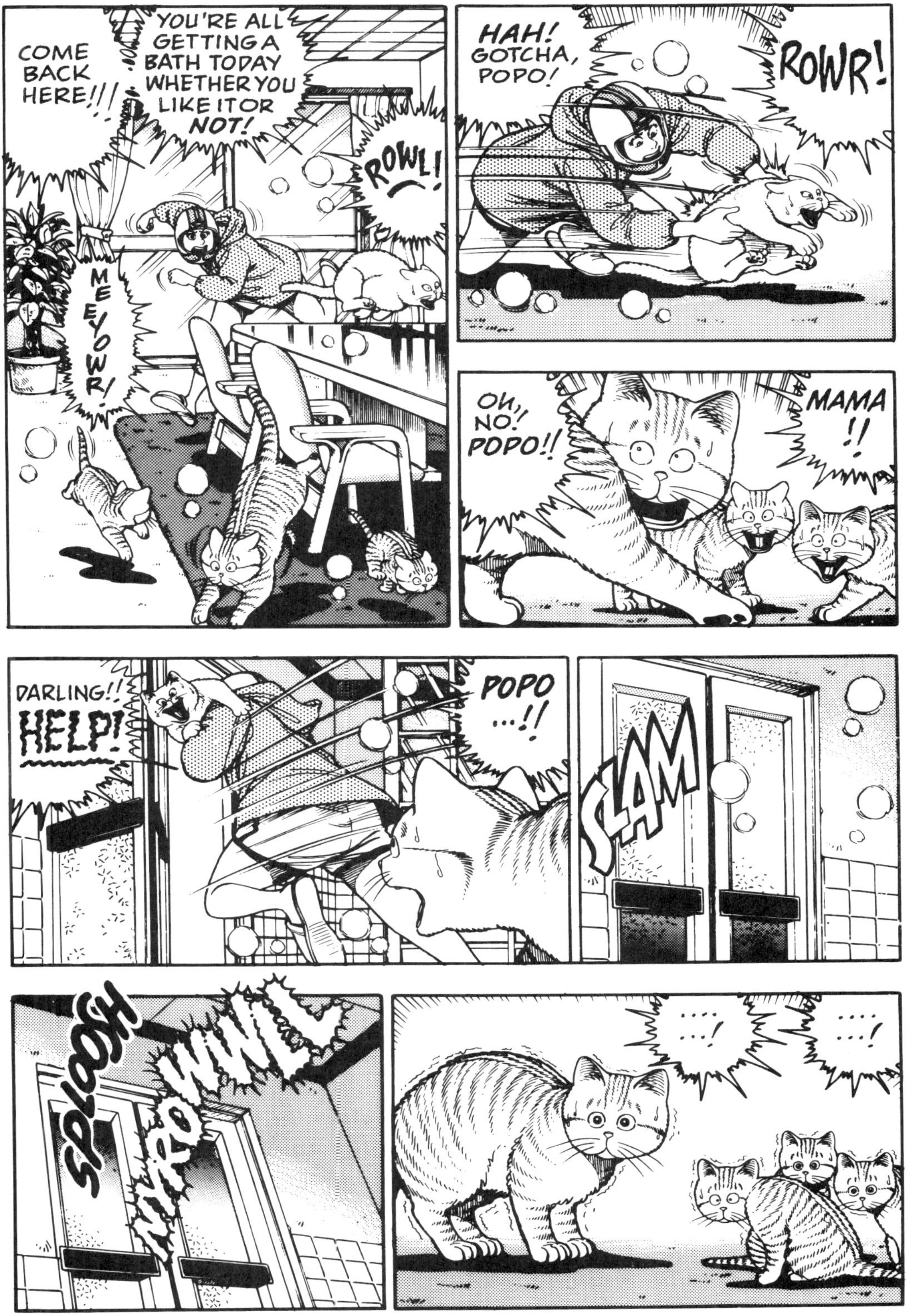
COME BACK HERE!!!
YOU'RE ALL GETTING A BATH TODAY WHETHER YOU LIKE IT OR NOT!
ROWL!
MEEYOWR!
HAH! GOTCHA, POPO!
ROWR!
OH, NO! POPO!!
MAMA!!
DARLING!! HELP!
POPO...!!
SLAM
SPLOOSH
YOWWL
....!
....!

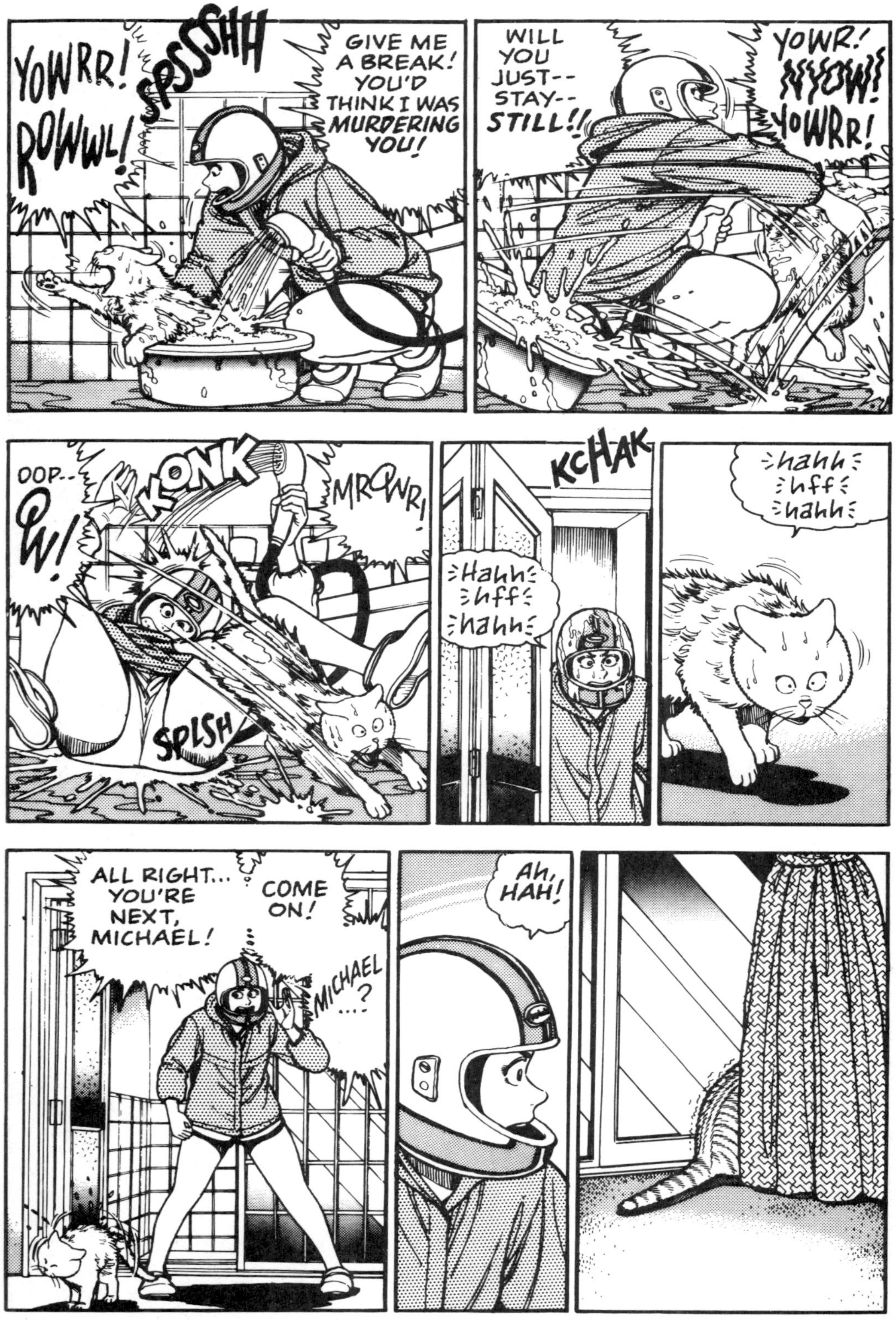
YOWRR!
ROWWL!
SPSSSHH
GIVE ME A BREAK! YOU'D THINK I WAS MURDERING YOU!
WILL YOU JUST-- STAY-- STILL!!
YOWR! NYOW! YOWRR!
OOP--
OW!
KONK
MRROWR!
SPLSH
KCHAK
Hahh hff hahh
hahh hff hahh
ALL RIGHT... YOU'RE NEXT, MICHAEL!
COME ON!
MICHAEL ...?
AH, HAH!

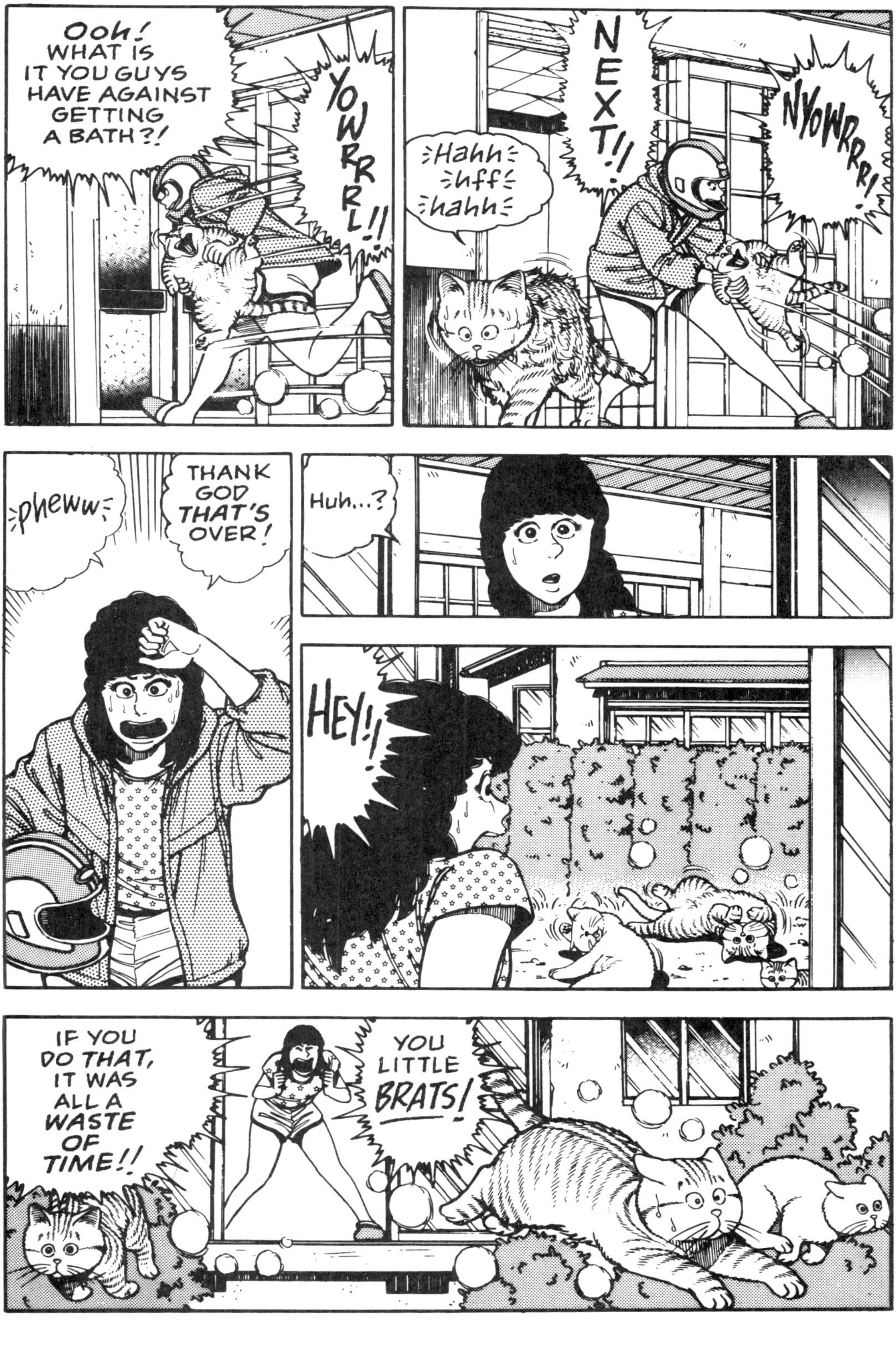
Ooh! WHAT IS IT YOU GUYS HAVE AGAINST GETTING A BATH?!
YOWRRRL!!
NEXT!!
Hahh uff hahh
NYOWRRR!
phewww
THANK GOD THAT'S OVER!
Huh...?
HEY!!
YOU LITTLE BRATS!
IF YOU DO THAT, IT WAS ALL A WASTE OF TIME!!

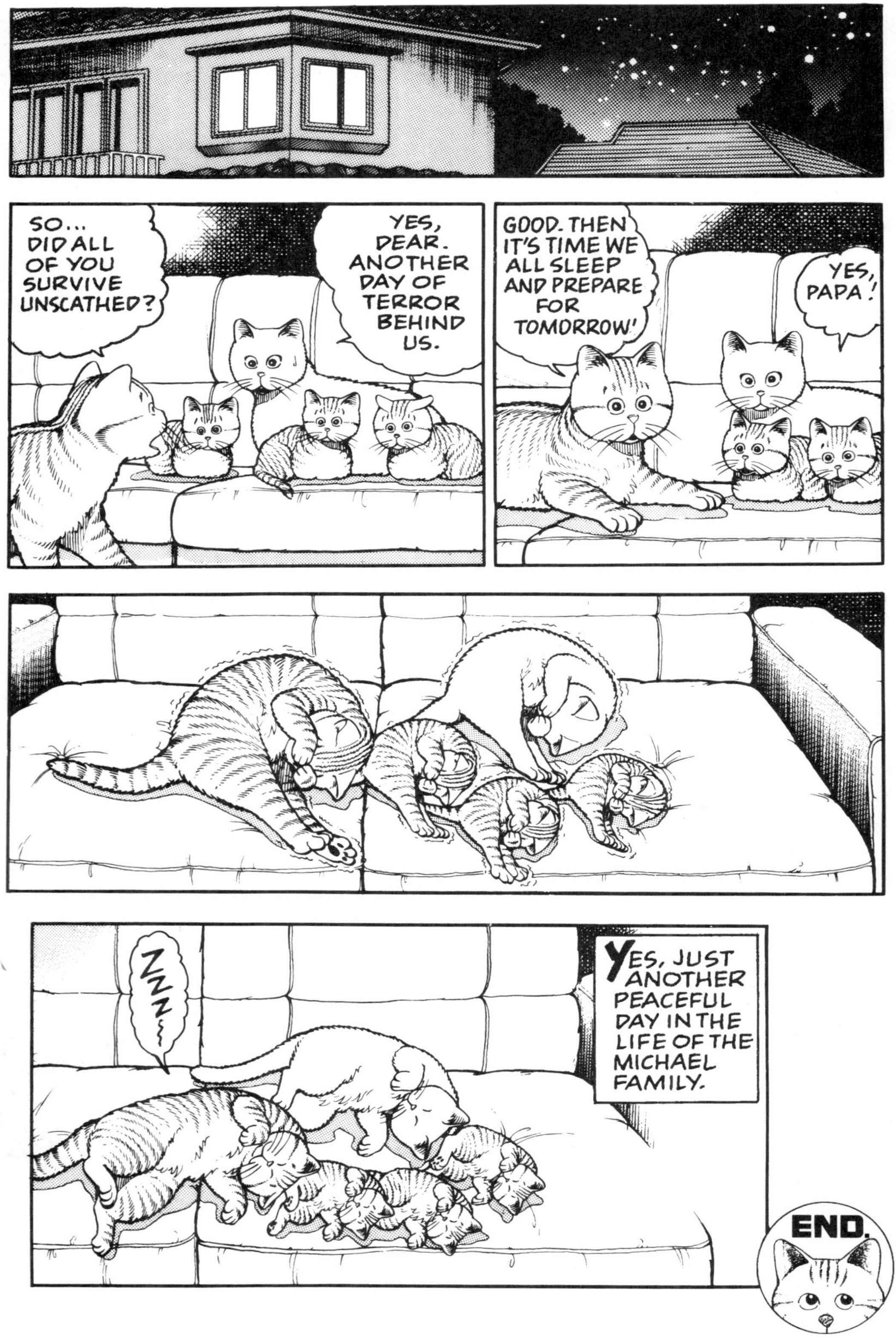
SO... DID ALL OF YOU SURVIVE UNSCATHED?
YES, DEAR. ANOTHER DAY OF TERROR BEHIND US.
GOOD. THEN IT'S TIME WE ALL SLEEP AND PREPARE FOR TOMORROW!
YES, PAPA!
ZZZ~
YES, JUST ANOTHER PEACEFUL DAY IN THE LIFE OF THE MICHAEL FAMILY.
END.

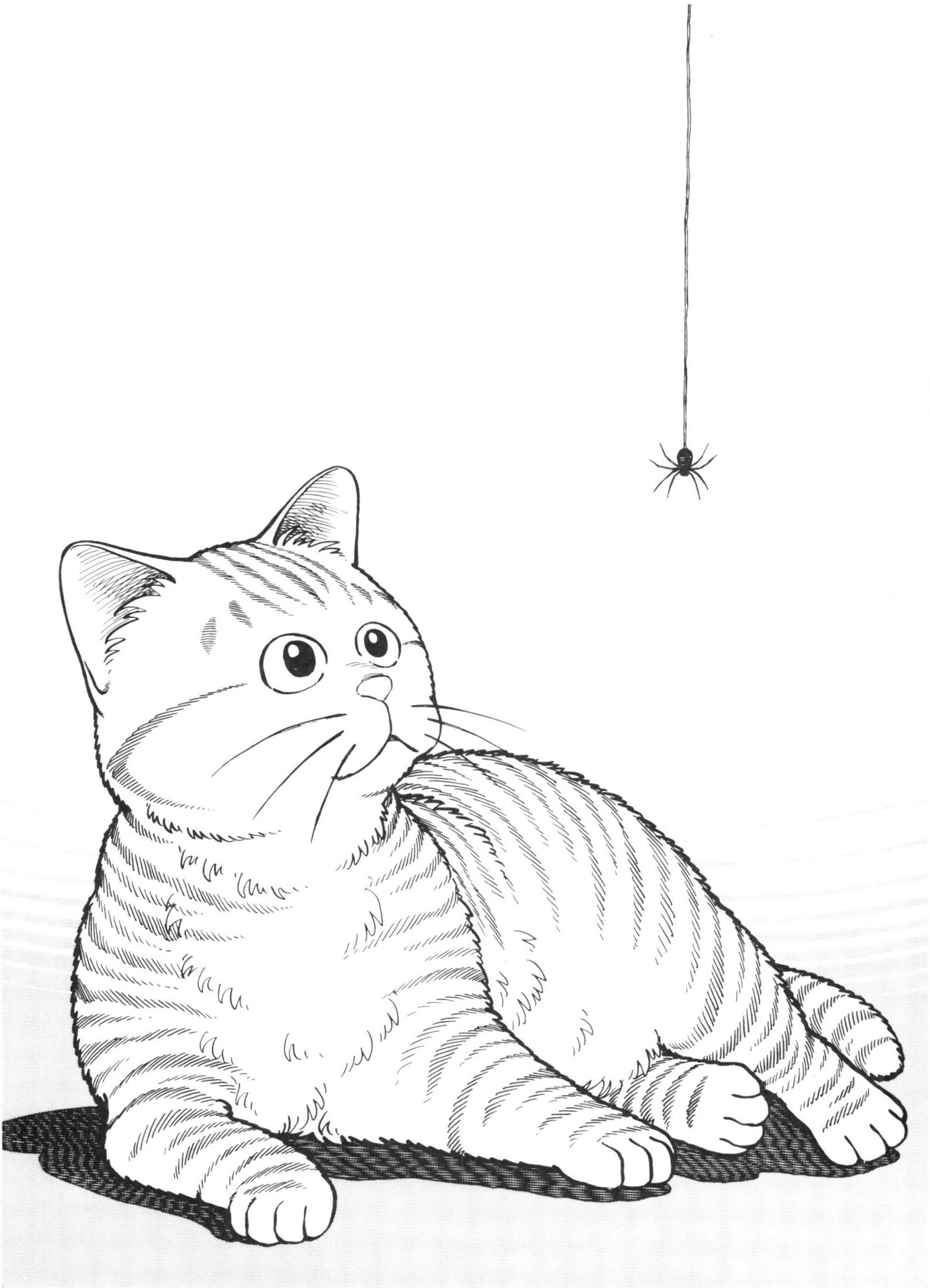

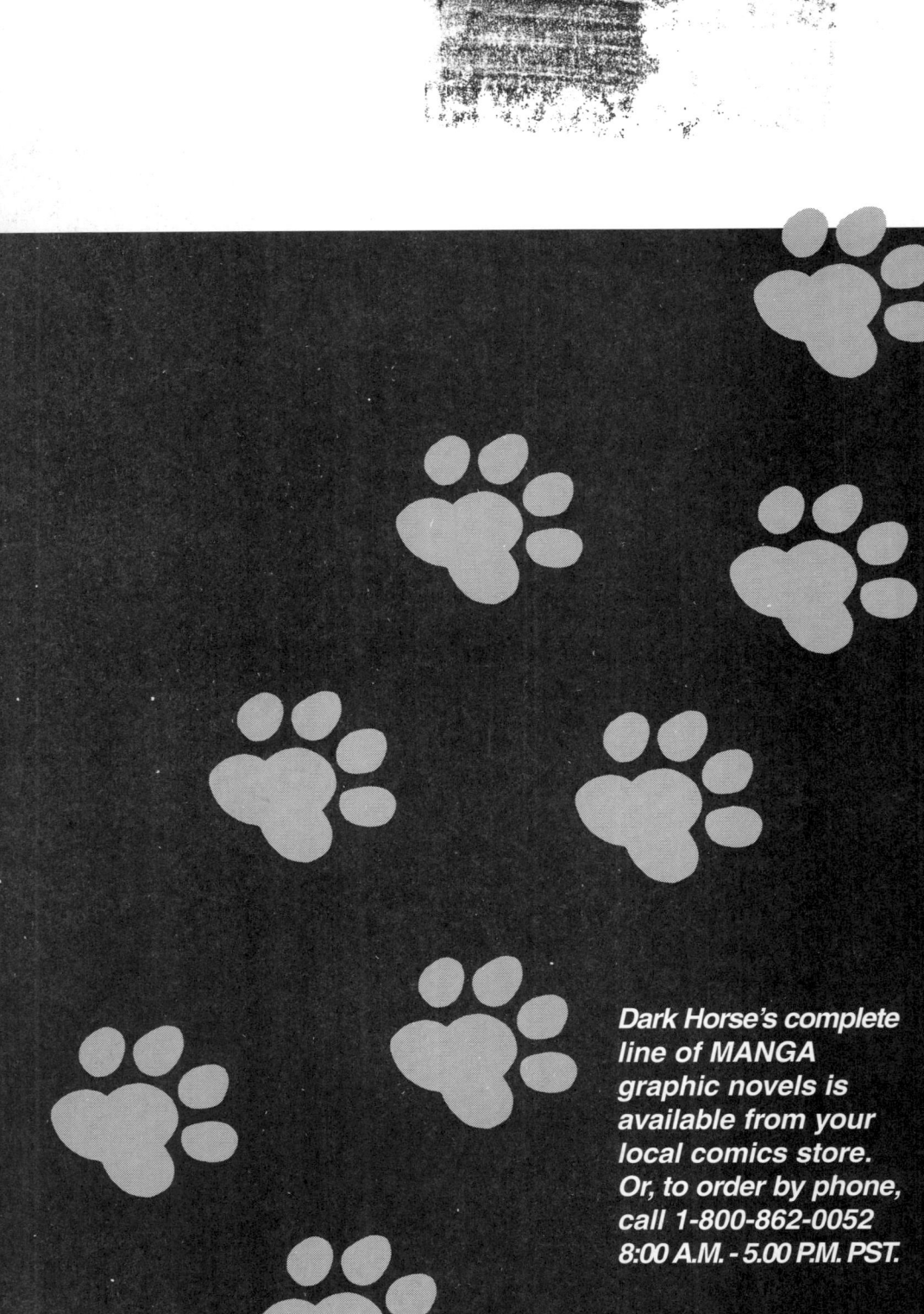

Dark Horse's complete line of MANGA graphic novels is available from your local comics store. Or, to order by phone, call 1-800-862-0052 8:00 A.M. - 5.00 P.M. PST.